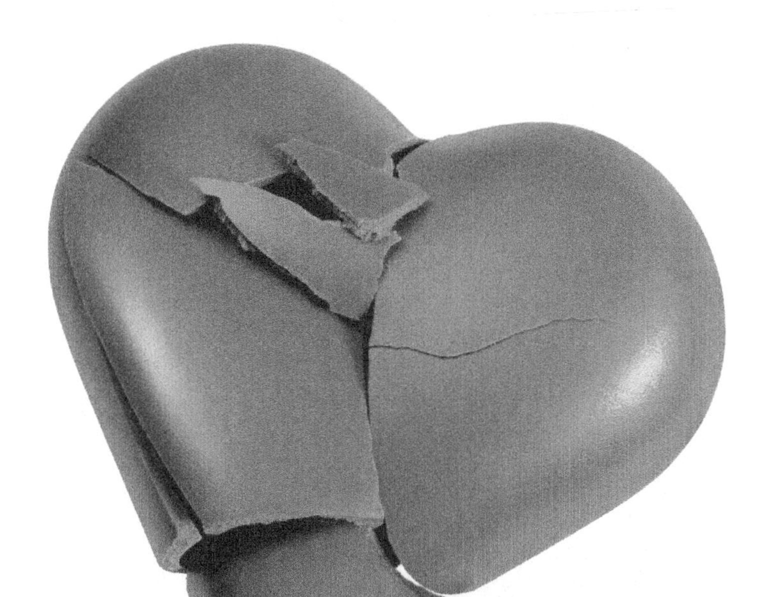

A September Day and Shadow Thriller

DARE OR DIE

Book Seven

AMY SHOJAI

Copyright

This is a work of fiction. Names, characters, places, and incidents either are the product of the author's imagination or are used fictitiously, and any resemblance to actual persons living or dead, business establishments, events, or locales is entirely coincidental.

First Print Edition, April 2023
Furry Muse Publishing
Paper ISBN 978-1-948366-58-8
Hardback ISBN 978-1-948366-59-5
eBook ISBN 9781948366571

FURRY MUSE
PUBLICATIONS
P.O. Box 1904
Sherman TX 75091
(903)814-4319
amy@shojai.com

September & Shadow Pet-centric Thrillers
By Amy Shojai

LOST AND FOUND

HIDE AND SEEK

SHOW AND TELL

FIGHT OR FLIGHT
Introducing Lia, Tee, and Karma

HIT AND RUN

WIN OR LOSE

DARE OR DIE

Chapter 1 – JACK

Jackson Glass picked up a picture, turning it around and around in his long, slender hands. As he traced Rina's face with his index finger the familiar ache boiled in the pit of his stomach. Memories haunted him. Decades had slipped by in an eyeblink, and tears welled. He'd worshipped her, a little brother tagging along just wanting her approval.

He gently set Rina's picture back on the polished black enamel desk, beside the bank of computers that lined the large room. The portrait, in soft pastel hues, offered the only concession to humanity in the entire apartment. Jack favored chrome, black or white enamel, and spartan furnishings. Even his workout equipment, black clothing, stark white hair, and pale visage reflected the austere nature of his life.

Rina had outshone his own extraordinary abilities—a genius beyond him—and gave it all up at the behest of her traditionally-minded husband. Ten years his senior, and barely twenty-five years old when she died! So much stolen from her. From them both. All because of Kaliko Wong.

The witch had killed his sister, and Rina's husband accepted the witch's lies. So, in a rage, with the hubris of youth, he went after the witch himself.

Like a snake grabbed by the tail, she struck with potent venom. He barely escaped. And because she couldn't reach him, his parents paid the price of his effrontery.

An orphan at barely fifteen, he vowed to play dead while planning future vengeance. He changed his name to hide from the world. His skills, even as a teenager, garnered top dollar and he sold his expertise to those requiring discretion and hard-to-find information. He built a network of like-minded overlooked talent, those either unable or unwilling to face the world. They connected electronically, never needing physical interactions. Safer that way.

From his invisible vantage, Jack watched Kaliko Wong and the organization she'd corrupted. She had destroyed everything that mattered to him. So, he wreaked havoc in small ways, disrupting plans, and recruiting insiders to his efforts, helping protect innocents like his sister. He watched and waited, electronic eyes, ears, and fingers tracked every move, chronicled each of the witch's criminal acts, documented her myriad sins. Only when necessary did he step briefly from the shadows to level the playing field, to give victims a better chance to escape her toxic manipulations. He analyzed, predicted, deciphered, and patiently planned, a chess master, playing the game for a final, ultimate sweet reward.

He had discerned a puzzling pattern. The witch targeted one woman time and again, a vendetta that escalated with each near miss. Jack helped thwart the machinations once, yet still the witch refused to abandon the persecution. What could merit such ire?

He tapped quickly on one of the keyboards, staring at the monitors for the response. His eyes widened, then he gritted his teeth. Jack didn't believe in coincidence. His sister's birthday, June 22, he considered sacred. But the witch had flagged the date, had something planned for her latest target.

Internally smiling—he rarely allowed emotion to alter his expression—Jack's fingers flew over the keyboard. He breached Kaliko Wong's private world effortlessly, but took care to hide his electronic presence, bouncing from IP to IP as a precaution. As far as anyone knew, Rina's teenage brother died of suicide over grief of losing his sister and parents. Only his alter-ego lived on in the ether of a virtual world, among other child-geniuses.

Fingers clattered the keys while his mind churned faster. He could hear the *click* in his mind's eye as each revealed puzzle piece slipped into place like a Rubik's cube. Soon, he understood the witch's plan, but not her motive. He had time. He'd already shown decades' worth of patience.

The possibilities quickened his breath. Alone, he buzzed around the witch, dodging in to land a sting here and there. But the concerted effort of a swarm could do more, perhaps even bring her down for good. Time to cultivate a partnership to de-fang the snake once and for all.

He wouldn't risk defenseless innocents, of course. But September Day was hardly defenseless.

Chapter 2 – SEPTEMBER

The quiet, soothing garden would soon bustle with activity as workers arrived to set up for the wedding, and September Day looked forward to this weekend being over. She had yearned for a happy ending for months, no, make that years. She and Detective Jeffrey Combs would build a life together. Nothing, not even her desires for privacy, would stop her from making this work.

Meanwhile, before all the strangers invaded the space, September calmed herself, communing with the scent of roses, and the soft panting breath of her German Shepherd, Shadow.

The flight of birds and their occasional songs broke the silence. Already the temperature had risen to uncomfortable elevations. September wore a sleeveless tank top, and loose shorts that fell midway down her thighs. She'd already worked up a sweat—or a glow, as her sister April liked to say—from running through the various hand-to-hand combat exercises she had practiced every day for the past several months. Her instructors told her that the more she prepared, that it became part of her routine, the better her responses would be. In times of emergency you didn't need to think; your body reacted instinctively based on the drills you'd practiced.

From an animal behavior standpoint, she understood the concept. The same was true for pets. Much training relied on building on instinctive responses. Turn innate behaviors into a game and the dog or cat enjoyed the lessons, then begged to repeat them.

She'd been reluctant to commit to a formal training program for herself. But after her near-death experience in South Texas at the painted church, Combs had convinced her. "If not for yourself, then for me. Otherwise, I'll die of a heart attack before the wedding."

September smiled. She'd enjoyed the exercises, the challenge, and it was little enough to please Combs. Once they married, everything would fall into place for the happily ever after she had searched for.

Lately her cousin Lia Corazon had challenged September to expand Shadow's repertoire. "The student teaching the teacher. Right, baby dog?"

He woofed and danced in front of her, enjoying the quiet morning as much as her.

Lia had trained her dog, Magic, to do all the skills a tactical canine officer needed. The young Rottweiler-German Shepherd mix knew all the basics, and much more. While his father, Shadow, could out-track him in finding missing animals, Magic's skill at identifying explosives, and tracking down and detaining bad guys couldn't be beaten.

Lia had quite a touch with training animals, especially Magic, almost to the point she didn't have to speak a command to have the dog perform. When September commented on the skill, at first

Lia looked confused, then hemmed and hawed before admitting she'd taught the dog hand signals.

Shadow already knew several hand signals, but Lia's skill with Magic inspired September to up the ante. So, over the past several weeks, she had added to Shadow's knowledge. He already knew that a fist meant to *sit*, and that her palm held out flat toward him meant to *wait*. Shadow loved to learn, so adding anything new made him happy. But lately they'd had little time to be together, just the two of them. She felt bad sometimes, because the dog hadn't asked to suddenly be part of a larger family, so their private time together was precious.

She'd also added talking buttons to Shadow's repertoire, or tried to. She'd recorded the various words and phrases he already knew, like *outside* and *play* and *car ride,* so he could paw the specific button to play the message and make his request. They'd had little time to practice. Besides, she usually knew what he wanted anyway—and you couldn't carry a hundred buttons with recorded words and phrases with you everywhere. Hand signals, though, worked anywhere.

"Shadow, ready?" She raised her right hand to the side of her face, extending her index finger to point toward her eyes, the hand signal for *watch me.*

He wagged, play-bowed before her, and barked sharply three times. September raised a finger to her lips, and Shadow fell silent in mid-bark. She held her arm out straight in front of her, palm parallel to the ground, and made a sweeping motion toward the ground. Without hesitation, Shadow flopped forward in the *down* position.

She gave him the thumbs up—*good dog*—gratified when he didn't move a hair from the position. Placing her right hand flat over her heart, September suppressed a smile at the dog's coiled energy, just waiting for the next hand signal. She swept her arm up and out pointing toward the far end of the rose garden—the signal for *go out*—and Shadow sprang to his feet and dashed away.

Before September could reverse the signal, extended hand sweeping back to cover her heart for the *recall,* Shadow snapped at the air. Even from the distance, she heard his teeth clack three times as though chasing some invisible aggravation. Probably honeybees that love the roses, or some other stinging critter. Not wishing to risk Shadow being stung, she gave him the release command—jazz hands, both hands held upright and shimmied.

He raced back to her, panting happily, and danced around her figure as she opened her arms wide to embrace his warm, furry body. "We've got a lot to do today, Shadow. Let me jump in the shower, then we'll run errands. Just you and me. Would you like that, good dog?"

He barked three times, watched for her to shush him. When she didn't, he barked twice more for good measure.

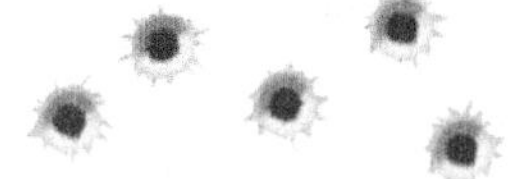

After shoving the SUV into park, September sat for a moment behind the wheel. She switched on the windshield wipers, pressed the juice, and watched them sweep away red dust, clearing the view of the sun-drenched exercise yard. You'd expect dewy grass for this early in the day, but native Texans knew better. Late June meant crunchy yards, unless one could justify watering the vegetation. Lia Corazon wouldn't waste her money that way, and probably considered September's roses an eccentric extravagance.

"I can afford it, at least until after the wedding." At her voice, Shadow's big black head popped up from the back seat. He stared into the mirror to connect with September's cat-green eyes. His tail thumped, and he stood, whined, then wagged harder when she smiled. "Baby dog, are you ready to do this?"

When he woofed affirmation, she swung out of the car and quickly released the German Shepherd from the ride. Shadow took a moment to stretch and shake and then leaned his shoulder against her. "I'm okay, Shadow." She wasn't, and he knew it, but saying the words aloud helped her focus on making it true.

She glanced over her shoulder at the vehicle with the scorpion security logo on the door parked at the end of the drive. September raised one hand to acknowledge the driver, one of a half-dozen in rotation that Combs had hired to keep her safe. She didn't recognize this one, keeping her under careful surveillance. Her jaw clenched.

A deep breath, hold for a count of five, and a slow ten-count release. She repeated the calming breath exercise three more times then strode to the small building. An adjacent attached area with dog runs held an assortment of canine boarding clients. As expected, when one gave voice, the entire kennel joined in the bark-a-thon.

"Chill out, dogs. I already fed you. Kinsler, cut it out." Lia's commanding voice had the desired effect, and all but one, a stubborn Sheltie, fell silent. A petite woman with frizzy goldenrod hair appeared in the doorway and saw September. "What're you doing here? Don't you have, like, way too much to do today?" She exited the kennel, taking care to latch the gate, before crossing to meet September.

"Busy day and weekend for you, too. I won't take much of your time." She gave Lia a brief hug. Lia had agreed to go above-and-beyond to help on the special day. The young woman barely came up to September's chin, but what she lacked in stature, Lia made up in attitude.

The younger girl dimpled. "Happy to help. Kinsler's peeved I won't give him special privileges, but he's been flirting with the Sheltie."

Kinsler, a tan and white terrier mix, belonged to Combs's kids. With the hectic wedding week schedule, followed by their honeymoon, September and Combs agreed to board Kinsler with Lia while the two kids stayed with Uncle Stan and Aunt Ethel.

Lia waved at the nearest kennel, where a floppy-eared black and tan dog lounged. "Besides, it gives me a chance to put Magic through his paces. He's a natural, but I need all the training we can get." Lia planned to make law enforcement a career. Meanwhile, Lia boarded and trained dogs at Corazon Kennels. "Want some coffee? I made fresh this morning."

That would've been several hours ago since Lia rose before dawn. By now, the coffee would dissolve rust. September wrinkled her nose. "Thanks, but I grabbed a mug-o-brew on the way over." A giant-size caramel macchiato with a double shot. September wished she'd made it a triple. She'd need it to get through the day and tonight's wedding rehearsal, especially after the most recent upsetting text, which threatened to derail all her plans. Tomorrow night would serve up another boatload of challenges. "I came out to double-check with you on the security plans."

"Your fiancé hired everyone and vetted them. I assume you're still speaking to the bridegroom. I just go where he points. Remember, you had to arm-twist him to include me." Lia stuck out her lower lip. "I didn't want to wear a fancy bridesmaid outfit, anyway." Lia had no need of frills and gowns—she turned heads whatever she wore, up to and including poop-smeared trainers.

"You can wear whatever you want, okay? April didn't want to wear the dresses I chose either." September's older sister prided herself on fashion sensibility and had taken over costuming the event. Costuming—that's how September thought of it. "April had everything planned, and I was tired of arguing."

September had asked her three sisters to be in the wedding party, more to fulfill her late-mother's perfect wedding vision than anything else. She felt closest to April, and as matron of honor, April would sing at the ceremony. Combs's daughter Melinda rounded out the bridesmaids.

Combs had tapped his Uncle Stan as best man. His detective partner, Winston Gonzales, and Combs's young son, Willie, would stand up with him. "At least Melinda liked her dress, and Willie's excited to oversee the rings. My dad took him to be fitted for a kid-size tuxedo." For once, Combs's kids were causing less trouble than the grownups.

Lia leaned closer, half whispering for effect, although they were alone. "Seriously, ask Combs about the security. Kind of overkill, if you ask me, obsessing over security when all we've got are rumors. He's even got a team covering the restaurant tonight for the rehearsal dinner. Between your friend Teddy handling cyber security, and your fiancé running surveillance on your property, I don't know what else they could do. Not to mention you're up to speed on self-defense—"

September held up a hand to stop the words. After her last adventure, she'd finally admitted coincidence had nothing to do with the upheaval in her life. Someone meant to destroy her. Yes, calm prevailed the past few months, but every time she'd relaxed her guard, something—or someone—swooped in to wreak havoc. So, the security team ran routine sweeps of her property.

She hated it. Hated living in fear. Hated putting her family and friends through the disruption and fear. Even her Maine Coon cat, Macy, usually quite tolerant of strangers, hated the intrusion and stress. Neither did his heart condition any favors. She suspected the cat took to the new talking buttons because they offered him more control to communicate his needs.

Living in fear was no kind of life. She'd locked herself away once before, hiding from a stalker who nevertheless found her. September vowed never to let anyone drive her into hiding again, especially now that Shadow kept her PTSD demons at bay. She also had other considerations beyond herself. She couldn't—*wouldn't*—let her chosen family, people she loved beyond reason, risk life and limb because they cared about her.

So she agreed to the constant watchful eyes, and doubled-down on honing important survival skills with self-defense classes. Knowing how—and when—to use firearms, hand-to-hand techniques, even defensive training with bo staff martial arts, meant hours in class, although September prayed she'd never need to use them. It had paid off, though, and she felt more fit and confident in her skin than ever before.

September couldn't wait to start the next part of her life with Combs. He believed the security would work and keep the danger at bay. But Combs didn't know about the most recent threats—or if he had received them, he protected her the way she now protected him.

Besides, if she told him, he'd postpone their wedding. And if that happened, they might never get married. She shivered, despite the nearly triple digits. The North Texas wind felt like a furnace.

Shadow leaned against her thigh and September dropped one hand to his brow. Her other plucked the cell phone from her pocket. "We need to increase security, whatever it takes. I'll contact Teddy. It's probably a fake threat."

Teddy called himself the geriatric hacker. His grandfatherly looks belied the skills that had saved her bacon more than once. He'd trace the text, confirm it legit or not.

"Tell your team. But don't tell Combs. Please. We can get this handled." She turned the phone around for Lia to see the text.

>Cancel wedding or everyone dies.

Chapter 3 – KALI

Kaliko Wong looked around the old three-story monstrosity with distaste. At her direction, one of her subsidiaries had sought an estate appropriate for a company retreat. In reality, she needed a hideaway—private, easy to defend, near her target—and chose this property on several acres of prime lakefront real estate. Thank goodness she'd only need the house for a couple of days. Kali hated the old yellow Victorian on sight, especially the kitschy name: Cat's Cradle Bed-and-Breakfast. Once this little errand was finished, she'd burn the place, along with the furry vermin that still haunted the building.

The house was sheltered by stands of cedar-oak, mountain ash, and a few pecan trees that still bore nuts every season. The lake—the property's best feature—abutted the grassy yard, complete with a newly refurbished pier. Brushy expanse on each side of the property hid the nearest neighbors, who would mind their own business if they knew what was good for them.

The dirt lane off the main road wound through the trees. Kali had her driver remove the Cat's Cradle sign from the roadway, making the turnoff virtually invisible. Even if you knew where to drive, the vehicle required good traction to make it through the ruts that the latest downpour had created. Fortunately, her driver, always prepared for every eventuality, had chosen a four-wheel drive vehicle, complete with a minibar. If the house got unbearable, Kali had a backup.

The driver had served her for years. More than a chauffeur, he doubled as security with many special abilities. She valued his discretion above all, but still took pains to reveal only the bits and pieces of her plan necessary for him to assist her success. His high salary cemented his lack of curiosity. He knew what happened to curious cats…

And it just might become unbearable if she couldn't flush out the vermin. The former owner kept cats, and boarders got to choose bedrooms based on their feline preference. Kali snorted. *Insanity.* The walls sported photographs of a variety of felines, with their names and attributes to help guests make their choices. Nebulae, a silver-furred striped cat that loved star-gazing; Sunset, a leash-walking orange cat; and on and on. She'd wanted the house, complete with furniture, but not the animals!

As soon as Kali entered the building, her nose stuffed up. She'd known immediately and complained but was assured the vermin had been evicted. Later, she'd punish the people responsible. She could put up with the discomfort for the few hours necessary, to finish this vital job. Over the years, Kali had experienced far worse than cat allergies. A cat couldn't kill you. At the thought, Kali the assassin laughed, then laughed some more.

Nebulae perched on the roof of the porch, meowing outside the master bedroom windows. She'd always enjoyed the comings and goings of guests in the old house, welcomed each with a warm purr, and snuggled into comfy laps. Nebulae especially enjoyed scrambling up the circular metal stairs from the big bedroom to reach the study. A telescope sat in the tiny room, pointed out the windows, for viewing the lake and surrounding grounds. And as a proper feline, Nebulae claimed everything seen from those windows as her territory. Well, she shared some with her buddy, Sunset.

He pawed the glass on the other side of the bedroom window, equally stressed by their new status. Neither one understood why their owner had rounded up all the cats and loaded them into carriers, then taken them away. Sunset had pawed open the lever handle on the front door during the evacuation. Nebulae squeaked through and escaped, but Sunset got trapped inside.

Now, new people inside the house moved around, but they didn't act right. The woman yelled and Screamed, even threw things at Nebulae, so she'd hidden in the shadows outside the house. But she missed Sunset. They usually snuggled together in a sunny window perch and managed the house together.

With all the other cats gone, and separated by the window, Nebulae didn't know what to do. She meowed again, and cheek-rubbed against the glass. Sunset returned the action. And then froze.

Steps sounded on the stairs, and Nebulae could hear them even through the closed window. Sunset's orange fur stood out on his body, shouting louder than a hiss his concern about the approaching stranger.

Quick as a whisker-flick, Sunset raced away from the window. He leaped up high to reach wall-mounted cupboards, pawed one open, and disappeared inside. Nebulae knew that was where the cats' feather toys and the red dot lived.

The stranger appeared in the doorway of the master bedroom, glaring around with a face that spoke of anger and fierce determination. Nebulae had learned to read human expressions. She wanted to meow again…maybe the woman would change her mind and let Nebulae inside? She hadn't eaten in forever. Hunger overcame caution, and she cried, pawing the window, pleading to return to her home.

When the stranger turned at the sound, her face told Nebulae to hide. And she listened, diving off the roof, to the soft shrubbery below. She'd try again later.

Nebulae didn't worry about Sunset. The orange cat knew all the best hiding spots in the old house. They'd spent much time together, holed up in cubbyholes. Sunset liked to leap out at people to surprise them and make them laugh with delight.

But Nebulae didn't think this woman would laugh. She hoped her friend stayed hidden.

Chapter 4 – SHADOW

Shadow pressed harder against September's leg and nosed her hand when she stroked his cheek. He eyed Lia, and his brow wrinkled. The words the pair shared made little sense to him. He only knew that they increased September's unease.

She smelled of sweet coffee, shampoo, and stress. The last a signal for a good dog to go to work. It was Shadow's job to keep her calm and happy, and head off the scary stuff that haunted September's dreams—and sometimes her awake moments.

Not so much as in the before-times. But Shadow stayed alert anyway. Sometimes the scary spells sneaked up on them both, like an evil, elusive squirrel dashing through the trees. It made Shadow's tummy hurt when September felt bad.

Sometimes scary specters from the past panted after Shadow's dreams, too. They shouted at him, chased him, pointed loud guns that hurt a good dog's ears, and stole his person away. He shivered at the thought, grateful when September rescued him with her soothing touch, rousing him from his midnight paw-churning whimpers of terror.

Except…now she slept alongside Combs instead. Shadow slept on a comfy floor pouf nearby, but it wasn't the same as snuggling tight against her warm body. The big man didn't want Shadow close at night. But that's when September needed Shadow the most. And Shadow needed her.

They took care of each other.

"What the…" Lia grabbed the phone.

Shadow knew that word, phone, from playing the name-game so often. Sometimes September asked him to *bring phone* when she couldn't find it. It never hid for long from his nose.

"Gotta be a prank, September. One of your jealous fans, that's all."

Shadow tipped his head and reached out to sniff Lia's shoe. It smelled of an enticing mixture of dog pee, dirt, and crushed kibble. Also, of Magic. Shadow liked the younger dog. Maybe they'd get to play tug. He'd like that.

September stiffened. "Most of the whack-a-trolls stalk my website and social platforms. A text feels personal." She hesitated, fingering her coffee-colored hair back behind an ear. "Same person, but different number each time. I've got three texts in the past four days, each one worse than the one before. I deleted the others."

"You gotta tell Combs."

September shook her head. Her heartbeat sounded like Macy-cat thudding down the stairs during zoomies. "He already wrapped me in bubble wrap with all his security. I have to do this myself, need to stand on my own. Combs can't be with me 24/7, not like Shadow."

At his name, Shadow nudged her hand again, and relished September's tender strokes on his tattered ear, the one the gun had bitten. "Shadow, I'm fine. Really." He watched as she took big breaths, listened as the thrum of her pulse slowed, and heartbeat steadied. But he knew better.

She pulled his tug toy, the one with the ball attached, out of her pocket and he came to attention. He watched closely, and when September showed her fist he sat down so quickly he scooted forward in the grass. She always asked Shadow for a *sit* or a *down* before the tug game began. He wriggled, waiting for her to throw the toy.

People often said one thing with words but meant something else. Their bodies never lied, though, and couldn't hide from a dog able to read everything about them. Shadow wagged just a bit, to tell September he understood. But his vigilance never wavered. Not even for the temptation of tug, one of his all-time favorite games. Combine it with a game of *bring*, and the game trumped even treats. Maybe not bacon, though.

She twirled the ball-on-a-rope around her head, let it go to fly through the air, and then swooped her fist to rest on her chest in the signal to *bring*. With an explosion of joyous energy, Shadow raced after the toy. He picked it up from where it had bounced on the hard-packed, sparse grass, chomping hard and shaking it back and forth, killing the ball-and-rope dead. Once he'd completed the ritual, Shadow proudly galloped back to September, and pushed the toy into her waiting hand.

September grabbed it, and held tight while he growled, then pulled and shook his end of the rope. When she asked him to release the toy—fist open—he gladly did so, knowing that would prolong the game. He tuned out the words as the two women continued to talk.

Their life together turned upside down when Combs and his kids came to stay. Shadow missed having September all to himself. She threw the tug toy again, and Shadow relished the hot air in his face as he raced to continue their game.

Twice more he fetched the ball-and-rope and September indulged his tugging habit. Finally, she put it away, so he circled around and nose-poked her in a tender spot. She shrieked, but it was a joyous sound, pretending to be upset. He knew, and play-bowed, hoping for a repeat of the game.

Shadow loved making her laugh by cold-nosing September to wake her up. Shadow adored playing the games she'd taught—he especially liked the *seek* game to sniff out lost pets. She'd been so busy lately, they hadn't played *seek*, or *show me,* or *bring* games in forever.

Instead, Combs directed strangers he called the *security team* that came and went from their big house.

September laughed more now than ever before, even without playing fun games. She especially laughed with Combs. Combs made her happy.

Would Combs make her so happy September wouldn't need Shadow anymore?

He whined under his breath at the thought, quiet so no human could hear, then yawned deeply to calm himself. The joy of the moment passed. No matter what, he'd never leave September. Not even if Combs tried to keep them apart. He knew September loved him—they were part of each other.

The crowded house didn't keep all the bad stuff away, even with more laughs. Shadow knew the haunts from nightmares sometimes sneaked into the light of day. Only a good dog stood between his person and bad stuff.

Chapter 5 – SEPTEMBER

September slammed the car door so hard Shadow yelped in surprise.

"Sorry, baby dog." She turned in the seat, and smoothed his throat, half smiling when he slurped her cheek. "Lia drives me crazy sometimes."

She hadn't convinced Lia to keep the texts a secret from Combs. Not yet a police officer, but Lia already held the law enforcement mindset. September kicked herself, wishing she'd gone to Teddy first. At least Lia promised to keep quiet until after September got some concrete information from the hacker genius. "No need to stir up dust if Teddy ferrets out a delinquent playing games, right Shadow?"

He barked, slurped her cheek again, and settled in his accustomed pose in the back seat. His nose left smears on the bulletproof windows. Combs had maxed out his credit cards upgrading her SUV, effectively turning it into an armored vehicle. He'd wanted bodyguards to escort her everywhere. They'd compromised on a discreet escort car, and her self-defense classes.

September started the SUV, returned Lia's wave, and drove away from the kennel. She saw the young woman load up Magic in her own vehicle, and gritted her teeth when Lia followed closely behind, eager to do her part with securing the property for the wedding.

September passed the escort car, acknowledged the driver's nod but didn't wait for him. The whole security detail managed everything so well she'd taken them for granted until this week. Now the visible signs of her minders were getting on her last nerve. "Sometimes, I just want to run away from the world. Let's hope Teddy can talk me down."

Shadow thumped his tail.

Teddy ran his consulting business from an RV he called Nellie Nova, allowing him to travel whenever and wherever he liked. She and Combs had invited him to camp out at their Rabbit Run Road address whenever he was in Heartland. The renovated Victorian had ample room in the field across from the big circle drive, and they'd already cleared the field for the wedding parking. She should have known how Lia would react and walked across the field to talk to Teddy first.

She had many appointments today, starting with meeting Arnold Stonebridge at ten to approve the bouquet roses—which had to blend with the ones in the backyard, a wedding present from her brother Mark—and ending with meeting April for a spa day—nails, hair, makeup—where she'd pretend she enjoyed it. She stifled a laugh. Her other two sisters, who lived out of town, were staying at Dad's house. They'd insisted on hosting a bridal shower two days ago, where they'd all plotted and planned how to doll up September for the big day.

September preferred no makeup, jeans, and cheap tops she didn't mind throwing away. Working with dogs and cats meant clothes covered with fur, mud, and worse. "My fault, I let all three of 'em arm-twist me."

Shadow tipped his head to one side, as if asking a question. That always made her smile.

When they pulled into the field in front of the house, Shadow wagged, and whined with quiet trills deep in his throat. The RV sat in its usual corner. Teddy preferred working late into the night and might not welcome an early morning visitor, which was why September had visited Lia first. But better to irk him than risk telling Combs before she had the necessary answers to inevitable questions.

Combs was theoretically working a half-day, although she'd left him in the back yard with the security team. Then they just needed to vault over the next few hurdles, rehearsal and dinner tonight, the wedding and reception tomorrow, to win a week away by themselves. Free from demands, or threats, just time to enjoy each other.

"C'mon, Shadow, let's go." She swung out of the car, then told him: "Window." He grinned, and moved to paw the inside of the door, waited until the window scrolled down, then hopped out. "Good dog, Shadow!" She hit her button to close his window again before locking the car. He'd learned the trick on his own, and it had come in handy more than once, so she'd put the behavior on command. Her escort pulled into the lot and parked beside September's car.

Together, they crossed to Nellie Nova. September peered through the window, noting Meriwether dozing on the dashboard. The orange and white Maine Coon cat's fur matched Teddy's new seat covers. September rolled her eyes. The old man had sure caught the smitten-kitten bug. She knocked and waited, glancing around. The middle of her back itched as she imagined cross-hairs focusing there.

Meriwether roused, blinked, and yawned widely. He hopped off the dash onto the passenger seat and head-bumped the glass when September placed her palm against the window.

"Coming. I'm coming." Teddy shuffled into view, a light robe hastily shrugged on over sleeping garb. He looked briefly surprised, but unlocked and opened the door without a word.

"Sorry for coming so early, and I won't keep you long." She pulled out her cell phone. "It's probably nothing, but—"

"I know why you're here." He gestured for her to shut the door as he walked back to the computer area of his tiny home. The big cat nose-patted Shadow when the German Shepherd sniffed him.

"You do?" Her brow wrinkled as she followed him. He sat at the small table and opened one of the laptops, then held out his hand. She gave him her phone and watch as he plugged it into a USB port to connect with his computer.

"Combs asked me to monitor internet chatter for any overt threats or communication about you. Quiet on all fronts for the past few months. That changed two weeks ago."

"Threats?"

He shrugged. "They're supposedly *warnings*." He drew air quotes around the last word. "They're sent from different IPs. I blocked 'em. Didn't seem credible, so no reason to get everyone wound up." He held up a hand when she would have interjected. "I notified the security team, and bumped up personnel, extra protection, the whole bamboozle."

Her phone beeped, and Teddy's eyes narrowed. He tapped the keyboard. "Given this hacker's skills, I figured he'd get a message to you directly if I blocked him, especially for a legit threat. Am I right?"

September nodded. "Three so far. The first two I didn't save." She'd had more than her share of media attention, so had tried to keep wedding information private, to no avail. Everyone wanted to know about the dog trainer hero who cheated death and cheer her happily ever after storybook ending. Or gloat if it fell apart. A lump grew in her throat. "I got that one early this morning. Lia knows, but nobody else."

"Okay. We'll let Combs know…"

"He'll cancel everything, Teddy. Please, all our plans, we've waited so long…" Superstitious, perhaps, but September feared this was their one chance to find happiness together. "Canceling means the trolls win."

"Can't keep secrets that put you in danger. We've been down that road before, September."

"I know, but…" Shadow nudged her with his nose, reminding her to breathe. September rolled her shoulders and neck, trying to release the growing tension.

"If it's bogus, all's well. Everything moves ahead just the same. But if not, we need to make plans." Teddy tapped a few more keys, scowling. "This hacker's good as me. And that's saying something." Teddy shoved wire-rim glasses back up his nose. "I see you didn't answer the earlier texts, either, and they all came from different numbers, probably all spoofed."

"So, a genuine threat? Or scare tactics to make us change plans, make us more vulnerable?" The team Combs and Teddy had put together made allowances for every contingency in order to keep family and friends safe during the festivities. "Even if we could, no other last-minute venue has the benefit of our prep work."

With Mom gone, the church wedding Rose had wanted no longer made sense. They'd planned a private event in the back garden at the Victorian, where security was already in place.

Teddy wrinkled his brow and pulled on his nose in frustration. "I can't track the guy! He knows I'm sniffing, just like Shadow on the trail." At his words, the big dog cocked his head. Teddy unplugged the phone and handed it back. "So why don't you ask him?"

Her eyes widened. "You mean text back and…"

Teddy grinned. "We may not know if he lies or tells the truth, but we'll learn something." He waved a hand at his array of computers. "None of this has helped so far. So go ahead. Text him back. Ask."

She fingered the phone. Biting her lip, she typed quickly.

<Who are you? Why the threats?

September waited. Her breath quickened. "There's an answer!" She scooted around the table to sit beside Teddy so they could read together.

>No threats. Warnings. Don't want you dead.

Her skin prickled, like icy fingers scraped her back. She let Teddy take the phone and type.

<Warning about what? Why do you care?

>Tell Teddy I admire his work.

September gasped, and Teddy grimaced. Another text followed immediately.

>We share an enemy.

She grabbed back the phone, speaking through gritted teeth. "I'm tired of this game. He knows us, but we don't know him." If he knew the name and face of her phantom tormentor, then share the information! She texted again, nearly stabbing the phone with her fingers.

<WHO ARE YOU? Name the threat so I can prepare!!!

>Name doesn't matter. Let me help. Together = better odds.

September wanted to shout at the messenger. Odds? She knew better, she shouldn't feed the trolls, but…

<Show your cards or fold. Why bet on you?

She and Teddy stared at the phone, waiting for the response.

>Ask Steven.

Chapter 6 – SEPTEMBER

September rubbed her eyes before giving Teddy a goodbye hug. "Keep me posted, and I'll do the same. Do you know what he meant about asking Steven?" Her nephew would turn nine years old next week.

Teddy hugged her back, then quickly stepped away when Shadow pushed between them. September shrugged. The big shepherd did the same thing when Combs hugged her. "Settle, we're okay, Shadow." Dogs only hugged during aggressive displays, or mating, so human dancing and hugging often triggered concern. "What could Steven possibly know about this?"

"You could ask him." Teddy took off his glasses and polished them on the hem of his shirt. "Not that he'd tell you." His white brows beetled as he replaced the specs.

"Or that we'd understand." Steven rarely spoke, and then only in cryptic rhymes. He interacted more with his mother, April, than ever before but his communication remained limited. "He does spend lots of time on his tablet. You don't suppose…"

Teddy stood in the open doorway after September stepped out

of the RV. "Anything's possible. I could poke around, see if everything from Steven's side passes the sniff test. Probably better to concentrate on more plausible avenues, though. Not much time left between now and the wedding."

She rolled her eyes. "Even less until tonight's rehearsal dinner. Sure you can't break away?" She checked the time. "Oh dang, I need to run. I'm meeting Arnold about the flowers."

"Go. Run along. Thanks for the invite, but I need to nail down that yahoo's credibility, or lack thereof." He grinned. "I told Combs to consider my efforts as a wedding present. I figure the two of you already have enough household gadgets and suchlike."

September laughed. "C'mon, Shadow. Car ride, let's go."

He loped back to her car, front paws dancing in the grass until she fingered the key fob to rolled down the rear window. "Kennel up." She swung behind the wheel as he launched himself from a standing start to sail through the window to the comfy rear seat.

She drove quickly, efficiently, while carefully keeping check on her mirrors and surroundings. The escort car fell in line behind her. Her trainers had drummed into her the necessity of monitoring her surroundings, wherever she went, until it became automatic. The lessons included listening to her gut; sometimes threats masqueraded as normalcy. Intuition often detected that out-of-the-ordinary *something*, that niggling at the edges of consciousness. Now, with the latest text messages taunting her, September's nostrils flared, as if she could sniff out the threat as easily as Shadow tracked a missing kitten.

Shadow offered one sharp bark in commentary as they pulled onto the road. "Not going home, not yet." Arnold had worked tirelessly to bring her garden to life and didn't want to cannibalize the roses for the bouquets, so she'd provided a list of colors. She worried her request took advantage of Arnold's generosity, but he insisted on making it a part of the wedding present he and Mark had put together.

Shadow stood directly behind her and rested his chin on September's shoulder. She reached up a hand to caress his ears. "Love you too, baby dog." His tail thumped against the door.

Stonebridge Gardening Center buzzed with activity, but few customers shopped this early on a Friday morning. September parked at the far end of the lot, backing into the slot to give herself an easy, quick exit should the need arise.

September pocketed her keys and called Shadow to her side. Although not trained in protection, she felt calmer and more secure with the big dog by her side—and shepherds instinctively behaved protectively. She glanced back into the parking lot to locate her escort car, only a scream away.

September and Shadow pushed into the glass-encased showroom containing potted combinations of ornamentals. Shadow sneezed, making September wonder what intriguing smells tickled his nose that she couldn't detect. Beyond the small room, the outside acreage featured a half-dozen open-ended Quonset buildings, each sheltering a specific assortment of plants, from ground cover to vining bloomers, fruit trees, and everything in between. Arnold appeared from a building, waved, and hurried toward her while mopping the back of his neck with a kerchief.

"Sorry I'm late, Arnold," September said as she walked with him to a workbench at the rear of the office space. "Busy time. I'm running last-minute errands all day."

The big man smiled. "No worries. We're all set on the flower front once you approve my choices. I chose roses different from those in your garden. Figured they'd make a more traditional presentation, and a pleasant contrast, to the riot of color in the surroundings."

She'd asked him to design the garden with a rainbow of rose colors, sizes, and fragrances. The garden was not only a beautiful recreation of the old Victorian house's original blooms, but also honored Arnold's brother Aaron, who had launched their gardening business but recently died. And they'd timed the wedding for peak blooming.

"Also, I wanted to ask you about bees," September said. When Arnold lifted his eyebrows she added, "Not honeybees. Those are fine, and I love that roses feed them and the hummingbirds. Some kind of stinging wasp has built a nest in the ground. They nailed Kinsler one day, and I'm afraid they'll disrupt the wedding. Combs wanted to spray, but won't that hurt the good bugs?"

"Sounds like yellow jackets. Mean beasties, they'll go after you just for stomping near them." He pulled a flyer that described a host of beneficial garden insects from a nearby display. "They do eat some of the bad pests like aphids. But yes, take care you don't kill the butterflies and ladybugs when trying to eliminate them. Probably easiest to just avoid the nest area for now. They can sting multiple times. Perfumes and fruit draw them."

"Check. No perfume tomorrow." She'd better warn her sisters. April especially poured on the cologne.

September smiled when he brought out two bundles of gorgeous blooms. None had fully blossomed yet.

As if expecting her question, Arnold explained, "They're refrigerated. That way they don't open too soon, and stay nice and fresh for the wedding tomorrow evening."

She lifted a yellow rose that had delicate pink and red edges to each petal. The other rose, a deep crimson, looked like velvet. September held it to her nose, inhaling. "Lovely, these are perfect." The red roses mixed with the white baby's breath would make up her bridal bouquet, and contrast beautifully with the pale-yellow and pink gown April had helped her select. Her bridesmaids' dresses, a deep green, would set off the yellow-with-pink rose bouquets for the wedding party. "I can't believe you found a yellow and pink rose that matches my dress."

"The red one's called My Valentine. Appropriate, don't you think?" He grinned. "And the yellow-with-pink, that's called Masquerade."

September felt icy fingers trail up her spine. *Masquerade.* A beautiful flower, but the name conjured feelings of *déjà vu.*

She felt Shadow nudge her thigh, and September almost suggested changing flowers—but instead offered a tight smile. Too late for changes. And the flower was stunning.

"Thank you, Arnold. Masquerade…that's perfect. I'll drop them off at the florist on my way to pick up the dress."

Chapter 7 – JACK

Jack took in the riot of color blossoming on dozens of rose bushes. The sun's glare hurt the back of his neck, despite the slathering of sunscreen he'd applied. His long hair, gathered into a tight single braid, was tucked down the back of his shirt. He turned the security company gimme-cap around backward for better neck protection. The property was thick with security.

Dark glasses hid colored contact lenses that corrected vision and camouflaged his true eye color. Otherwise, Jack's severe light sensitivity hobbled his ability to function, although he did well enough even with his eyes closed. After years of practice, he'd prepared for any contingency. Jack welcomed the chance to test his body and his mind.

He'd created a resume, padding it with work experience that held up only because of his skills with computers. But his physical prowess and special training would ace any test. Combs, a big man, still only reached Jack's chin. Years of self-defense, weapons practice, and unnamable skills put Jackson Glass in a league beyond most of the members of even the elite ensemble filling the garden.

Jeff Combs stood on the patio talking to the head of security. Jack knew about Combs. He had a reputation as a straight shooter, a thinker who could close cases, though most of his rep arose from interactions with his bride. Combs thought his beloved had terrible luck and had only recently enlisted formal security measures.

The team had kept the property under surveillance for weeks. So far, they'd documented nothing out of the ordinary. But Jack knew their enemy had ways of getting things done. His own investigation revealed when, but not how, tomorrow's attack would come.

Four new members, including himself, joined the security team this week. Jack congratulated himself that the warnings he'd sent to September had opened the door for him to slip through. This meeting was a final run-through for the upcoming celebrations. Now he had a front-row seat to Kaliko Wong's end game.

He had to keep September safe, at least long enough to convince her to join him in de-fanging the witch. He intended to punish Kali personally.

"Over here! Found something." One of the team members, a frizzy-haired blonde girl with a sniffer dog, yelled from outside the rear fence perimeter of the garden. "Magic just alerted. We've got a bomb."

Chapter 8 – SHADOW

Their quick visit to pick up flowers ended with September's heart racing. Shadow often anticipated situations that caused her distress. Other times, the emotions ambushed them both. She got in the back seat of the car with him so he could climb into her lap, his warm weight anchoring her to the here-and-now to keep scary things at bay.

Once her hands stopped trembling, she pushed him off and got behind the wheel. Shadow wished September would lower the car windows, so he could drink the smells as they rode the wind. He pawed the door button, but it wouldn't work. Sometimes—he didn't know why—the button stuck and refused to move. Other times it scrolled open with the barest of paw-taps.

The car smelled strongly of the flowers in the front passenger seat. He sneezed, then sneezed again. Not unpleasant, but Shadow could sniff flowers at home anytime, just by visiting the back garden. Now, she carried them in the car, too? Sometimes people did strange things even good dogs didn't understand. They knew things dogs didn't, though, so she must have a good reason.

He enjoyed visiting Arnold. The man smelled of green things, of bacon, and dirt. Sometimes he shared the yummies with Shadow. At the thought, Shadow's mouth watered, and his tummy rumbled. Maybe September would stop at one of the drive through places that handed out treats for good dogs. He'd like that. A lot!

When September pulled the car up in front of a small shop, he thought he might get treats. But she gathered up the box of blooms. Shadow stood in the back seat, waiting for her to open the door or window. She no longer left him locked in the car. They traveled everywhere together, even if the trip was only five paw steps from the car and back. He liked that. A good dog's job meant staying with his person, to keep her safe.

"Quickly, Shadow. We're in a hurry." She thumbed the key fob, and he hopped out the open window before it scrolled all the way down. Shadow watched as the car that followed them everywhere pulled into a slot across the street. September waved at the driver, so Shadow knew everything was okay. He followed September across the sidewalk to the glass-fronted shop.

As she opened the door, bells jingled like the wind chimes at their house. More flower smells. Shadow sneezed again.

September strode to the front desk. "I'm here to drop off the wedding flowers."

"Name?" The brisk woman at the counter tapped on the computer keyboard and cocked an eyebrow.

"September Day. It's the Day-Combs wedding, tomorrow night. This includes the boutonnieres and other items ordered."

The woman made clickety-click sounds and nodded. "Right. Arnold called." She pulled the box closer and whistled. "He sure knows how to pick 'em." She tapped some more. "Sign here. They'll be ready tomorrow afternoon. I close at five."

"My sister April will pick them up." They started for the door,

September grinning at Shadow. "Told you, a quick trip. She'll make something for a good dog to wear, too." Her satisfaction made Shadow's tail wag. "Now down the street to get the dress."

He wagged, not understanding, or caring what the words meant. He knew lots of words. But not all of them. It was more important she sounded happy and included him in the conversation.

"Excuse me, one moment please? Could you clarify a detail for me? The bride's always right, but if it were me…" The woman raised her voice to call them back.

September turned, hand still on the half-open door. The cool air in the small shop spilled out into the warmth of the summer day. The June sun warmed Shadow's dark fur. "I wrote everything down. And so did Arnold."

Shrugging, the woman reached under the counter. "Delivered yesterday with instructions to add them to the Day-Combs flower arrangements. But the blue's all wrong for your color scheme, and too dainty to fit with the roses. The note said to ask you."

At September's gasp, Shadow's hackles rose, making his skin prickle.

"Forget-me-nots?!" She staggered and sank to the floor.

Chapter 9 – SEPTEMBER

September's arms hugged Shadow close, shivering as much from anger as terror. She ignored the shop owner's worried exclamation and waved off her offer to call 911.

"No, I'm fine, just a bit dizzy." Shadow licked her face, and she squeezed her eyes shut and let him, then pushed him away to stand.

"I agree with you. The blue flowers won't work. Throw 'em away." At the woman's stricken expression, September added, "Or use them for someone else." She licked her lips. "Who sent them?"

The florist looked at the card. "Says from you. Maybe one of the wedding guests wanted to surprise you with a gift?" Her scowl dug furrows in each side of her mouth, probably worried this gaff would cost her the job.

"Nope, not me." *Somebody playing an ugly joke.* But to say it out loud would make it real. September took a deep, steadying breath. "Do whatever you want with the blue flowers. Like I said, my sister will pick up everything tomorrow."

September held the door open for Shadow. *Somebody knew about the forget-me-nots.* Only a few people knew about them. Combs for one. And her sister April. Had news reports included a mention? Whoever sent them knew September considered the dainty blooms as a threat, a warning, or a promise to destroy her. That's what Victor had always meant by the flowers. He'd used *forget-me-nots* to remind September of her shameful past.

Victor Grant died in prison. Murdered. She'd been glad.

September's brisk walk turned into a jog to the end of the block. Shadow loped beside her, tongue lolling with excitement. It took everything she had not to race to her car and speed away. She'd overcome gas-lighting sadists before and refused to allow a bunch of wilted flowers and an anonymous text to dictate her plans. Teddy was on the job. Lia said Combs had beefed up security for the wedding. The guy lurking in the car across the street was there for her protection.

Her flushed face welcomed the cucumber-scented cool air of the formal wear boutique. September would have been satisfied with a private JP ceremony, wearing jeans—okay, maybe not jeans, but informal attire. She'd done the whole white dress and veil thing before. That part of her life, like a dream, she'd relegated to the "before." September wanted her future happy-ever-after to look and feel as different as possible.

When her sisters insisted on "helping" find the perfect dress, September agreed only if they followed her guidelines. Nothing revealing, something simple, and no dark hues. She wanted color. Pastels accented with bright splashes. Yellows with pinks or reds. A palette to match the blooming garden and her hopeful soul, promising a future filled with beauty, happiness. A color-filled new life.

"September! Right on time, my dear." An enormous man with wavy black hair, and a massive beard braided with beads, threaded his way between the displays of sparkling gowns. "Please, to the back, I've got your dress ready. I can't wait to see it on you!" He pursed his lips at sight of Shadow. "No touchy the fabric, doggy, there's a good puppy."

She stifled a laugh at Shadow's ear twitch expression. "He's a good puppy, for sure. No worries."

Sebastian knew that, but she understood his fussy concern for the beautiful clothing. As they wove their way through satin sheaths, silk brocade, sequins, and beaded bodices, she noticed some of the price tags and blanched. Her sisters had paid for her dress. Otherwise, September wouldn't have dared step inside the shop.

Sebastian had measured her months ago, consulted with her on fabric color and dress style, and he'd come to her house for a preliminary pattern fitting. However, he wanted the creation to surprise her—guaranteed to wow her and Combs.

"My sisters approved the dress?" They had to, before paying for the completed gown.

"Oh my, yes. And the attendant gowns, too, just you wait, they're so lovely. Understated of course, nothing to upstage the bride. Lovely sleeveless blue-green sheaths." He leaned forward to whisper, "Designed with some give-and-take in the fabric, if you know what I mean." He left his assistant in charge of the front and led September to the back fitting area. "By the way, not to be nosy or anything, but your sisters' names? Did your parents have a thing about the calendar?"

She shrugged. "Something like that." They'd been named for their birth months with the older twins, May and June, followed by April. It had been a burden during grade school, but she'd grown used to it.

"Voila!" He opened the double doors to the private area with a flourish, then stood back, hands pressed together, mouth open with anticipation.

September gasped. He'd placed her wedding dress on a mannequin in the center of the room. It was everything she'd hoped, and more. "Perfect, oh Sebastian, that's gorgeous!"

A fitted long-sleeved silk sheath glowed a pale yellow at the bodice, then deepened to a rosy hue at the hemline—very much like the Masquerade rose's petals chosen for the bridesmaids' bouquets. It featured an asymmetrical neckline, with the fitted bodice flaring at the hips to fall in gentle folds to the ground.

Layered over top of the sheath, a translucent, textured floor length organza spilled in billowing waves. Flared bell sleeves reached nearly to the floor. Down the front of the bodice and covering most of the sleeves, Sebastian had sprinkled a garden of pale pink to crimson floral appliques. It looked like a dozen roses had shed petals to confetti the gown.

"I love it!" She grinned and threw her arms around his massive frame.

His ears turned red, but he patted her back before pulling away. "Let's get you into this. It should fit like a glove, but we want to check things out before you dance down the aisle." He tipped his head to one side, gazing at her up and down. "The undergarments make a difference, though. You could be a model, but even the professionals wear the right foundations. I don't suppose you brought special undies?"

She wrinkled her nose. "Knew I forgot something. But it should be fine. I haven't gained weight since we measured." In fact, with all the training, she'd lost nearly eleven pounds. Her trainer said she'd gained muscle instead. "I'll take it anyway. I'll try it on at home. Promise."

Tsk-tsking and shaking his head, Sebastian called the assistant to help him cover the gown in a protective garment bag. "The shoes, don't forget your shoes, Cinderella." He motioned to a pair of matching yellow sandals—had his helper package them up—and insisted on carrying the whole works to September's car.

"The back seat?"

September shook her head. "That's a lot of dress. Not enough room for it and Shadow." She stroked his head. "No offense, baby dog, but you're not using my gown for a bed."

Sebastian shuddered. "I should think not! The back of the SUV then." He carefully situated the garment bag on top of myriad duffel bags of canine equipment, and a cat carrier she always kept as a just-in-case. "Now, hang that up immediately. I won't be responsible for snags or wrinkles should you fail to treat my work with the respect it deserves." He winked. "And have a marvelous wedding. You'll make a beautiful bride."

Chapter 10 – JACK

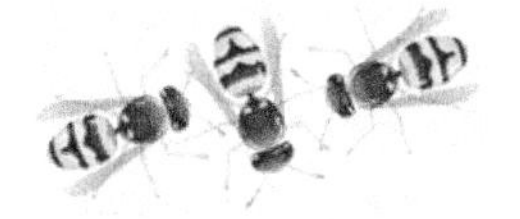

When his phone vibrated, Jack plucked it out of his pocket to read the text.

>Got dress. She didn't try it on.

Damn! After he'd dug out that little nugget about the blue flowers, Jack had bet they'd stop the coming train wreck. But she'd picked up the dress as planned. The backup could still work. September needed to postpone the wedding, at least long enough for him to make his pitch.

Detective Combs and the explosives expert, now outside the rear garden fence, had raced to rope off the area around the hidden bomb. The team leader barked orders, and all the members moved to predetermined positions. It surprised Jack they had someone with the expertise to defuse an IED. At least Combs had prepared for such an eventuality, and took the threats seriously—though he didn't know how far out of his depth he was.

Their mutual enemy had the expertise to plant a bomb, although she favored a sniper weapon. The witch rarely used subtlety. He'd known her to use knives, garrotes, and poisons. The witch liked blood and enjoyed punishing her enemies up close and personal. She must be losing patience.

This tangible threat worked in his favor. If September refused to heed the warning, her fiancé's professional caution could offer stronger persuasion. And as the groom, he could no-go the wedding as easily as the bride.

"What the hell, Lia?! What were you thinking?" Combs's anger, tinged with not a little relief, boomed through the air. The explosive's expert, scorpion tattoo on his bulging biceps, reappeared through the rose-rambled gate.

The blonde girl followed, with her dog in tow. She carried the IED, or what looked like one.

"I told September. And I told Teddy, too." Lia huffed. "Sorry you didn't get the word, Combs, but you told me last week to stop bothering you and run everything through Teddy."

Disgust painted his face. "At ease, everyone. Lia ran a training exercise with her dog." He cranked his neck, and everyone could hear the crackling sound.

Lia cradled the fake bomb in the crook of one arm while holding the leash of the massive black Rottweiler with the other. "I've run exercises with Magic every day, sometimes two or three times, through the search area. He'll get bored or frustrated, or just switch off without an occasional find. So I planted something. Before the big day tomorrow, I wanted him sharp." She spoke swiftly, with passion, and blinked hard but contained any tears.

Tough kid. Reminded Jack of Rina, before she got married. His lips tightened.

The rest of the team made noises of disapproval, but Jack stayed silent. If Combs had any inclination to postpone or cancel events, he hid it well. And Jack couldn't suggest it himself, without raising questions he didn't want to answer.

Combs blew out a breath. He looked wound up, more than wedding day stress. "I'll circle back with Teddy, Lia. You get ready for the rehearsal dinner tonight and put that mutt's nose to better use. The venue won't let us in until just before the dinner, so you're primary on clearing the place. Then the evening team handles the perimeter. Got it?"

She nodded, then looked at the dog with pointed but silent communication. Magic's panting mouth snapped closed, and his drop ears came forward, as if hearing a spoken command. As one, they whirled and padded back through the garden to the rear of the house and disappeared through the patio door. Moments later, Jack heard a truck engine roar to life.

Combs turned to address the group. "My apologies. She's a relative of my fiancée, great with dog stuff, but clueless with procedure. I count on you to act in your professional capacity." He pointed around the area. "Your company has provided excellent coverage for several months now. Some have been with us from the beginning and are posted where needed. The rest got called up this week for extra coverage."

Jack nodded when the man acknowledged him. He made note of the others, wondering how Combs vetted them, and planned his own look-see.

"Based on our assessment, the threat remains despite no overt escalation." Combs cracked his knuckles, a nervous tic to relieve stress. "We've got three teams on rotation: one team covers the house, another the grounds—they're working their assignments as we speak—y'all supplement the third team." He stared at the newbies. "You report directly to me, and provide eyes-on protection for September on site here, or whenever she leaves the house."

Nodding, Jack approved of the plan. He'd done his own

homework. September hadn't left the house more than once a week, and never at the same time. Her trainers came to the house. The gardener came here. Even the wedding gown designer consulted with her at the old Victorian home. The few times she left, when Detective Combs could break away from his job, he accompanied her.

But with the wedding imminent, she'd either gotten careless, or had had enough of her minders. So they'd increased the car surveillance. He knew today she was running all over Heartland completing wedding errands, with only one minder keeping watch. What would they do after the wedding? Lock up the house forever? Jack's teeth ached at the thought.

"The rehearsal and wedding are inside the house, and tomorrow the reception is here in the garden. We'll need all hands for those events. Coverage at the gate, vet anyone before they come inside, at the door to the house itself, also the surrounding fields, and especially the back garden. We've had the fields mowed an acre around to remove any cover for interlopers, but we still need to watch for the unexpected. Understood?"

Nods all around.

"Those not already on duty, familiarize yourself with the property. Reconvene on the patio after lunch."

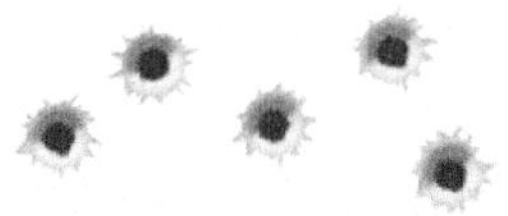

"Lia's on her way to the restaurant with her dog. That's more of a soft target. I'd like an all-call tonight, but the space won't allow for everyone. And I couldn't convince September to host a cookout on the patio." He rubbed his eyes, a groom's normal stress multiplied by the situation. "Fortunately, we only have a handful of folks attending the dinner."

"How many?" Jack had to ask. At least Combs understood they risked more than just the bride by putting on this party.

Combs closed his eyes a moment, as if counting. "Ten, maybe a dozen. Security will outnumber the wedding party."

Still too much risk. Teddy might know computers and understand how to intercept warnings, but he did not know how vindictive and determined—and invisibly—the witch worked her black magic. The last information Jack intercepted doubled-down on the need to eliminate September Day, but also added her immediate relatives to the hit list. Once married, Combs got a laser leveled at his head, and so did his kids. Jack still hadn't figured out the reason and needed more time.

Tonight, at the rehearsal, he'd talk September into joining his cause. Once he figured out the *why* behind the vendetta, he'd use that to persuade the bride to listen to reason.

And if that failed, Jack had one more trick up his sleeve. The bridal gown designer had a gambling problem. So, he paid off Sebastian's debt for a small prank, but the bride delayed the surprise by not trying on the dress. It could still work, last minute, but better a pissed off bride than a dead wedding party.

Combs checked his phone, shoulders hunched. "Lia's at the restaurant, and they won't let her in." He pushed hands through his hair. "They got a bomb threat."

Blowing out his breath, Combs texted while still talking. "That tears it. Restaurant closed for the duration. So, no rehearsal dinner." He smiled without humor. "Safer all around, keeping everything here where we can control access."

But could they? If Jack had multiple targets, he'd want them all in a single compact location, too. Combs might have just played into Kali's hands and didn't know it.

"Sir, have you informed the escort? With the extra threat, I'd recommend additional security and getting September…" At Combs's sharp look, he amended his words. "Perhaps it would be better if your fiancée return to this secure location earlier than planned."

"You're Glass, right?" Combs crossed to him. "Jackson Glass, retired special forces. Teddy Williams gave you high marks, said you came with the strongest recommendations. I sent a text to September's escort. Once they respond, I'll message September." He grinned. "She'll probably be relieved, but her sister won't enjoy having the spa time cut short."

Jack's neck relaxed. He had created a believable backstory and credentials if Teddy Williams didn't doubt them, at least not at first glance. It had to hold up long enough to get next to September. "Has the escort checked back?"

Combs glanced at the phone again, frowning. "Nothing yet." His brows lowered. "Wait, a call from Gonzales." He glanced at Jack before adding, "That's my partner." He stepped away to answer, listened a moment, and then put the phone on speaker. "I've got the team here, Gonzales. Give it to me again."

"A patrol just reported in, after response to a concerned citizen's call. They found a body, a John Doe, dumped in a culvert south of Heartland. No visible COD, stripped of all identification, including clothes."

Sounded like something from the witch's play-book. Random, or the killer wanted Heartland's finest focused elsewhere.

"Dead guy has a scorpion tattoo like the Scorpio Security logo. So, we sent a picture to the company, and positive ID just came back. Combs, the man worked on September's escort detail. Somebody's using his uniform and credentials to infiltrate the team."

Chapter 11 – SEPTEMBER

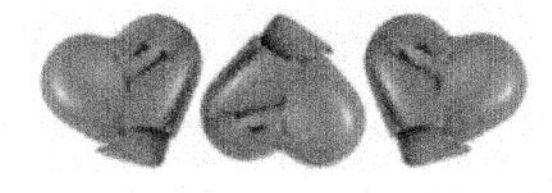

September wanted this day over. Having multiple women swarming around her was unnerving. The last time she'd had her hair cut and styled, Mom made the appointment and insisted on the makeover—to cover the spot where she'd nearly been scalped. Since then, her hair had grown back and fell well down her back. "You can trim the ends, but I like it long." So did Combs. She smiled at the thought.

"Sure you don't want some highlights? That'd make the white streak less noticeable," asked the stylist.

The girl doing her nails—deep rose to complement her dress—stroked her hand. "Relax! Don't pull away, it'll mess up the lacquer."

April giggled, sitting two chairs over with her own hair done up in pieces of foil. "You could get a temporary rinse. Scare Combs out of his sour expression for once."

September considered it. "He's not sour, just has lots on his mind." So did she. Maybe they should've paid for a his-and-her's Botox treatment. She dimpled at what Combs would say about the notion.

Shadow, relaxing on the floor beside her chair, rested his head on her bag beneath the manicure bench. She took the go-bag everywhere, just in case. September hated the thought of using the gun, but now felt naked without it nearby. Shadow sneezed, then whined. He wasn't used to all the chemical odors. Neither was she.

"I warned Doug. He doesn't like surprises." April batted her blue eyes. "But mixing things up can spice up the relationship." She wiggled eyebrows suggestively at September.

"Doug agreed?" She figured April's husband would prefer her "Barbie Doll" looks to something more in keeping with the thirty-something mom. September had never been a fan of her brother-in-law, but Doug had gained points by sticking with April during her health scares. "I always thought you were a natural blonde, at least when we were kids. How long does a color change take?" Her sister had already been at the salon a couple of hours by the time September arrived.

"No time limit on perfection." The stylist shrugged. "Ya have to strip out color first, then…well, it takes several steps, but another half hour should do it."

April fluttered her fingers to speed up the drying of her own nails. "Sure, as a kid I had blonde hair. But it got darker over the years, and I got help to keep it that way. For your wedding, I thought we should look more like sisters, you know? Since I'm your matron of honor." She blew a kiss. "I really am honored. And I hope you love the song."

Her sister had the voice of an angel. "You make every song sound wonderful." September picked up one long twist of her dark hair. "Temporary color, really? How temporary?"

April squealed and clapped her hands. "Do something funky. Add pink streaks to match your dress!"

September laughed. "On my wedding day? I'm not that brave any day of the week." She had plenty of notoriety without drawing attention to herself with trendy styles. "Maybe some highlights. Something subtle? And temporary!" She glanced in the mirror at the young man finishing up her trim. "What do you think?"

He grinned. "I can make that happen. Except for that white streak in your hair, that's natural. It would take color differently."

"I like my skunk stripe. Don't mess with that." September sat back and let him work his magic. Their mother, Rose, would have been in her element, directing each detail of September's wedding. April had risen to the challenge, though, and after the facial, eyebrow attention, and mani-pedi, September felt pampered and polished, prepared for the big day.

Her text buzzed, and she reached to answer. The girl grabbed her hand again, tsk-tsking that she not ruin the manicure. "Okay, I'll wait." September rolled her eyes, but still looked at the phone as another text came, followed by a flurry of three more. Teddy. Combs. Combs again.

April's phone erupted at nearly the same time. "What's going on?" She'd moved to another station and now reclined with her head in the sink.

The front door rattled but didn't open. The stylist and assistant had blocked off the entire afternoon, and, at September's request, locked the shop door. Through the glass, September saw their security escort bang again on the door to get their attention, pantomiming unlocking the entry.

The assistant squeezed oil on the nails of both of September's hands and pointed to the sink. "Wash there." She crossed to unlock the door.

April struggled to sit up. "What's going on?" The stylist soothed April to keep her wet hair over the sink. "Hey, watch the water spray, not in my eyes!"

September hurriedly washed her hands and dried the sparkling nails. She collected her phone to read the texts, the most recent first. It came from the anonymous source.

>Security breached.

She would have discounted the warning, but for the text from Combs echoing the warning. She glanced at the door again, where the assistant had inserted a key in the door, and her eyes widened. "Stop! Don't open." She dashed across the salon and grabbed the nail girl's arm, spinning her away from the entry.

The young woman gasped, and scrambled away, rubbing her bruised arm. September didn't bother apologizing. She stared at the slender figure through the glass, now pounding the door with one fist. The lithe woman wore the familiar Scorpio Security uniform, but September noticed long, brightly polished fingernails filed to sharp points.

September whirled, and wadded the damp towel in her hand before hurling it across the room to get the other cosmetologist's attention. "Call 911. April, we've got to go. Now!" She didn't know all the security personnel, but she was sure she would have remembered any of the team sporting claws.

The clawed woman shouted. "You're at risk. Need to move you to a secure location. Jeff sent me." The dark-haired woman tipped her head to one side with a half-smile. "Got his warning, didn't you?" She *tap-tap-tapped* on the glass with her nails, then reached toward her belt.

If September had had any doubts, the woman's words quelled them. Nobody called Combs by his first name.

Shadow roared, placing himself between September and the threatening figure. "Good dog, Shadow! Come-a-pup, with me, baby dog!" He spun, still snarling, and raced back to her side.

April struggled to sit up, wet from her processed hair running down her face. "What the hell, September? Your bodyguard's going to spoil your spa day." April wrapped the towel around her head. "Everything ruined!"

"Never mind that. Just get the hell out of here." September's training kicked in. She'd parked out front, but the text from Combs said he sent help. They just had to get out of this trap. She shouted at the stylist who hovered over her sister, wringing his hands. "You have another way out?"

He nodded, pointed, and stumbled to the back, leaving April to struggle out of the styling chair on her own. The junior assistant scrambled in his wake.

A muted shot shattered the glass door. A clawed hand reached through the breach and turned the key to open the door.

April screamed. "September, they're shooting!"

"Get out of here, April!" She shrugged the go-bag over one shoulder but had no time to reach her gun inside. If she was to die wearing sparkly nails, yoga pants, and wet hair, she'd go out fighting. *I am so freakin' sick of victimhood!*

September grabbed the bottle of nail dip powder in one hand and a squirt bottle of solution in the other. As the fake security guard climbed through the shattered glass door, September squeeze-sprayed and flung the contents of both at the woman's face, then whirled and raced to the rear of the building.

Screams of pain and frustration sounded behind them but that distraction wouldn't delay a professional for long. The employees had already run out into the alley behind the salon. As September and Shadow raced out the back door, she saw the stylist and his assistant turn the corner, running as fast as they could, brightly colored smocks flapping as they raced away. April shivered, hugging herself, and leaned against the wall right outside the door.

"Let's go, April. We can't stay here." September grabbed her sister's arm and urged her down the narrow alley.

"Why does everyone hate you, September? Why won't they leave you alone?" April's teeth chattered. The dark dye from the interrupted processing streaked her cheeks and neck with black Gothic tears that matched their mood. "I thought the bodyguard was supposed to protect you, not break through a freaking glass door to come after us."

She had no answers. "She could still come after us. Keep moving. Combs sent help." But until the promised rescue appeared, they'd circle around the block to reach her armored car.

April struggled to keep up, stumbling in the stylish high heels that boosted her height to nearly even with September. They linked arms around each other's waists and quickly reached the end of the alley. September pulled up short. She carefully peered out to check for danger.

Shadow panted beside them. When he looked back with a low growl, September knew they'd run out of time. Without further pause, she yanked April around the corner with her. Dust and shattered brick pinged against the building, evidence of silenced gunshots, and her sister squealed. They ran down the main street, feet pounding the brick sidewalk.

As they ran, September fumbled for her keys. More pings and brick shards spat on their heels. They ignored the red light and raced across the street, but September could see an empty parking place where she'd left the car. "Where'd you park, April? My car's gone."

"The other direction." She gasped for breath. "Where's Combs? I'd love to see his sour mug about now."

Sirens wailed and several police cars sped down the street. September raised a hand to flag one down. She stopped with surprise when her own tricked-out SUV pulled up in front of them, Combs in the driver's seat as if April's words conjured him.

"Get in." Combs craned his neck, scanning the surroundings as she climbed into the passenger seat. April and Shadow piled into the rear.

"How'd you get here so fast?" September ducked down in the seat, peering out the window and expecting to see the slim woman open fire at any minute.

"I hope they catch her and throw the book at that woman." April huffed, still dabbing her face and wet hair. "She shot at me! At us. Lord knows what I'll look like for the wedding. Oh, my hair…and nails ruined!"

Combs didn't look at her. "Bomb threat at the restaurant, so they canceled the dinner. We found your security detail dead. And now this attack." Tires squealed as they sped out of town, racing back to the secure fortress of a house on Rabbit Run Road. "Enough is enough, September. We cancel the wedding."

Chapter 12 – KALI

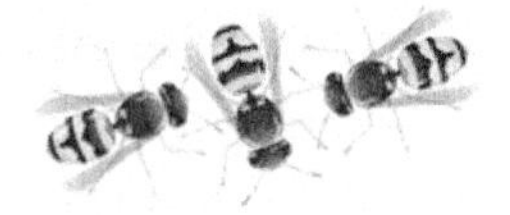

Kaliko Wong rubbed one slim arm across red, weepy eyes. Her bleary vision focused long enough to make out the SUV speeding away with her quarry. Sirens wailed, and she darted back down the alleyway. She needed to ditch the stolen uniform before the local yokels caught a clue.

She'd sent several agents after September Day over the past months. An adversary hardly worth her attention, she'd thought, and easily squashed by the skilled crew at Kali's beck and call. Yet repeatedly, despite a truly gasp-worthy lack of training, September escaped death.

Time for Kali to take care of the gad-fly herself.

Reaching a dumpster, Kali stripped off the uniform shirt, and shucked out of the slacks, stuffing both into the trash. Underneath she wore dayglo form-fitting biker shorts and a tank top. Once mounted on the bicycle she'd stashed nearby, with helmet hiding long black hair, she stood out as a dedicated cyclist, not an assassin on the hunt—with a gun nested in a fanny pack.

She'd known of September Day for a while, but only recently

learned that the woman was a nemesis she'd thought long dead. Kali's business associates suspected the truth, and they'd bury her should the facts come out.

Kali wanted no more excuses for failure. Back in the day, her skill as a creative assassin won her acclaim in all the right circles. That's how she'd met her husband. And how she'd inherited his empire on his untimely death. She smiled, dabbing again at her streaming eyes.

By monitoring her target, Kali knew about the recent upgrade to a security service. The woman's escort died before he hit the ground. They wouldn't find the injection site easily, either. His dispatch whetted her appetite—Kali had long starved for the up-close wet work she adored. She wanted to savor September's death, and see the woman's green eyes dim as she breathed her last. But she couldn't resist a bit of cat-and-mouse play at the door to the salon. What simpleton indulged in a spa day with death threats all around?

Yet, once again, September had slipped through her claws. She'd read the reports of how this creature, this nothing of a person, had bested some of the most highly skilled operatives in her employ, all without formal training. But clearly, the recent defense classes upped her skills. *Should have shot her immediately.* The next opportunity, Kali wouldn't grant herself the luxury of up-close satisfaction.

She couldn't wait to leave this sauna-hot, bug-infested Texas village and return to the luxury of her penthouse accommodations. It had taken her decades to climb the ladder, grab the power she deserved by the neck, and make things happen. Kali refused to consider anything less than winning this contest.

To lose meant death, and she had no intention of failing. Dead was dead, no matter how it happened.

Chapter 13 – SEPTEMBER

September squeezed her eyes shut, trying to hold back the emotional aftermath of the escape, bracing herself as Combs zigged and zagged through the narrow Heartland streets on the way home. Shadow yelped when they hit a pothole that slung him against the door. September turned as far as the seat belt allowed to both comfort the dog and herself.

April, however, was having none of Combs's plan. "You can't cancel the wedding. I mean, you can, but it won't keep those people away. Will it?" She directed the pointed question at September. "Our sisters' families took time off work and traveled for the occasion." She leaned forward to put a hand on September's shoulder. "So sorry, sweetie. Seems like you two will never have any peace until law enforcement tracks this creature down." The pointed jab landed where intended.

"Don't you think we tried?" Combs growled, shoulders hunched and white knuckles gripping the wheel. "As much as we'd like, Gonzales and I can't co-opt the entire Heartland Police Department. Teddy brought in the best team he could find. We have no motive, no suspects. Hell, when your mother died, she took a lot of answers with her. And Tee's not doing much better with Chris's notes. We're running blind."

September flinched at the mention of Rose's murder. Her death remained fresh, but also was the reason April survived, thanks to Mom's kidney donation.

"Hey, chill everyone. I'm sorry. It's my fault, thinking I could have a normal wedding." September stared at Combs, trying to hide her disappointment. After all, a man paid to protect her had died. "You're right. I've been selfish. We're putting everyone at risk. The kids, our friends and family…"

Combs grabbed September's hand, and squeezed, relief clear in his voice. "I want to get married. I do, you know that. But with a target on your back, I want to keep you safe more than I want to get married. We can reschedule when things calm down."

"Reschedule *when*? Don't you see? Things won't *ever* calm down! Not until this creature gives up, gets caught, or…I don't know!" September pulled her hand out of his grip and crossed her arms hard across her chest. Her go-bag at her feet—filled with survival and defensive tools—offered a stark reminder of what the future held. She wanted to pound the dashboard. "I just want to get married to my best friend, is that too much to ask?" She took a big breath, trying to figure out how to salvage the impossible. "We don't need a fancy dinner tonight. Everyone will be at the house for the rehearsal anyway. We can order pizza or something."

"Get married tonight instead of tomorrow." April leaned forward in the seat, delighted laughter tinkling. "It's brilliant! Then take off on your honeymoon before the baddies know you're gone." She tapped Combs's shoulder. "Stop by my apartment so I can grab my gown."

Hope swelled. "I already have my dress." September hooked a

thumb toward the rear of the car. Shadow barked at her tone, and she added, "Yes, we've got the flower pup, too." She hadn't wanted to handle the potentially hurt feelings of choosing one niece over another for the honor so took the coward's way out. "Even if the official bouquets aren't ready, we have plenty of extra roses."

Combs blew out his breath. "We're not risking a stop anywhere, April." He scowled, his sour expression so common it had etched deep worry lines between his eyebrows. "Only the wedding party, not all the guests, planned to attend the rehearsal."

"We have a few hours to call everyone. Our sisters are already at Dad's house." April laughed again, clapping her hands. "September, it'll be fun. Everything's already set. We'll thwart that ghost stalker and have a blow-out of a wedding, anyway." She blew a raspberry at Combs. "I'll just ask Doug to bring my dress over when he drops off Steven on the way to the airport. He can't come anyway, has a business meeting all weekend."

Combs shook his head. "Gonzales and I have a death to investigate. And we need to assign you a bodyguard, not just an escort." He alternated staring out the windows and checking the mirror.

"But you're off duty until the end of next week." September raised her voice. "If Winston and his wife can't come, I'm sorry. But this could be our only chance to get married." She softened her words. "Don't let outsiders ruin this for us. At the house, we can keep everyone safe." She hesitated. "If we need to postpone the honeymoon, we can talk about it. Please? For us."

His jaw tightened, but he nodded stiffly. "Okay. Since you asked so nice."

Already on her phone messaging people, April's fingers flew. She squealed with delight. "Guess what? The caterer can bring everything, too. We can have the reception in the garden just like you planned." She beamed.

September sat back in the seat. If she hadn't pushed, Combs would have given in to the simple choice and locked them both away for safety's sake. She'd already postponed happiness for too many years.

Tonight, all her dreams would come true.

Chapter 14 – JACK

Jack's fingers flew, tapping in detailed instructions to the remote team intent on ferreting out the witch's motive. The unlikely crew, scattered over dozens of states, all had their own reasons for joining his cause. The goal—destroy Kaliko Wong's empire—drew closer with each genius insight.

For him alone, another imperative rose above all else: Neutralize the witch, not just her crime syndicate. Jack had no illusions about what that would entail. He'd lived a gray life for so many years that going out in a blaze of color appealed to him, even if bloody crimson was the primary hue.

He had only a few hours left to prevent the house on Rabbit Run Road from becoming ground zero. Jack didn't know what form Kali's attack would take, so pressed his team to narrow the options. Short of a space-alien force-field, Kaliko Wong would always assert her will.

Before Combs had raced to rescue his bride, he'd told the security teams to increase surveillance of the house and surrounding property. When Lia returned from the restaurant with her bomb dog, she'd swept the inside of the house and the outside. Again.

But Jack worried it wouldn't be enough.

The first of Jack's extensive network checked in with a chilling observation.

>No eyes on target. MIA past week. Nobody talking. Either scared silent or no need-to-know.

Damn.

The witch had left her nest in New York City for the first time in ages. That was telling. With plenty of agents to assign to dirty work, Kali lived an opulent and very public lifestyle. She conducted worldwide business with impunity and deniability, behind a screen of legitimacy, from the glittering high rises of the city.

To breach that facade, Jack had recruited a team member to work from the inside. The young woman, an assassin trained by Kali herself, owed the organization a debt. She wanted out, and Jack's plan promised freedom.

Takes one to kill one…

Many had personal reasons for switching sides. Those who agreed to do the witch's bidding got paid very well for the lifetime contract—until Kali no longer needed them. At least three who had been assigned to kill September met violent ends when they failed. Kali, like her namesake, the goddess of doom and destruction, wreaked bloody vengeance.

What had the bride done to piss her off? Knowing the answer would give Jack ammunition to enlist September, and maybe Combs, to his cause. But so far, the motive remained hidden. His best team members continued to cogitate on the problem.

Quickly, he messaged the private message board reserved for the *twice exceptional* team members. He logged in, using his Kid Kewl identity, a persona that used rhymes to engage and disarm the innocents who frequented this virtual playground. None of them knew his real name. That kept them safe and protected Jack as well. They could locate the witch. Once found, he'd put his recruited assassin back on Kali's tail.

He typed the first message, alerting any on the message board he needed help.

<We're still lacking. Need phone tracking.

It took less than a minute.

>WW has lots of burner phones. But she got sloppy. :P One pinged north of Dallas.

Jack scowled. Some of them used WW, or wicked witch, to identify Kali, either for fun or because they understood the danger of naming an adversary. If her phone pinged north of Dallas, that meant Kali came here to direct the operation herself.

Must have tired of her minion's many failures. He cocked his head, thinking. In New York, an army beholden and fearful of Kaliko Wong kept her untouchable. Leaving her viper nest made her vulnerable. He couldn't waste this opportunity to find and eliminate her. He replied, the rhymes coming easily from practice.

<Clickety-click, find her quick.

While the phone nerd narrowed the search, Jack messaged his assassin and booked her on a flight into DFW. With a little luck, she'd arrive in five hours. At the wedding tomorrow, with his assassin in place, he'd have a real shot at taking out Kali—pun intended—hopefully without collateral damage and without needing to enlist September's reluctant help.

Next, he direct messaged another member of the bulletin board. "Follow the money," he muttered. If he couldn't physically neutralize her, he'd cripple the Wong empire financially. He thought Tracy had just the skills for the assignment. The girl had been tracking the organization's accounts for some time, just waiting for Jack's instructions on how to use the information.

<Tracy, Tracy, working steady? Numbers ready?

Almost immediately came the first reply.

>Number juggling. Very fun! Soon.

He smiled. The witch could afford to hire the best minds to shelter income, hide finances, and funneled much of the organization's income into untouchable accounts. He'd learned that the State Department worked tirelessly to untangle the rat's nest of income streams, yet nothing stuck to Wong. But they didn't have twice exceptional savants on their team. If anyone could ferret out useful financial information, Tracy could.

The message board pinged again, this time without prompting. All the message board members had special talents, made even more extraordinary because of their youth. This note came from one of the youngest, the most talented of Jack's crew—as brilliant with computers and data as Jack himself.

>Found a mess about a test. Wich scares the airs.

Jack wrinkled his brow. The boy's posts always mimicked the Kid Kewl rhyming syntax. Jack considered it either a hero-worship affectation, or perhaps echolalia. Some neurodivergent people used unique coping mechanisms. That made communication difficult. He typed quickly.

<Please clarify. Tests for bad guy?

He had asked the boy to find any odd activity in Wong's inner workings, especially on or around six months ago. That coincided with the attack on September in South Bend.

>Wich just cares about airs. Now gotta go. Dad sed so.

He blew out his breath and rubbed smooth the furrows in his forehead. The boy couldn't spell worth beans, and half the time left Jack wondering what he really meant. Before he could compose another rhyming query, Combs sent an alert to the entire Combs security team.

>Everyone ok, but some woman shot up the spa. Wedding moved to tonight.

Son-of-a…

Jack quickly updated the assassin, hoping her plane had no delays, and to jump on an earlier flight if possible. He'd deal with deciphering the message board notes later. With the wedding moved up by twenty-four hours, they had less than five hours to prepare.

Chapter 15 – SHADOW

Shadow followed closely behind September as she paced back and forth in the music room: piano to the desk, and back again. The big stringed instrument called Harmony stood up in its velvet box next to the piano. He knew their names because September taught him with the name-game. Shadow knew lots of words. He was smart that way.

He hated guns. Sometimes his ear tip stung almost as if the bullet's bite had returned. That woman in the shop in town shot at September, and at Shadow too. It was a good dog's job to protect September from guns, and the bad people that shot them.

September pulled out the rolling chair, sat down in front of the desk, and swiveled back and forth before standing up again. He padded after her as she talked on the phone with different people, one after another. Shadow heard their surprise when she told them her message—always the same terse message—and he recognized some voices.

The other dog's scent lingered. He didn't like Magic sniffing around his house. Even though he knew the police dog and enjoyed playing with the youngster at Lia's kennel, he didn't like Magic intruding, especially when Shadow wasn't there. Magic had left paw-scent *everywhere* in the big house, even on Shadow's bed. How rude.

He whined, more as a worried comment to himself than for attention. But at the sound, September stopped talking into the phone and slipped it into her pocket.

"Oh, baby dog, I know you're upset. Me too." She knelt on the hardwood floor and opened her arms.

Not needing a second invitation, Shadow pushed into her embrace, breathing in the perfume of September's signature scent. Her hands combed the fur on his neck and back, and he squeezed his eyes shut with delight, snuggling hard against her neck, tail lashing the air. Shadow hated when dog friends tried to hug him, even in play, but he relished September's touch. This was home. He pushed his face hard into her bare shoulder, poking his muzzle beneath her armpit where she smelled the strongest. Bliss!

She giggled and pushed him away. "That tickles, Shadow. You have an icy nose, even with ninety-degree temps outside."

She stood when April hurried into the room, her shoes click-clacking on the hardwood floor.

"The caterer has a cancellation, so they bumped us ahead in the schedule. They'll deliver in an hour." April wrinkled her nose. "Combs wants nobody else here—agreed—but that means it'll be a self-serve buffet." April teetered on her tall shoes. "Doug will bring Steven early, too."

Shadow's ears flicked at his boy's name. In the before-times, Shadow took care of Steven. But now he helped September. They belonged together.

"I canceled the string quartet." April sighed with disappointment. "Don't worry, I'll still take care of their payment.

We can leave their mini-stage in place, and I'll stand there for my solo. Doug will bring my speaker and connect to Bluetooth for the online MP3." She sat on the edge of the desk and removed first one shoe then the other to massage each foot.

Shadow wondered why she wore the funny shoes. Not like September's simple flat sandals. At the thought, he nose-touched her bare toes, now covered with some odd color on the nails. He wagged when she absently stroked his brow.

April made a funny noise with her mouth. "Some food isn't ready, so they'll swap out as needed. I said yes when they asked about adding banana cream pie, yum!"

"Remember to avoid that back corner of the garden. Yellow jackets like food, and we don't want the guests getting stung." September hugged April, and Shadow whined at the action. He didn't like it when people hugged, but he guessed it was okay if September wanted to. "I'm just grateful we got anything. Most of the guests said they could still attend. Don't know what I'd do without you! Thanks for saving my wedding."

Grinning, April hugged her back. "You know how I love a theatrical production. We've got to pull out all the stops on your big day." Her phone made a noise, and she glanced at it and nodded. "Since Combs won't let us leave the house, Mark agreed to run over to pick up the wedding bouquets between meetings at his glass shop. I told him she closes at 5:00 and he said no problem, but he may skid in on two wheels." She laughed. "I think our brother's finishing up your wedding present."

September smiled softly. "He already gave us the present. I thought you knew. Mark partnered with Arnold Stonebridge on the garden redesign. So it's perfect that Mark delivers the wedding bouquets."

Chapter 16 – JACK

Jack kept watch inside the front door, glad that the team leader had noticed his pale skin and assigned him indoors, as September rushed about from room to room, cell phone attached to one ear, and the woman's sister flitted about with manic energy. He'd felt relieved when he overheard that not all the guests could attend tonight's event. The fewer that came, the better they could protect everyone.

He knew Combs would have nothing to do with targeting anyone, even a killer, and would fire his butt should he smell even a hint of what Jack had in mind. Without direct law enforcement affiliation, September offered the more persuadable option. His text warnings had primed her. But each time he tried to talk to September, she got called away. With only minutes here and there to persuade her, he couldn't move the needle. If only he could offer her a concrete motive, he knew she'd consider his plan.

But Jack knew her type—his sister had had the same weakness.

September might discount her own danger. Hell, she'd dodged

death more times than a cat with nine lives. But she wouldn't risk others. Tap into her desire to protect family, and she'd buy in to his plan, with or without the motive. Together, they could defeat the witch once and for all. *Then* she could get married and have a normal life.

But if she insisted on getting married tonight—well, he'd try again and might still recruit her. If she lived.

His com-unit buzzed, and he acknowledged the guard stationed at the front gate. "Got a kid here with his dad. Douglas Childress says he's got a delivery for his wife April and is dropping off the kid to his mother. ID legit. Confirm?"

He checked the list out of habit but didn't have to. Jack knew all about the family. "Let them in." Jack strode to the foot of the winding staircase. "Ma'am? Mr. Childress and Steven are here."

"Coming." April danced down the steps, calling back up to September. "Doug's here with my stuff. I'll bring up my dress, but where do you want the speaker for the music? It's kind of big."

"Patio if it needs an outlet. Otherwise, on the mini-stage where you sing. Use the golf cart if you want." September remained out of sight, doing whatever brides do before their wedding.

April dimpled at Jack. "There are wasps outside, so we switched the reception and ceremony. Food inside, and wedding in the garden. The bride enters on the stairs and proceeds out the patio doors. What do you think?" She waved a hand at the ribbon-festooned railing and banisters.

"Nice." *Dammit.* He wondered if Combs approved the change. Jack preferred keeping everything inside the solid brick walls. Jack retreated to the door. He thumbed his com-unit. "Please screen the electronics Mr. Childress is bringing in. Use the golf cart for transport."

"Copy."

April's mouth pursed. "You won't have to take it apart, will you?" Her hand patted dark hair, finally dry, although she'd complained off and on about it, loudly, to September over the last hour. "I'm not a fan of a cappella singing. Bad enough I had to cancel the musicians."

"Doing my job, ma'am." He crossed his arms, kept his expression neutral, standing silent and solid in front of the door.

When the doorbell rang, he peered out the stained-glass sidelights before stepping aside to let April open the door. "Thanks, honey." She took the garment bag from Childress and lifted disapproving eyebrows at the zipper, which gaped open.

"Guy at the gate had to look. Check it for stains. He hadn't washed his hands in a while." Childress urged a slight blond boy before him into the house. "This whole thing's more trouble than it's worth. Why can't they just go on living together?"

"In or out? Sir." Jack waited. The wide-open door offered a clear shot into the house, to view the interior—or worse, should someone be so inclined.

Childress offered a curt nod. "Out. I can't attend the wedding. Sorry again, April." He leaned in and gave her a quick peck on the cheek. "They're still checking out your speaker, said they'd bring it in after." He looked down at Steven, started to stroke the boy's head, but stopped himself. "You take care of your mom, okay?"

Steven didn't look up from his tablet or acknowledge his father's words.

"Oh, he'll be good. Steven's always a good boy, and we look out for each other. Right, Steven?"

This time, the child nodded once. Up-down, a quick jerk.

Childress grimaced, turned, and left.

April saw Jack's expression. "Steven likes things said a certain way. His dad doesn't always remember. Right, Steven?"

Again, the up-down nod.

"Let's go upstairs. You can watch everybody from the window. Right, Steven?"

This time, a sharp head shake, side-to-side, precisely three times.

A bit of exasperation filtered through April's lilting voice. "You can play with your tablet in the guest room while your aunt and I get ready for the wedding. The other kids won't get here for a while."

No response.

"What d'ya say? Let him stay." Jack spoke quickly, deliberately sing-songing the rhyme.

She glanced at him, wrinkling her brow. "But…"

"I don't mind, leave him behind." Jack kept his expression bland but noted Steven's quick flitting glance. "I believe in Mister Steve."

April laughed, the sound uneasy. "If you're sure he won't be in the way. He doesn't like crowds, or loud noises, or breaks in routine, or…" She leaned down to her son. "Over there, choose a seat at the table. A great place to look at your tablet, and monitor things here with Mr. …?" She glanced up.

Jack offered a slight smile. "Great place for cool kids to hang out." He added softly, "Steven can call me Kid Kewl."

Steven looked up, made brief eye contact, eyes wide, and trotted to find a perch at the table.

Jack wasn't surprised when moments later his phone buzzed.

>Really Kid Kewl, or April fool?

Jack gave a single nod, sharp up and down, without looking up.

Chapter 17 – SEPTEMBER

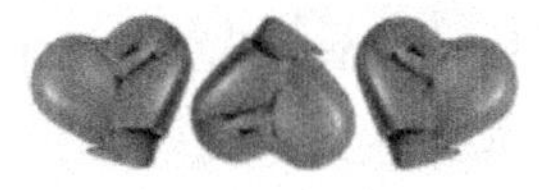

"Can anything else go wrong?" September let the wedding dress drop to the ground in a colorful jumble of fabric. The yellow-to-rose silk sheath didn't fit. Yes, she'd lost weight, but it seemed that the added muscle had increased the size of her thighs and biceps, and the silk had no give. "Blue jeans after all." She dropped on the bed and lowered her head into her hands. Shadow stuck his nose between them to lick her face.

"No, absolutely not." April picked up the under-dress and draped it over a nearby chair. "You will not get married in jeans. Besides,"—she fingered the organza overdress—"betcha this will fit just fine." Still on the hanger, the fragile appliqued fabric added a garden of color to the room.

Absently stroking Shadow's face, September pressed her forehead into his neck. "So much trouble for a brief ceremony. Did I tell you that Jack Glass, the new security man, pressed me to cancel altogether?" She bit her lip. "Maybe we should."

"Don't even say that." April grabbed the wine glass from the dresser and pressed it into her hand. She sat beside her on the bed.

"You're getting married in fifteen minutes! To the love of your life, right? Dad's waiting outside the door to escort you down the stairs, where the bridesmaids are ready to begin the procession. Besides, Combs, with all his security friends, made sure everything's safe. You've had stalkers before and faced them down."

September shuddered, and Shadow pressed closer. "But this time, they also threaten my whole family." Especially Combs, maybe because he represented the police? Jack didn't explain when he revealed that little nugget. She looked at the glass. Maybe the wine would calm her nerves. She downed it in three quick swallows, shuddering at the taste. Leave it to Combs to try to protect her from the worst of the news.

But April refused to back down. "Screw 'em. Nobody knows why this person targeted you. Married or not, seems like they've got it in for you. So why not get married? Isn't that what you want? To marry your sour puss?" Her attempt to get September to smile didn't work. "Besides, they've got a whatdyacallit, APB out on that woman who attacked us. She won't get anywhere near here." April wrapped an arm around September's shoulders and squeezed. "I'm living my best life now because of you."

September glanced through the connecting door to the other bedroom. Steven had moved upstairs when the guests started to arrive and now sat cross-legged on the bed playing with his tablet. All April ever wanted—a husband and kids.

Macy snuggled next to the boy. Lately, the cat had taken a liking to Steven, maybe because he never stared or tried to grab the Maine Coon. Steven appreciated the cat's non-demanding presence and acted fascinated by Macy using the talking buttons. September wondered, not for the first time, whether to suggest a similar technology to help Steven communicate. But that was up to his parents, not her.

April saw her watching the boy and cat; her voice became soft. "I want a best life for you, too. A happy family, with Combs, and kids—well, maybe furry kids, if that's what you prefer. Whatever you two choose. Don't you?"

Small voice. "Yes." Then louder. "Of course. And it's my wedding day. Can't let some crazy lady derail my life." She shrugged off April's embrace and stared at the gown. She couldn't stop her voice from trembling. "My beautiful dress…"

"You'll still wear it, the important part anyway." April bounced up off the bed, crossed to the closet, and pulled out her sleeveless blue-green attendant dress. "It's a little big for me, and probably a couple of inches short for you. But you're wearing flats. And it stretches. Try it."

Standing, September let her sister slip the sheath over her head. Rather than fitted silk, the elastic material clung to her curves, revealing more than she liked. "I don't know, April…" She tugged at the material that cupped her butt.

"Not finished yet. Here." April slipped the organza over September's head. The translucent fabric spilled over her bare arms and allowed the blue-green under-dress to tint the outfit. Rather than a yellow field as planned, the blossom appliques now grew on a field of green. "The color matches your eyes."

September stood in front of the mirror, turning this way and that, and a faint smile blossomed. "It actually looks okay." Then she frowned. "What will you wear?"

"It looks spectacular! And I don't have your muscles, so betcha your yellow and pink dress works just fine for me." She crossed to try it on. "Nobody but us will know the difference, since the matron of honor often wears a different color from the other attendants." She slipped on the silk dress. She took a few steps, holding up the over-long front of the dress. "I've got stilettos. It'll look fine."

September crossed and hugged April hard. "Once again, you're a lifesaver!" They looked at each other in the mirror, arm in arm, one tall and slim in green, and the other petite and curvy in yellow. With April's dye job and September's spur-of-the-moment highlights, they looked more like sisters than ever before.

A knock sounded on the door, followed by their father's low voice. "Everything okay? Melinda and the girls are lined up, along with Willie. April, how's September?"

She took a deep breath and smiled at April. "I'm ready, Dad."

"Oh, don't forget the flowers." April dashed to the bed and picked up the two bouquets Mark had delivered. The larger one, for the bride, featured the velvet red My Valentine blossoms, while the remaining attendant bouquet contained the yellow-with-pink blooms. April eyed the two and shrugged. "You pick, it's your wedding and doesn't have to match the dress."

Smiling, September chose the smaller bouquet of Masquerade roses. "You're wearing the yellow, so only right to complete the ensemble with the bouquet planned for it." She gathered the wide yellow garland, decorated with half a dozen roses in full bloom, and slipped it over Shadow's head on top of his plain leather collar. No corny tuxedo for him; he'd scatter the petals instead of a flower girl. He grinned, anticipating the trick they'd practiced. September opened the bedroom door and waited for April.

April called to her son in the adjoining room as she slipped on her high heels. "Honey, stay upstairs with the cat. You can watch from the window, right Steven?" He nodded but didn't look away from his tablet. She softly closed the bedroom door.

September watched April walk with the elegant tread of a beauty queen to the top of the stairs. Her other sisters waited in line on the stairway below, with Combs's daughter, Melinda, leading the way. Willie waited impatiently with their rings, eager to do his duty. Someone flashed pictures. She thought it might be Mercedes, Detective Gonzales's wife, or her brother Mark. Both had offered, and she didn't know or care who April had tapped.

September grasped her father's arm, stilled her nerves, and waited for the recorded music to begin the procession. Shadow took his place on her other side, yawning and licking his lips with the same nerves she felt.

Chapter 18 – MACY

Macy liked Steven. Steven ignored Macy, the way a polite cat would. He turned away sideways, sat on the floor, and made himself small like a cat, signaling no threat. And he waited for Macy to make the first move. Macy purred and stroked his coffee-colored fur against Steven's leg. Usually he wouldn't touch the boy. Macy didn't like uninvited touches, either, other than from September.

Since the big man, his noisy kids, and their—*spit!*—little dog Kinsler moved in with September, Macy had learned to stay out of reach. Macy and Shadow understood each other. But Kinsler refused to listen or learn from a wise cat's lessons. So, when this boy visited, Steven's calm silence offered relief. The boy never grabbed Macy's fur or chased him the way the others did.

Intrigued, Macy had watched the boy from afar. Over time, Macy drew closer when the boy visited. But even within touch-range, the boy never presumed to invade Macy's personal space. Mostly, the boy stared at the object he held in his hands. September did the same with her phone.

Macy stared at interesting things, too, mostly to see if they moved so he could chase, pounce, and bunny-kick them—like his stuffed mouse toy. But after you raced around the house, thumped up and down stairs, and dragged a stuffy around, a cat needed a nap.

The past weeks kept Macy's house filled with strangers tromping through rooms, leaving doors open—he'd escaped into the garden twice—and making more noise than any sensitive cat wanted to hear. Today, so many strangers came and went that September's voice filled with tears.

He'd wanted to stay in September's bedroom, nap on her pillow where her richest scent remained. But when the boy's mother arrived, he didn't like April's loud voice, so instead slunk into the next room. When Steven arrived and curled up on the bed with his stare-object, Macy leaped from his perch on the bureau to the bed. Steven nodded his head—sharply, up-down—but otherwise ignored Macy just the way he liked. So, Macy curled up on the comforter that matched his coffee-colored fur, right next to the boy's bent knees, and purred the song of his tribe. Macy dozed, the purr soothing himself and Steven, as he heard the boy's breathing and heart rate steady.

Macy roused when the boy's mother spoke. "Honey, stay upstairs with the cat. You can watch from the window, right Steven?" He nodded but didn't look away from his stare-object. She softly closed the bedroom door.

Music from downstairs made Macy's ears twitch, not lovely music like September brought into the room with her cello. Loud music, accompanied by laughter and people talking, floated up from the back garden.

Macy dropped his head onto his paws. The tip of his bushy tail flipped, expressing his opinion of noise, strangers, and all-things un-catlike.

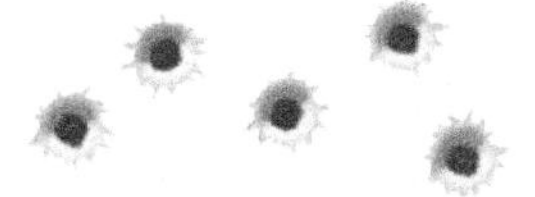

Shadow yawned, and it turned into a whine. He licked his lips, staring around on high alert. Too many people in his house for comfort. They all wore strange outfits, laughed too loud, and smelled of strong odors that made a dog sneeze.

He didn't like all the flowers, either. They smelled funny, not like the ones in his garden outside. But if September wanted people to carry a bunch of flowers, he wouldn't object.

He waited impatiently for the crowd on the stairs to descend to the living room area. They walked slowly in an odd cadence with the music, one at a time. It took forever. September's brother Mark stood on the landing, pointing and flashing a light at people, and calling for them to "wait right there."

The *wait* word made his fur itch. Shadow didn't like waiting. What a waste of time when they could hurry on to exciting things. If dogs were in charge, things would move more quickly to get to the good stuff.

Finally, only September and her dad remained, with Shadow by their side. The stairwell narrowed as it curved, so a good dog couldn't stay next to his person as he wished. September sent him ahead, as they'd practiced. But Shadow whined, and waited for the light flashes to end, so he could pad closer and rejoin September.

The low murmuring grew louder as they finally reached the landing, crossed the room, and walked out the double doors to the brick patio. The garden spread before them. At the far end, in the center of the garden fence stood an open archway dripping with blooming roses. A quickening breeze made them dip and dance. Shadow heard the music swell, and he saw lots of people waiting on chairs in front of the arbor. His hackles rose at the mix of strange people and smells.

September knew. She dropped her hand to his head, and Shadow felt better. She paused just before they crossed off the patio into the garden and stared at the pale man guarding the entrance. He had a gun—Shadow knew that smell.

September stiffened, and turned away, walking forward so quickly her father and Shadow hurried to catch up. She smelled of excitement and nerves. Shadow turned back briefly to lift his lip in a silent warning at the pale man with the hidden gun. He didn't like guns. Or people who made September nervous.

Ahead, the people in chairs stood up when they appeared and walked down the pathway between them. He saw Combs standing with Detective Gonzales and Willie on one side of the flowered archway. On the other side stood in a bouquet of ladies, each smiling bigger than the last. April carefully mounted steps to the miniature stage behind them. She bent to fiddle with the speaker, and the music got louder.

September's pace quickened. Shadow could hear her heart match the pace.

The wind breathed hot hair against their backs. September tapped him on the head, and he looked up to her smiling face, understanding the *go out* hand command sending him ahead of her. He padded quickly forward and looked back, anticipating the trick signal. When she briefly shook her head, grinning broadly, Shadow mimicked the behavior. He stopped in place and shook himself hard. The blossoms on his fancy collar shattered and scattered in a carpet on the grass.

The audience of guests murmured and laughed with

appreciation, and Shadow grinned and wagged. He liked to make people smile, especially September. She gave him the thumbs up *good dog* signal. Maybe now he could get rid of the obnoxious flower collar.

They paced slowly in time to music approaching the knot of waiting people. Combs stepped forward, a wide grin lighting his face. September's dad spoke some words and stepped back to the chairs. September raised her bouquet with one hand to push mussed hair from her face.

A black four-legged wraith appeared out of nowhere. Paws churned toward the wedding party.

Shadow stiffened and danced ahead. He placed his body between September and the Rottweiler.

Lia raced in Magic's wake. "Bomb! Bomb, get away, bomb, get down!"

Magic skidded into his sit-stay alert, bowling into the cluster of brightly garbed bridesmaids.

The women shrieked and scattered, dropping bouquets. April froze, hiding her face in her bouquet. Combs laced one arm about September's waist and flung her away back up the aisle. She fell to the grassy pathway, halfway between the wedding bower and patio. Shadow straddled her figure, barking—at what he didn't know.

Gonzales grabbed Willie and tossed the small boy into the crowd of onlookers. He reached up to help April from the dais.

September screamed, fighting to get clear of Shadow. He wouldn't let her. A good dog's job was to keep his person safe. He grabbed the fabric of her dress and tugged, pulling her back to the house and away from the scary turmoil.

The percussive blast knocked him off his feet, striking him deaf, blind, and dizzy for many heartbeats. When Shadow finally staggered to his feet, screams echoed in a choking mist of blood-stink. Hot summer wind painted a rainbow-colored arabesque of petals against the blazing sunset.

September was gone.

Shadow whirled, searching, searching. Only his nose worked—blood, so much blood, her silly shoe there—but he couldn't find her.

He howled.

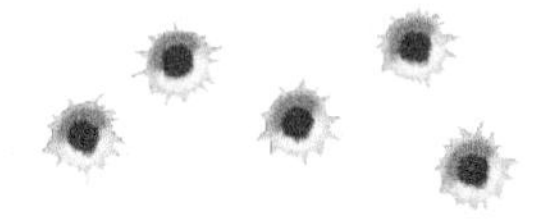

BOOM!

Screams. Window shook. Cracked. Shattered. Glass tinkled as it fell.

Macy shrieked. He levitated off the bed. Danger! Noise!

Fear filled the air and coursed through his body. Fur stood at attention, making him look even larger than his eighteen pounds. Hot wind from outside brought a tainted stink. Grease. Greenery. Blood.

The boy keened, clapping hands to his ears. Steven rocked back and forth, trembling, wails growing.

The calm evening turned inside out, transforming the familiar room into a place of horror. Macy couldn't think! Must escape! Protect himself from threats all around…

Macy slunk off the coverlet. He dove under the bed, crawling to the furthest corner, grateful the comforter fell to the floor to hide a cat's presence.

Seconds later the boy followed him, mouth open and panting, eyes wide and unfocused. Macy hissed, then Steven's scent—known, familiar, safe—registered. He crept closer, pushed his big head beneath one of the boy's arms, purring, purring to scare the fear away.

Chapter 19 – JACK

"Get her away from here." Jack guided September's compliant, giggling form out of the golf cart into the trunk of the waiting vehicle. So pale, so lovely... The wine doctored with GHB worked its magic. He'd gambled April wouldn't drink, due to her transplant, but needed this just-in-case option. Guests had already placed multiple calls to 911 and soon the house would be swarming with emergency vehicles. They'd want to question her—question everyone—and her staying here risked more lives.

He was sure at least one was dead, but he hadn't stopped to count the wounded as he removed September from the fray. He'd warned her, dammit! The "prank" with the dresses should have stopped the wedding. But it may have saved her life.

As she stirred, he reached into the trunk, grasped the flimsy fabric of the fancy overdress, and ripped it away from her body. He tossed it on the ground while he slipped off her remaining sandal. She laughed. Jack smoothed the hair from her face with one gentle hand. The date rape drug left victims giddy and happy—perfect behavior for a bride—and very pliable, just what he needed to keep her safe. The effect would last about two hours, and, if lucky, she'd have no memories of any of this. Time was not their friend. He slammed the trunk lid. "Back roads only. The more trees, the better. Wait until the first ambulance arrives, then go." That might add some cover from drones. "I know where to find you."

He wadded up the sandal in the colorful fabric, revved the golf cart, and sped back to the side garden. Most guests ran toward the patio and house, so he'd used the kitchen-side garden entrance. He had dogs to fool, as well as people.

The security team was managing the devastation, keeping the injured from moving, and getting the ambulatory out of the way. Jack waded through scattered debris, picking his way through pieces of tattered clothing, shredded vegetation, and worse.

Screams had given way to soft sobs. Lia stood at one side, frozen, hand clenched white around Magic's leash. The dog cried softly, pressed hard against her thigh. Somewhere else, another dog's deep bark sounded, as if searching for something. Or someone.

The overwhelming scent of motor oil—*my God, the witch used C4*—mixed with roses and coppery blood-stink made Jack want to throw up. A white-haired man with glasses joined Lia—Teddy Williams. He'd seen pix of the guy. Teddy tried to put comforting arms around her shoulders. She shrugged him off.

Good, the old man had survived. Teddy could still prove useful.

Overhead, a drone passed across the darkening sky, no doubt with a spy camera trained on each telling detail. He'd got September away just in time. Others remained at risk, though, until he took advantage of the confusion. Jack wanted the drone footage to see only the evidence he provided.

Jack stuffed September's dress and shoe under his shirt until he reached the worst of the carnage where the mini-stage had collapsed. An older woman let out an anguished howl and dropped to her knees. She cradled an unconscious, bloody form. Maybe Combs? Hard to say.

The old cowboy beside her pulled out his gun, aimed, and shot at the buzzing drone. Jack tried to wrest his gun from him and couldn't. Jack raised his voice. "Get under cover! Everyone into the house. Now! Anyone able to move, get inside. They're not finished." A second drone appeared with the first, this one clearly armed and ready to continue the job. A short, sharp burst of gunfire sprayed from the drone. The man in the cowboy hat crumpled, and the woman screamed, "Stan!" She looked around frantically, arms still around Combs, but yearning for her injured husband. "Somebody help us!"

Security personnel converged. Together they moved the ambulatory injured toward the house.

Jack heard Combs moan as he was moved. So not dead, at least not yet, but Stan didn't look so good. "Help him, Doc Eugene, please help him." The woman grabbed the arm of another guest, who looked shell-shocked, like the rest of them, but appeared able to render medical aid.

"Where is Winston? Has anyone seen my husband?" A petite woman wrung her hands, a fancy purse swinging from one arm. "He's a detective, probably helping." She took a big breath and yelled, "Winston!"

Jack grasped her wrist to stop her from moving toward the bodies still lying beside the collapsed stage. "I'm sure he's helping the injured. Wait for him in the house. Please."

The drones crisscrossed the area over and around the house in a clear search grid. Looking for their ultimate target, or a confirmation of a kill. They wouldn't leave until they had it.

Jack pushed to where the bodies lay. At least two, maybe more—hard to say. His jaw tightened, seeing the stained yellow silk still clinging to one form. Whoever operated the drones likely knew the bride would be wearing yellow, and hopefully didn't know about the last-minute change. So he unfurled the embroidered organza fabric and covered the woman's nearly unrecognizable form.

He was dropping September's shoe when eighty pounds of black fury flattened him. The shepherd snatched the shoe, pawed, and sniffed it thoroughly, then dropped the sandal and barked and snarled so close to Jack's face he could feel the hot breath and saliva spray.

Sirens wailed, drawing near. "Lia, get Shadow. He's going crazy." Teddy's distinctive voice cut through the cacophony. The old man's voice choked on a sob and then steadied. "I'll hold Magic's leash, but you need to get Shadow, he's found her body. Oh, God help us, we couldn't protect her. September's dead."

Jack covered his face from the dog's assault with one forearm. Beyond the snarling dog, the drones glimmered and danced in the sky. One zoomed away, but the other swooped closer. They'd seen and probably heard Teddy's heartfelt lament. Checking mission status. Fingers crossed that the witch believed she'd succeeded. It zoomed away, as one of the security guys peppered it with gunfire.

Lia trotted forward, face dirty and no longer holding back sobs. "Shadow, good boy, Shadow. Come-a-pup, we've got to go."

The black shepherd's howl joined in a counterpoint duet with the sirens. Shadow screamed his fear and anguish. He barked one more time, directly in Jack's face, turned to Lia and barked at her, then sped away from the garden with its wreckage of pain and tears.

Chapter 20 – KALI

Kali watched the live stream from the last drone. "Closer. Confirm target." She spoke with sharp authority to the unseen operator. She had slipped a sundress over the form-fitting biker gear, and tossed the bike in a dumpster when the black vehicle picked her up.

The car now sat high on a hill in a hospital parking lot, one of dozens. Nobody would approach in such a place or question the running car that kept the AC blowing cool air. As the only medical facility in Heartland, she'd get a closeup view of any survivors ferried to the emergency ward.

Impatiently, she leaned forward to better view the drone's camera feed as it swooped lower to reveal the devastation. She caught her breath and smiled.

While Kali preferred the surgical precision and thrill of up close and personal elimination, September had left her with no choice. She'd escaped once too often. Nobody could survive that bomb—and she was to blame for any collateral damage.

Kali could have eliminated the entire wedding party, heck the entire assembly, but generously spared family and friends by using the highly targeted IED. Yet even the tiny amount of explosive caused a damaging percussive wave, possibly lethal to anyone too close in the garden. So she wanted to confirm who survived, and plan accordingly.

The video feed showed a central impact area. A motionless figure wearing a colorful and now blood-stained dress made Kali's grin widen. That matched the description they had of the bridal outfit. In addition, three men lay on the flower-strewn grass, obviously thrown some distance from ground zero by the wave blast. One rolled back and forth, holding hands to his ears. The others didn't move.

Security swarmed the area. Too little too late. She also recognized September's brother, Mark. He wandered around the garden, shaking his head, orbiting the blast area like a plane afraid to land. She laughed, clapping her hands, and nearly spilling her drink. He knew! He knew what he'd done. Oh, how delicious!

"Monitor the brother. Keep me apprised." The drone operative acknowledged her command.

She knew all about Mark, knew his weaknesses and pressure points. Now she'd given him plenty of reason to hate himself, enough to end his life. If he didn't do the deed quickly, she'd make sure someone helped him take that last step. Clearing up all the pesky details took time but would pay well in the end.

A young woman, blonde hair escaping a headband, shouted and pointed at the drone. Her black dog barked and lunged from the end of a leash, but Kali had no audio. It didn't matter now. She'd find out the identities of the other casualties soon enough. One of the security men looked familiar.

Kali frowned. "Get me a closeup on that man, the one next to blondie."

The camera zoomed in, panning slowly, and settling on his pale face. He wore a hat, but it couldn't hide the white ponytail. Could it really be him? If it was, he'd let his hair grow, matured from whip-thin, sickly boy to this buff specimen with snowy hair and complexion.

The screen went blank. Someone shot the drone's camera, possibly brought down the machine. No matter, it wouldn't trace to her. She bought and sold influence, and her clients included cops, from small-town to national influence. Nobody could touch her, and most knew better than to try.

She closed the laptop and settled back into the leather upholstery, taking another sip of celebratory champagne. The game just got more interesting. Kali smiled and sipped, waiting for the ambulances to arrive. She had people inside the hospital to feed her info.

Chapter 21 – SHADOW

Shadow retraced the route he and September had trod. He dashed so fast, grass-covered clods kicked up as he dug his paws deep for purchase. The garden gate nearest the kitchen door stood wide open. All the strangers guarding the entrance had left, running to find the source of the loud BOOM that still left a good dog's ears muffled with hurt.

Testing the scorching breeze, he turned one way and then the other. There! Her scent still clung to vegetation, as though September ran her hands through petals. No scented path marked the brick walkway though. That man carried her this way. Her scent had covered him, and he had her funny shoes…where had he left her?

He nosed the kitchen door, discounted it, and raced around to the front of the house, following the pools of September-scent that caught in eddies here and there. Despite the crowd in the back garden, no cars clogged the circle drive. He'd seen security people waving cars away, so they parked in the field across the road where Teddy's RV lived. Shadow galloped toward the garage. Maybe she'd got in their car?

But the closed door said otherwise.

In the distance, wailing sirens neared. Shadow raced to the big green gate at the front of the empty circle drive, still closed but no longer guarded. Her scent lingered here, too, where she'd pushed past. Thankfully, the gate hadn't latched afterwards.

Quickly, he squeezed through, lifting his nose to the gusting wind. His chest hurt, and his ears felt stuffed with water like after a swim. He didn't like swimming. At the thought, Shadow shook himself, hoping to clear out the water feeling. That made him dizzy and he staggered a bit.

A big truck with the screaming siren appeared far down the country road, looking too large to pass through the tree-lined car path. Shadow whined. Sirens meant bad things. He wasn't sure if sirens made bad things happen, or just sniffed out trouble and appeared afterwards.

"Shadow! Shadow, come-a-pup. Come, good boy. Please!"

He glanced over his shoulder at Lia. She stood in front of September's house, hugging herself. He liked Lia, trusted her. But she wasn't September. He had to find his person. Maybe Lia would help?

Taking a few steps back toward the girl, he barked once, twice, and then again. People knew things that dogs didn't. That man took September away, then came back. Maybe Lia could make him bring September home.

Shadow had to find September. Stay with her. That was his job. Shadow barked again. He stood in place, but his paws danced with impatience while he waited for Lia to come near.

She reached for his flower collar, and he ducked away, managing to shrug out of the oversized gadget. It still smelled of flowers. He didn't like flowers very much anymore.

"Please, Shadow, stay with me. I'll take care of you. She'd want you safe. September…" Her voice broke on the name, and the girl fell to her knees, sobbing.

Shadow leaned forward. He licked the wet salt from Lia's face. She loved September, too.

But not as much as him. He accepted Lia's hug for four heartbeats before he pulled away.

The breeze puffed and September's scent rode the eddy from across the road. Without looking, he followed his nose and yelped when his tail clipped the front of the wailing truck. It yelled a horn at him, too, but his muffled ears barely noticed.

Lia jumped up and ran to the vehicle as its siren wound down. She pulled the gate open wide to welcome the siren people.

Ahead of him, down a narrow pathway between parked cars that smelled like guests from the house, Shadow rushed toward the beckoning scent. At the far end, a nondescript vehicle sat with windows down, engine running. He slowed his paw steps as he neared, dodging behind the car when the driver peered out the window at the noisy siren. When Shadow reached the rear of the car, September's scent engulfed him, and his tail waved with excitement. He nosed the metal—still hot from the summer sun—and knew he'd found her.

Whining, he put paws on the trunk, scratching at the metal. She made no sound, but her scent covered the edge of the metal, and more poured out from inside the hidden cavity. He scratched some more, paw-thumping the car. Maybe he could make it open? Paw-thumping made windows go up and down. Anything might happen if he pawed it the right way. And September needed him!

The car rolled forward on the grass. Exhaust snorted out the rear end like it ate something bad. Shadow jumped down. In the mirror, he could tell the driver saw him. Her eyes widened.

He knew that face. Not his favorite person. Not someone he could trust.

Confused, he barked and yelped. He paced beside the car as it picked up speed, bumping along in the field on its way to the smooth car path. Once it reached the road, Shadow knew a dog's four legs couldn't keep up. He couldn't let the driver run away, not with September inside.

Shadow saw the beaten-down grass where cars took turns driving into the field to park. This car would travel that same path. And a good dog's four paws could leap and bound faster over grass and ditches than the driver's small car.

Despite the ache in his lungs, Shadow increased his trot to a gallop, running faster than the little car. The driver glanced at him again and again, yelling words he couldn't hear, and would have ignored even if he could.

The car slowed to bump down and back up the ditch at the side of the road. Shadow timed his leap perfectly. If he couldn't get the trunk open to get September out of the strange car then he'd catch a ride.

His black form cleared the open rear window with a hair's breadth to spare. He landed with a solid thump in the back seat. The car sped up onto the pavement, the driver staring in the mirror at Shadow.

Shadow stared back. And growled.

Chapter 22 – JACK

No more drones haunted the sky. A fire truck and three ambulances crowded the drive in front of the house, with a host of police cars blocking further access. Jack's plan had paid off.

The backyard looked like a tornado had spun through the event, with chairs scattered and broken. Twinkle lights installed for the reception competed with fireflies. The scent of roses mixed with oil, blood, and vomit. Screams had subsided to sobs, as family members and friends clung together, crowded on the patio to watch EMTs crouch over the injured. They hung on every finger twitch, every moan that signaled someone still lived.

Many of the attendees suffered minor scrapes and bruises, either from the panicked stampede or from the explosion. Some would need embedded sticks or other debris removed. More serious than any visible injury, Jack knew the risk for concussion and lung injury was high, even among those at the back of the crowd.

He'd manned his post at the side garden gate near the kitchen, watching from a distance, until Lia sounded the alarm. She and her dog somehow avoided injury, as if Magic somehow told the girl when and where they should take cover. Jack took advantage of the confusion, reached September within seconds of the explosion, and whisked her away to the waiting golf cart.

The lion's share of attention focused on four victims. A woman's body, misidentified as September, clearly took the brunt of the explosion. But three cops, one retired, also suffered life-threatening injuries either from the bomb, the drone strafing, or a combination of the two.

The police waited, giving the EMTs every opportunity to save lives. They champed at the bit to collect evidence and had already cordoned off the altar and stage area to keep foot traffic to a minimum. And September's office had been commandeered to question survivors, one by one.

His warnings hadn't been enough, never mind they'd been ignored. Jack should have predicted the drones. And the bomb. He still didn't know how an IED got past them. If not for the bomb dog's alert scattering the wedding party away from the blast, more might have died.

One after another, gurneys carried motionless figures away. Only two needed IVs and medical support, at least for now.

"Winston? Oh, Winston!" The petite brunette wailed. She shook off restraining hands and rushed to the last gurney, shrouded in a blood-soaked covering. Combs's partner hadn't made it. A brother-in-blue took charge of the detective's widow, escorting her to the waiting ambulance.

Gonzales had saved Willie Combs. He'd tried to help April and died for his efforts. Now the little boy shivered in his sister's embrace. The two kids, clearly in shock, stared with tear-drenched faces as EMTs rushed their father to another of the waiting ambulances. Lia kept a tight grip on Melinda's shoulders.

Melinda resisted, turning to an older woman. "Aunt Ethel? Will Daddy be okay? And Uncle Stan?" She whimpered. "Why'd anyone want to hurt September?"

"They're heroes, they can't die!" Willie's lower lip trembled but he held back tears. "Where's Shadow?"

Lia hugged Melinda harder. "Shadow got upset and scared, too. I told you he ran away from me. I'll take Magic out later and track him down." Her dog's ears pricked at his name, and he leaned against Lia's leg. "I hope Shadow will come to another dog. But right now, he's hurting, upset, and confused. Just like the rest of us."

"Take them inside, Lia, and stay with them, please." The white-haired woman's stoic expression didn't falter. She'd been a cop's wife for decades, and it showed. Ethel clutched her husband's cowboy hat and turned to Teddy standing nearby. "I'll go with my two fellas to the hospital. They're both tough." Her expression didn't change. "Watch out for the kids will you, Teddy?"

"Always." Teddy stayed on the patio as the rest of the wedding party slowly filed into the house.

They wouldn't want to leave. Jack knew the feeling. With any disaster aftermath, you held your breath—figuratively or literally—trying to stay inside that bubble where you last felt normal, afraid to pierce the protective cocoon and experience the harsh new reality with all its pain.

Jack waited, wanting to speak to Teddy alone. The man didn't miss anything. He could help the cause or derail everything. "Know anything about dogs?"

Teddy didn't look at him, just took off his wire-rim glasses and polished them on the hem of his shirt. Jack recognized the action as a way to give Teddy time to think. "I'm not an expert by any means. Not like Lia." His head jerked toward the door where she and the kids had disappeared. "September's the real animal expert."

"May she rest in peace."

Teddy ducked as if slapped. "About that. Funny how things work out. Not funny ha-ha, but funny weird." Teddy reset his glasses on his nose. "When somebody new comes into a security team at the last minute, I hope to hell they get properly vetted. Usually they do. When it's someone I care about, I poke around a bit, too, go deeper." He glared at Jack. "After looking you up, I have more questions than answers."

Jack took that as a cue to leave.

But Teddy caught his arm. "Thing about dogs—and like I said, I'm not an expert—Shadow's unique. Lia saw the shepherd run off. Shadow walked September down the aisle but ran after the blast?"

"Dogs get scared of noises. It happens."

"Not Shadow. That dog's been through hell and back, always by September's side. He's faced down more scary stuff than I've seen in a lifetime. And I served." He drew himself up to his meager height, but barely reached Jack's shoulder. "That service dog never willingly strays more'n three steps away from September. Ever. You think he'd leave her? Alone…like, like that…" Despite himself, Teddy's voice broke.

Jack gently shrugged off Teddy's hand. "I'm sorry for your loss." The man clearly had doubts, but no concrete knowledge. "Who knows what kind of behavior losing his partner might cause?"

"I know. I know! But dammit, a poor woman got blown to bits over there. It can't be September, or we'd have a grief-stricken maniac dog on our hands." Teddy glared, eyes brimming over with grief.

Teddy knew nothing, could prove nothing. Like all the

grieving, he searched for alternatives to his new painful reality. Jack strode away, but heard the man break down into sobs.

Before he could leave, Jack answered the official's questions, told them more than they wanted to know, and got an admonishment to stay available. He kept September's survival to himself, for now, as he couldn't rule out Kali having spies listening to every word. Jack needed the cops and September's family to believe that he and the security team had failed to protect her, or the group.

Jack's jaw tightened, regret palpable, but his plan only beginning. Teddy might still play a part in taking down the witch. But until then, September had to stay dead.

Chapter 23 – SEPTEMBER

September dreamed she and Combs were floating together on a boat. They'd planned a honeymoon cruise, but the bumps, dips, and rush of wind proved anything but soothing. They'd talked about white river rafting, but she'd vetoed that idea. The trip had to work for Shadow, too. Had Combs surprised her after all?

She opened her eyes, but everything stayed dark. Not a midnight cruise at all—wouldn't she see stars?—and you don't curl up on your side in a kayak. "Combs? Where are we?" She roused enough to realize she was lying on a rough carpet, head resting on a stinky spare tire.

Memory returned in a rush so hot and painful that September cried out. Her head pounded in rhythm with her pulse, and the heat of the enclosed space made her lick dry lips. How long had she been out? She'd walked down the aisle on her father's arm, Shadow proudly leading the way. Then Combs dashed forward, flinging her away from danger when Magic signaled a bomb alert. Shadow above her, a loud noise—then falling into inky darkness…

What had happened next?

Abruptly, she tried to sit up and banged her head against the low ceiling. Her body responded with a wave of pain and nausea. September moaned, clutching her stomach.

Shuddering, she practiced calming breaths, concentrating on what she did know. The movement and tire told her she rested inside the trunk of a car. Hot, so very hot. Heatstroke was a real risk when stuck inside a metal box. She felt all around, discovering the dimensions, as the car bounced over a bumpy road.

What had she done to deserve such attention? Had people she loved been hurt because of her?

The car slowed and turned on to an even bumpier pathway. September moaned and finally threw up but didn't feel any better. She felt battered, more bruised than she would expect from riding in a car trunk. Her body ached and her nose ran. She swiped the wet away, grimacing at the taste. Blood. Whoever put her in the trunk had worked her over first. At least her hands and feet weren't bound. She'd wait for her chance: when the trunk opened, she'd escape.

She searched for the emergency release, standard on modern cars, but couldn't find it. An older vehicle, for sure. She brought up her knees to kick out one of the rear lights—maybe an alert police officer would stop the car—but pain shot through her bare feet on the first impact. When and how did she lose her shoes? Her hands scrabbled and clutched, searching for something, anything, to use as a weapon. Nothing. No tire iron, or anything loose in the trunk.

The jarring ride came to a stop, and September held her breath, straining to hear anything. Her ears felt muffled, but with a distinct ringing in one. She pinched her nose and blew outward, trying to equalize the pressure like on an airplane during a descent. Her ears popped, but she still couldn't tell how many people might be in the car.

A dog barked. Her head throbbed. The bark sounded again. Not any dog—Shadow!

She tried to yell at him, but her lungs didn't work right. She couldn't catch her breath. September flailed and pounded on the trunk. She braced herself and kicked at the back seat, searching for a weak spot. Maybe Shadow could dig through to reach her. She stopped, unable to continue or think clearly, hearing Shadow bark and yelp his own fear and frustration.

"Shut up already." A woman's voice growled, but not at September. "You're not part of the deal, can't stay here, gotta get out now." A long pause. "Don't you dare bite me, or you'll be sorry!"

Shadow howled.

September squeezed her eyes shut and prayed. *Please don't hurt my dog!*

Chapter 24 – TEDDY

Teddy couldn't stay in this house of grief any longer. He blamed himself. He should have—somehow, some way—predicted what happened.

Lia sat on the sofa beside the kids. Out of respect, the police gave them space and hadn't interviewed them yet, not that the children could add much. The officers had more than enough information from the rest of those in attendance.

Teddy wrapped his arms around Melinda and Willie, then squeezed Lia's shoulder as he passed by. She clutched his hand. "I swear, Magic cleared the whole place of explosives before the ceremony. Twice!" The dog leaned against her, whimpering, ears slicked down as if feeling just as guilty as Lia. But dogs, and humans, couldn't predict the future.

"Magic alerted in time to save many people." He patted her hand and moved on. Teddy guessed the lethal explosive arrived very late, after Magic had cleared the premises. The bomb experts would try to figure out what happened. They'd log who arrived when, and what came with them, to create the timeline and opportunity.

"Flowers." Lia's eyes looked unfocused for a heartbeat before looking back up at him. "Magic says…well, he alerted on a bunch of flowers that smelled wrong."

Teddy shrugged. Flowers covered the whole backyard. And he'd seen Lia and her dog sniff-explore every nook and rose bush.

"I mean the bouquets, Teddy. Not the outdoor plants. Somebody booby-trapped September's bridal bouquet." Tears welled. "I can't believe she's gone! She wriggled out of so many horrible crises. And Combs…" She glanced at the two shell-shocked kids and hushed her voice. "Ethel said she'd call with news"—she looked around the room—"but I promised the kids we'd go to the hospital for a while. They want to be near their dad. I think they need that."

"Where's the rest of the family?" Teddy looked around the house. September's father, siblings, and their spouses and kids were nowhere to be seen.

"May and June wanted to get their kids and dad away from here. All but April were staying at his house." She stroked Magic's broad, muscled neck and smoothed his silky ears.

"You saw Shadow take off. How did he act? Scared? Upset for sure—"

"How do you think he acted?" She breathed heavily, but kept her voice low. "He saw his person killed. Dogs experience shock and grief, too. And they react in just as many ways as people do." She blinked hard, then added, "He wasn't scared, though. He was on the hunt. Tracking."

Teddy raised his eyebrows. "Tracking what? Who?"

"Looking for September, Teddy." Her voice filled with sorrow. "Pets sometimes search for lost loved ones after they've died. Especially if they don't get to see the…the body." She hiccupped a sob. "That happens with pet friends, but with owners too. I think Shadow didn't want to believe she's gone. Same as us. So, he ran off to find her." She wrapped her arms around Magic, shuddering.

Teddy shook his head, not really buying it. Lia ascribed to all sorts of woo-woo thinking, at one time claiming Magic talked to her with pictures she saw in her mind. Teddy patted her hand again and limped to the front door. September arranged for a golf cart to transport guests from the field parking space to the house, and he'd welcome a ride about now. In times of stress, the bullet injury in his leg still bothered him, and today his cup of stress runneth over.

He'd left his computer and his phone in Nellie Nova and couldn't wait to get back to the RV to make some inquiries. As in life, September's death swirled with too many questions. She'd survived every attempt on her life, often due to luck more than anything else. That luck just ran out.

He needed to evaluate what impact his dear friend's death had made in the cyberworld, look for chatter on the dark web, check out the gossip, separate concrete from speculative threads. Careful inquiries could track down the persons responsible. He'd make it his life's purpose to bring September's killer to justice.

Teddy threaded his way past the police cars and the one ambulance still waiting, maybe to collect September's body. He gulped. He didn't want to be here for that. He kept his eyes on his feet, placing them carefully once he reached the uneven field, on his way to Nellie Nova sitting in the far back corner. Breaking a hip on his way to the vehicle wouldn't help.

Many of the cars had left, and the beaten-down grass and tire treads left bald spots in the field. He noticed a paw print, and then another in a dusty area. Shadow? Yes, Lia said the dog raced away across the field. Teddy sighed, fearing for the dog's safety. And if

Teddy felt bereft, how much deeper must be Shadow's anguish?

There, another paw print. Absently, Teddy tracked them across the barren field. Here, a yellow sandal someone shed as they fled the area.

September would want friends to care for her beloved four-legged partner. But Shadow had proven repeatedly that he could take care of himself.

Teddy reached the RV, unlocked the door and climbed inside. Meriwether trilled and padded quickly to meet him. "Meri, what will we do without her?"

He sank into a chair and welcomed the big feline into his lap. September's cat Macy also would need help. "Lord help us, Meri. What the hell happened? I failed her. I should have stopped it, somehow." He buried his face in the cat's fur and sobbed.

Chapter 25 – KALI

Kali's stomach growled—mayhem always made her hungry—and she wanted a bathroom, a shower, and a change of clothes. But first, she wanted an update.

The last ambulance had arrived fifteen minutes ago and she'd watched the parade with satisfaction. Four ambulances: the first two screaming in with sirens blasting and lights strobing the darkness—the survivors—the last two ran silent, the victims' fates already determined. She wanted confirmation that September's remains reposed in one of the two silent ambulances.

Once the hospital publicly released the information, Kali could press her advantage. She ran everything about Wong Enterprises, but nay-sayers within the organization watched her every move, looking for advantages and leverages with which to sway her decisions. Removing September eliminated a potentially powerful tool they could no longer use.

Her disposable phone tweedled. "Tell me."

"Two dead. Two critical."

She already knew that. "Who's dead? Who's critical?"

A pause. "Winston Gonzales DOA. Hold on…" Kali could hear raised voices, barked medical orders, and muted sobbing, the audio soup of a hospital emergency room in crises. "One of the criticals just coded."

"Who is it?" Kali wanted to crawl through the phone and strangle the speaker. She'd paid good money for in-the-moment intel. But money only got you halfway there. Kali always got better results with threats. Her hand grabbed the edge of the leather car upholstery, claws cutting deep. "Tell me."

Something in her voice shook loose the speaker's reticence. "Some big guy. Old, with thick white hair." Another pause.

Not Combs, dammit, so didn't matter. "Send me names. I don't pay for generic descriptions or speculation." She jabbed the disconnect button and raised her voice to the driver. "Driver, take me to my house."

She'd prefer to stay in Dallas accommodations, in the Wong suite of rooms kept just for her. But until she confirmed this little errand fixed all outstanding issues, best that she stayed near this backwater village. Hired help had failed her over and over, most recently in South Texas. "I don't like the south. Not at all."

It took twenty minutes to arrive. Kali braced herself as the car rocked back and forth in the rutted gravel drive and tree branches scraped the sides. At least her driver could easily guard access to the narrow private drive. Kali liked privacy.

The burner phone again rang, another source checking in. This operative called herself Diva, and Kali hadn't got her under an exclusive contract. Diva hired out to anyone willing to pay her extravagant fee but had proved her worth repeatedly, providing accurate intel ahead of anyone else.

"What do you have?" The car pulled up to the garage of the pale-yellow house. She didn't wait for the driver to open her door.

"Word out already about an attack on a cop wedding, cops dead and others in critical condition."

Kali grinned. Good, the stuff Diva planted in advance paid off. The public would believe the attack targeted the police. "Which cop survived?" She waited impatiently as the driver joined her on the porch and unlocked the front door. She rushed into the house, dashed up the stairs, and hurried to the master suite. Kali kicked off her shoes as she rushed to the bathroom. She set the phone on the vanity, punched it to speaker phone, and took care of her discomfort. She glanced out the second-story window, taking in the glimmer of moonlight reflecting off the obsidian lake.

"Combs. Injuries sustained from the blast. Lots of bets on whether he'll make it or not. Maybe he'll die of a broken heart cuz his girlfriend died."

"Yes!" Kali pumped her fist, the exquisite relief doubled from emptying her bladder. "That's confirmed?"

Diva didn't hesitate. "Not yet. Presumed, only. Authorities waiting on DNA before confirming identity. But her family and friends, hospital staff, and local gossip all agree she's gone. I can increase the chatter to that effect."

Satisfied, Kali stood to turn on the shower and shed her clothes. No need to pay her hospital insider when Diva could get better information, quicker, from her digital aerie on the east coast.

"Traditionalists believe she's gone." Diva spoke quickly, almost as if she knew she'd lost Kali's attention.

"Perfect." *That should escalate the resolution, and confirm transfer of assets, monetary and esoteric. She'd waited months for this.* "Your compensation will arrive as usual." She disconnected.

Almost immediately, a text arrived from a different source.

>Interested parties targeting alternate.

Hissing, Kali grabbed the phone and texted back quickly.

Something she'd anticipated but hadn't expected so soon.

<When? Do they have him yet?

>Chatter only. But prepping.

Kali thought for a moment. Whoever came up with the best leverage first owned the game. This also confirmed September's death. If the attack aborted the vows, Combs no longer mattered. He'd probably die from injuries soon enough. The alternate target in her competitor's control posed problems for her end game.

>Secure asap.

She set aside the phone. The alternate target wasn't like September—who would break before she'd bend to Kali's will—she'd already corrupted Mark. He had delivered the bomb, so she could use his guilt to her advantage.

Kali climbed into the shower, turning the hot water to high until the exquisite pain made her cry out with satisfaction.

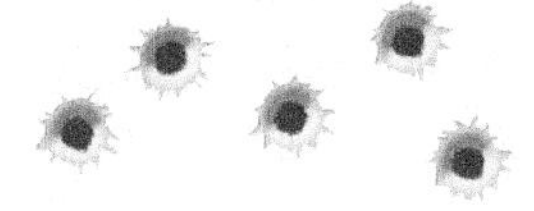

Nebulae watched from the porch roof, staring into the bathroom as steam fogged the window. The stranger, now in the shower, made odd sounds—something like cats fighting. People often did strange things that made no cat sense.

She purred when Sunset hopped up on his side of the glass and pushed his cheek against the window. For a moment, the pair trilled and bunted against the barrier. Then Sunset hopped down.

Nebulae knew what the orange cat planned next and didn't need to see. Sunset enjoyed water games, especially making the toilet flush… and people shrieking when the water changed.

Chapter 26 — JACK

Jack had driven halfway to the rendezvous spot when he got a message from the assassin. He'd arranged for her "Diva" alias, and fed her the information she needed to satisfy Kali. While he fully trusted nobody but himself, he needed help, and someone on the inside like her helped enormously.

Now she'd shown a crack in her practiced armor. September's dog had found them, and instead of dumping Shadow, she had a proposal.

Kali had eyes everywhere. The team managing internet chatter could finesse the story September's beloved dog disappeared after her death—of such stuff legends are born—but not if a similar dog appeared partnered with a similar woman they wanted to keep hidden.

No, the dog couldn't stay. But…they could use Shadow as leverage with September. She'd do anything to keep him safe. Put Shadow in reserve, away from September, but where others wouldn't recognize him and ask questions. To do that, though, she'd need help.

>Good idea. Will make arrangements.

Once she helped him with the witch, September would get her dog back. Meanwhile, Shadow would go for a doggy holiday.

He pulled off the highway, drove around neighboring streets, and chose a church parking lot. In his experience, cops checked cars sitting too long in parks, or even fast-food joints. They also had cameras monitoring businesses and public places. A neighborhood church turned the other cheek. By the looks of this one, it had little chance of any video monitoring.

Jack pulled out his laptop, booted it quickly, and found what he needed. It took no time at all to create the documents. A fake background for a dog wouldn't lift eyebrows. Within ten minutes, he'd inserted a newly created record into the doggy daycare database. According to the log, the black shepherd/collie cross visited twice a year, acted fussy around strangers, and cried and barked a lot during the first days. In the past, he'd tried to dig out of the kennel, and would need extra security to keep him from escaping. Jack couldn't afford to have Shadow escape and be rescued by a Samaritan. Jack checked the website to ensure he'd covered all the bases and debated when filling in the name. Couldn't use Shadow, that'd raise too many flags. But the staff should have something to call the pooch that he might respond to.

With a smile, Jack input the four-letter word: Baby. He'd heard September use the nickname several times in their limited time together.

The kennel wouldn't open until tomorrow morning, but Quinn needed to drop off Shadow immediately. He found the owner's name—easy-peasy—and placed the call.

"I'm trying to reach the owner of Pauline's Paw Palace, the dog daycare center."

"Speaking. But we're closed."

"I understand that. But we have an emergency, and I hope you can help. I'm calling on behalf of one of your longtime clients, who was unexpectedly called out of the country because of a family death. I'm the neighbor—and if it matters, I also work with the sheriff's department." He gave her a fake name that would stand up to an internet search or even a phone call. It never hurt to throw in some additional clout. "My daughter's on her way over with Baby, the dog. I would consider it a personal favor to the department to make an exception and open at this late hour. The owner left additional funds to compensate you for your inconvenience."

She blew out her breath. "What's the owner's name again?"

He rattled off the made-up client and listened to the clackity-clack of fingers on a keyboard.

"Here it is. Oh, poor Baby, he must be distraught. I see he's not a happy boarder, anyway."

Jack nodded, although she couldn't see. "The dog had already spent most of the day alone by the time I got the message. My bad, it's been a horrible day. You don't want to know." He cleared his throat. "Should I call my daughter to turn around and wait until the morning? Guess we could stash Baby in the garage, but it's kind of hot tonight—"

"Give me a minute. I have staff on site 24/7. I just need to let 'em know. Tell your daughter to come on down and we'll make Baby as comfy as we can until his person gets back."

He disconnected, satisfied but still disgruntled. Usually he planned better. People often mystified him, and non-humans puzzled him even more. Jack had bet Shadow wouldn't leave the bloody aftermath of the blast, that the wedding dress would fool him, at least long enough to get away with September. The dog earned grudging admiration for finding September in the car.

Jack needed to talk with September ASAP, and manage the

narrative. Teddy Williams probably already had his nose poked into discovering everything about Jack. And if Teddy didn't believe the fiction of September's death, that could alert the witch to look closer, too.

He also wondered about Steven. How would the boy manage his grief? Hard to say with people on the spectrum, like himself. He hadn't planned things to go this way, but the guilt piled on to what he already shouldered. He'd recruited several of his team from the Kid Kewl message board, many genius-level intellectually, even if emotionally and physically immature. Before meeting Steven in person, he hadn't realized just how young they were.

He shut the laptop and started the car, but before he left the church parking lot his phone blipped. A text from Tracy, his number-jumbler.

>Numbers numbers numbers! Racing there to here and here and here; sighpress bunches!

<Numbers slumbers? What about zeroes? Any heroes?

The kid was brilliant, but it took time to tease out her meaning. What the hell did "sighpress" mean? And time continued to tick-tock away. They would expedite the autopsies in the attack's wake. That would confirm identification, probably within 24 hours.

>Numbers moving, zooming here to there! From everywhere, but all to sighpress

<Money moving? Lots at stake, it's not fake?

>Lotsa bucks, lotsa loot, lotsa cash, lotsa $$$. Number jumbling totals change change change, up and up and up and doesn't stop.

He sat back, mouth dropping. Couldn't be a coincidence. Word of September's death had triggered money transfers from around the world. To sighpress. She had to mean Cyprus, a known haven for money laundering. Tracy monitored the witch's accounts and could calculate totals without thinking. That she couldn't keep up floored him. The money funneled as a tribute into the witch's account. Besides the money, he shuddered to think what other influence she'd gained.

Jack pressed the gas and left black rubber marks in the church parking lot. He needed to dig further, and find out the WHY behind targeting September Day, especially if Steven couldn't. Because that could influence September's decision, or even help enlist Teddy to his cause.

Chapter 27 – SHADOW

The girl stopped the car on a gravel lot and got out. Shadow whined. He'd given up barking, especially after September's voice fell silent. The driver kept the windows closed, and try as he might, Shadow's paws couldn't find the magic button that made them open.

After the door slammed, he watched the slight form trot toward a distant building. Lights came on, and other dogs barked. Shadow's ears twitched. Many dogs, by the sound of it, lived at this place. He pressed his nose to the window, whiffering scent to better read his surroundings. The door of the building opened, and the driver stood briefly with the tall stranger. She accepted a looped cord, made a gesture that stopped the stranger from following, and hurried back to the car.

She put her hand on the rear door handle. Shadow growled. He recognized the slip-leash, and his ears slicked back. The driver hadn't let September out of the car, and Shadow had no intention of leaving without her.

The barking and howls from the other confined dogs

increased, and Shadow's hackles rose. Some sounded sad, others angry, some just excited, but all shouted their frustration at confinement. It reminded him of Lia's place, where lots of strange dogs spent time in separate kennel runs.

The driver unlatched the car door with one hand, holding the open loop of the leash ready with the other. Shadow backed away, lips lifting in a silent warning. No! He wouldn't leave the car, not without September. His tail pressed hard against the other window. Snarls bubbled deep in his chest.

Backing off with a frown, the girl pursed her lips, then smiled. She whispered.

"I know what you want. But this is the best I can do. Work with me, okay?" She stepped away from the open door and took a few steps to the rear of the car.

Shadow's brow furrowed and growls abated. He licked his lips. September waited inside the trunk. Would the girl let her out? He had to see… He leaped out of the car, paws skidding on the pebbles, and whirled to reach where September's scent was strongest.

The leash slipped over his face and tightened around Shadow's neck. He screamed and dug in his paws.

"Need help?" The figure waiting at the building started toward them.

September's hoarse voice cried out from inside the trunk. "Don't hurt my dog, please don't hurt him!"

He had to help her, stay with the car, take care of her. That was his job! But the noose tightened as Shadow struggled.

His captor yelled, "Stay back. You'll make it worse." The girl drew Shadow after her, trying to soothe him with quiet words. "I won't hurt you. I promise." She tapped on the car trunk, leaned down and whispered urgent words. "September, your dog's okay.

Calm him down, so he won't get hurt. It's my job to make sure neither of you gets hurt." She paused, then added, "You'll be together again soon. For now, do the right thing to keep your dog safe. Please."

A pause. Then the soft voice from the trunk. "Shadow." The voice, HER voice, so soft people couldn't hear. But Shadow heard his name, spoken with tenderness, with regret and worry. His heart wanted to explode from his chest.

He cried, and lunged at the trunk, standing on his rear legs to paw-thump the metal. Small cries whimpered from deep inside, making his tummy hurt.

"It's okay, baby dog. I'm okay. Go with her. Chill, Shadow, chill." Her voice broke, and she sobbed.

With a cry, Shadow dropped off the trunk of the car. When the leash tugged at his neck, his head drooped nearly to the ground. Ears down and tail tucked with dejection, he slunk at the girl's side to the building with shouting dogs and many kennels.

He stood silent, looking back over his shoulder at the car, as the girl passed the leash to the waiting stranger. Shadow refused to budge until he saw the girl drove the car away, with September still inside.

Shadow tipped his head up to the night sky and howled one long ululating cry. Then he reluctantly followed the stranger into the boarding kennel.

Chapter 28 – SEPTEMBER

September prayed she'd done the right thing. Curled up inside the trunk she'd had little choice, but she couldn't bear the thought of Shadow in a stranger's power. The girl's voice sounded so familiar, but a name eluded her.

Thirst made her tongue stick to the roof of her mouth, and she wondered if she had received a knockout drug as well as being affected by the blast. The smell of her own vomit kept her stomach roiling.

Her brain didn't want to work. It hurt to take deep breaths, her head pounded, and one ear felt like a devil had embedded a pitchfork in it. If her kidnapping had something to do with the death threats, she didn't understand why she was still alive.

The car slowed then turned so fast her body rocked to one side. Now off pavement and on gravel, the bouncy movement making her teeth click. With nothing to clutch for stability, each bump and swerve knocked September's head against the side of the trunk. Pain bloomed to greater fury, and her eyes filled. Where was Combs? And the rest of the wedding party? She whimpered.

A sudden stop, and immediately a car door screed open. The trunk unlocked with a click and September froze. A figure, silhouetted against a distant, bright light, lifted the trunk lid and bent over. September shrank away, hands fisted to defend herself.

The figure stepped back, hands raised in a placating gesture. A smaller silhouette spoke with the driver's voice. "You can get out now. Nobody here to see, but we need to get inside quick."

September realized the small stature of the driver meant somebody else must have carried her to, and deposited her in, the trunk. She knew that voice, but her pounding head kept her from connecting the dots. She squinted at the taller silhouette. "Combs?" She struggled to sit up, wanting nothing more than his arms about her. She fell back into the trunk, dizziness overtaking her.

"Let me help. No, I won't hurt you." The man's low voice also tickled her memory, but she couldn't see his shaded face. Ice-white hair spilled over his collar. One bare muscled forearm quickly wrapped about her shoulders, the other scooped beneath her knees. He lifted her out and set her gently on the uneven ground beside the vehicle.

"I know you. One of the security guys Combs hired." She blinked, eyes still straining to focus. "You wanted us to cancel the wedding?"

"Jackson Glass. Yeah, we met earlier."

The girl driver made a sound of disgust, probably at the vomit smell, but slammed the trunk. She hurried ahead to the open door in a small cottage.

September tried to take in her surroundings, noting scraggly trees and the sound of nearby water, to prepare for her eventual escape. Quickly, he guided her inside. The door shut behind them and she heard deadbolts. Wooden blinds kept the low lamplight captive inside the dwelling. Jack urged her to another room, but she struggled to escape his muscular arms. "No! Let me go, don't shut me in again!"

He stopped immediately and stepped away. Without his support, September struggled to keep her balance in the suddenly whirling room.

After the oppressive temperatures of the trunk the air conditioning felt icy. She hugged herself. "What's going on? Where's Combs? And where'd you leave Shadow!" She whirled and took two unsteady steps toward the girl before grabbing a tabletop. She started to fall, and the girl pulled out a kitchen chair and shoved it under her butt.

The face finally clicked in September's memory. "I know you. Charlie Cider." She hissed the name. The kid's hair looked different, but the tattoos were the same. She'd saved Charlie from some bad actors in South Bend, and this was the thanks she got.

"You're mistaken. My name's Quinn Donovan."

September drew in a breath. That name also tickled her memory.

The girl sat in another chair, and nodded at the guy with white hair and pale-as-ice skin. "We just do what we're told. Kid Kewl is the answer man."

Kid Kewl sounded like a child's idea of a superhero. "So call your answer man. Messing with people's lives brings down all kinds of trouble. Especially messing with the police." *Where was Combs?* She hugged herself again. "Would somebody please tell me what's happening?" She stared at the man, but couldn't quell the tremor in her voice.

He kept his distance and modulated his voice to a deep, soothing baritone. "Ms. Day, you want answers, and so do we. You knew about the threats. That's why Detective Combs hired extra protection, me and others, and why you moved the wedding to your home."

She nodded, then winced when it made her ear hurt worse. She felt a hot trickle of wet run from her ear down her neck. Blood.

Quinn handed September a tissue, and pointed at her own nose. September dabbed the blood away from her upper lip and then held the tissue to one ear. "What the hell happened?" Small voice.

Jack's lips tightened. "A bomb."

He kept talking, but she couldn't hear anything except a weird buzzing sensation after those two potent words. She talked over the buzzing, explaining to him why he must be wrong. "Security cleared everything to keep everyone safe. Only family and close friends, everyone I trust. I saw the reports. Even Magic—"

He stopped talking. His eyes met hers, and she wanted to reject the overwhelming sorrow reflected in his expression.

She remembered Lia's scream and Magic alerting. And Combs grabbed her and flung her backward, toward the house. Then everything turned to black.

"A bomb?" Her lip trembled. "Combs? Please, where is he? And my family, my friends—" *Chosen family, people who she'd come to love as her own.*

"Combs hired me to keep you safe. The witch has surveilled you for months but only got active recently. We didn't expect a bomb, but I used the disruption to get you out—away from the drones." His matter-of-fact assessment sounded like a computer analyzing data. "We're lucky. Could have been more victims."

Victims. Plural. "How many?"

He looked at her but didn't answer.

"Tell me! Who got hurt?" She tried to stand, but the room spun, and she sat again, hard, bruising her tail bone. "I deserve to know!"

Quinn looked at Glass, began to speak, but he held up a hand and gave a slight head shake to stop her words. "People were hurt. But so far, only one confirmed dead."

"Who?" *Oh God, oh God, oh God, all her fault her terrible fault. What had she done?*

"Right now, the only confirmed victim is you." He forced a smile that looked pained. "We need to keep the world believing you're dead for as long as possible."

Chapter 29 – TEDDY

Teddy parked his RV in the hospital lot and took a deep breath, squaring his shoulders. His phone continued to ping with updates, queries, and shocked comments from colleagues and friends. He knew from his preliminary review of online chatter that the attack at the wedding hadn't ended the danger. Now, other family members, and especially Combs, had become targets.

He didn't know why. Yet.

With grim resolve, Teddy stepped out of Nellie Nova, blocking Meriwether when the big cat wanted to follow. He couldn't protect September, but by God he'd keep safe everyone else she cared about. Combs—if he survived—his kids, September's father, and her siblings.

As he hurried to the entrance, Teddy worried what he'd find. He had stood at the rear of the gathering, so other than an earache had come through the attack unscathed. Because of the garden design the guests had watched from a distance. The wedding party, those closest to ground zero, had suffered the most grievous injuries. Teddy fought back tears, time enough for emotions later. He needed to assess any continued risk and ensure nobody else suffered from the devilish assassin.

The help desk directed Teddy to the correct floor, where he joined the worried throng of family and friends. That included Captain Felix Gregory, Combs's boss, and several other police friends. He made a mental note of those in attendance, as well as a few glaring absences. He nodded at Lia, who sat in a far corner with Combs's kids. They'd beat him to the hospital. She whispered something to them and left them clutching each other to meet him.

"No word yet on Combs." She wiped her eyes with the back of one hand. "If only I paid closer attention to Magic's alert—"

He hugged her to him. "No, Lia, you and your dog saved people today. I should have insisted they cancel the wedding."

She pulled away. "Look at us, competing for who messed up the worst. September would say *crappiocca happens.*" She attempted a smile but crumpled into tears again.

He fought his own tears and cleared his throat. "Go back to the kids. Think you could convince 'em to wait somewhere else? Your place, maybe?" The hospital waiting room, echoed with tragedy, offering little hope.

Lia shrugged. "Already suggested that. Melinda's as stubborn as her dad."

Teddy saw Captain Gregory excuse himself from his conversation and thread his way through the crowded room to join them. Lia stiffened, as though she expected a dressing down from her future boss, but he gripped her shoulder and forced a smile. "Where's that dog of yours? He deserves a medal."

She looked stricken. "Magic is with Doc Eugene, getting checked out. Excuse me." She dipped her head and hurried back to the two distraught kids.

Teddy watched her retreat. He hadn't thought of it, but it made sense to have the dog evaluated for possible injury from the explosion. The veterinarian, another longtime and trusted friend, had stood at the back of the ceremony. He'd seen the man aid the injured in the aftermath. Doc Eugene would put Magic right.

Teddy shook the captain's offered hand, both gripping hard as though that would shield them from expressing emotion. "Lost a good man today. Winston Gonzales started on the force before he met Mercedes and got married. Now his kids have no daddy."

Teddy craned his neck to meet the man's thunderous gray eyes. "Feels personal for me, too."

"I got two more of my own in there." He jerked his thumb vaguely toward the emergency room door. "I've known Stan Combs for over thirty years, before his bum ticker forced his retirement. There's nothing in the world I wouldn't do for him, or Ethel." He scrubbed one rough hand over his face. "Ethel's with Combs now. They won't let her near Stan. He's in awful shape." He worked his jaw. "Don't think he's gonna make it."

"I got no words." Teddy took off his glasses, polishing them on his shirt. "Still gathering intel. Gotta be something I can do." He shoved glasses back in place, and held up one hand, expecting protests from the by-the-book officer. "I'm not asking permission. I'll dig up what I need anyway, just offering to share." When Gregory started to speak, Teddy plowed on. "Seems to me your best folks, the ones with insight into this mess at least, can't tell ya anything. Get much from the witnesses?" Not that he expected any of them would know anything. "I work with the security team Combs hired—"

"Yeah, they did a fantastic protection job." The sarcastic words, followed by an expletive, prompted scowls among those waiting. Gregory modulated his tone. "My people interviewed the *team*, as you call 'em,. They had no clue what went down. None of them got their britches dirty—nary a scratch. Makes ya wonder."

Teddy glanced across the room when Lia got Melinda and Willie up and moving. He raised a hand, and they gestured back, Melinda looking sullen with a jutted chin. Willie's expression reminded him of a beaten puppy, bewildered by the world's unwarranted cruelty.

Lia paused as she herded the kids out the door. "Doc Eugene called. Somehow, Magic got through with only a couple of scratches. We'll pick him up on the way home. Call me!" She held her phone toward Teddy with an emphatic gesture. He nodded.

Gregory directed Teddy outside the waiting room for a more private discussion. Quickly, Teddy brought him up to date with the limited information he'd had—more suspicions than concrete facts—prior to the wedding.

"Yeah, shoulda-woulda-coulda." Gregory sighed. "But neither Combs nor his bride had any intention of letting *anything* stop their wedding. Matter of pride with 'em. Plus, they'd both dodged danger so often before…"

Teddy agreed with Gregory's assessment. Pigheaded Combs and September thought they were invincible. "We had nothing concrete. Don't know how we could've stopped the assault. Hell, we still don't know *why* they were targeted." Teddy related the recent increase in dark web chatter, plus the odd text warnings September received from the anonymous troll.

"You think Combs needs protection?" Gregory reached for his own phone. "That'll take some effort, depending on his injuries." He hesitated. "Whoever orchestrated this attack seems to have virtually unlimited resources. Intelligence, funds, foot soldiers? And we don't know who or why?"

"Working on that." Teddy's phone pinged again.

Gregory snorted. “Heartland doesn’t have the resources for 24/7 protection. Oh, our people will line up to help—they attacked our own!—but we’re already stretched thin. Most rural forces are.” He checked his own phone. “Press conference in twenty minutes. God I hate this!”

“Hold that thought.” The text message again came from the person who had warned September this morning. *Not ignoring it this time.* He scanned the thread. His face reddened at the tone—chastising him for ignoring the warning, getting people killed. True enough.

>Believe me this time. Protect Combs, he’s next.

Teddy texted back his understanding.

The captain tipped his head at Teddy, eyebrows raised. “What?”

“The insider who warned September confirms Combs also on the target list.” He didn’t like trusting an anonymous text message, but… look what happened the last time. The person’s suggestion couldn’t hurt, and might save, Combs’s life.

He shared a plan with Gregory, and the captain smiled for the first time. “I like the way you think. But better clear it with Ethel first and talk to the doctors. In my experience, neither like fudging the truth.” He took a breath. “We don’t know who’s after Combs. So, nobody—and I mean absolutely no one—but you, me, the docs, and Ethel can know.” They shook hands again.

Teddy left the hospital to follow up on the chatter the text messages mentioned. He’d watch Captain Gregory’s press conference later. Whoever targeted the wedding would watch, too, and hopefully back off enough to give Teddy—and his mysterious texting partner—time to even the slate.

Chapter 30 – JACK

Jack felt satisfied he'd convinced Teddy to join his effort, even if he had held back certain information. He knew the old guy could eventually unravel his identity. Before that happened, Jack needed to get September on board with the plan, which would cement Teddy's help.

They had a common enemy. Together, with Jack's team and September's friends, they could bring down the witch *and* her empire. And maybe get a small taste of revenge into the bargain.

He was so close…

September had moved from the small kitchen table to the overstuffed sofa in the living room. She huddled beneath a crocheted comforter, still shivering even though he'd adjusted the AC to more moderate levels. The shock, he figured. But he couldn't risk taking her to a hospital.

Dust coated much of the room. Jack had rented the place when he launched this ultimate effort against the witch. Only a few places in the Heartland area had private properties that fit his needs. He'd used a different name on the paperwork, of course.

Grabbing a couple of bottles of water from the cooler he'd brought, Jack sat across from Quinn at the kitchen table. Her history read like many of those caught in Kali's web. Used and abused by those who raised her, she tried to escape but knew too much to get away clean. She'd been rescued by September, and championed by Teddy, before disappearing—only to reemerge as Quinn the assassin, with better skills courtesy of Kali's organization, and a new purpose in life.

He'd watched her for several weeks before approaching. Quinn had no qualms about eliminating bad actors in the world. But she had no taste for liquidating innocents, unlike Kali's indiscriminate bloodletting. Her desire to escape Kali's leash meshed well with his own goals. "You updated the witch?"

"Diva told Kaliko what she wanted to hear." Quinn took the water, opened it, and drained half with three quick swallows. "She'll get confirmation soon enough on the news. Not sure how that helps." She nodded toward the living room and dropped her voice. "You don't know September like I do. She's a force of nature. Once she gets her bearings, how ya going to keep her hidden? Unless shackled, she'll be gone by morning."

He didn't answer, not directly. Better Quinn didn't know the next step, so her honest reaction helped convince September. "Wong's compatriots already reacted to her death." He gave air quotes around the last word. "We need to figure out *why* they need her dead, but it's opened up the financial floodgates."

Quinn wrinkled her nose, and took another slug of water, arming away the sweat from her brow. "She wanted confirmation, but if cash already flows, maybe proof doesn't matter anymore. They can't un-send the funds, can they?"

"The accounts probably require some kind of password confirmation to access. They'd hold that back." He knew the game, each side offering a glimpse of a promised prize, waiting for the other to blink first. He sipped his water and glanced at September's tragic figure. He needed to have a big, unpleasant conversation with her, but she wasn't ready. She needed to mourn the loss of her hopes and dreams first. Her only chance for a future meant aligning with him. He had to convince her of that. He'd waited years for this. He could wait a little longer, until the press conference…

He looked up when September rejoined them in the kitchen, the comforter still snugged around her shoulders and over the wedding dress sheath, which hugged every curve of her lithe body. Her bare feet padded silently, painted toenails the only cheerful aspect in her appearance.

"Thank you. I guess." She nodded stiffly, first at Jack, then Quinn. "But I need to go home, find Combs and get my-my-my…" She wobbled, and Quinn jumped up to guide her to a chair. Quinn glared at Jack, and mouthed, *toldja so.*

Jack shook his head. "Not a good idea—"

Her chin jutted out. "I heard you talking. What does Kaliko Wong have to do with any of this? I've heard that name before. Some kind of criminal, right?"

He raised his eyebrows. Maybe she knew more than he realized. "We believe Wong Enterprises hired assassins to target you."

September's mouth dropped open. "Me? Why?"

"The million-dollar question." Quinn crossed to the counter and boosted herself up to sit on the edge. She opened the faucet and refilled her water bottle.

Glancing at Quinn first, Jack returned his focus to September. "You recognized Quinn as Charlie from South Bend. Quinn was at the painted church, remember, you just didn't know they were the same person." He held up a hand when the girl would have protested. "Hang on, Quinn, if we want to work together, we got to come clean and trust each other. Okay? Right?"

Grudgingly, Quinn shrugged and took a slug of water like it was whiskey.

"I tried to help Charlie, so did my friend Teddy Williams, but she disappeared on us. Not even a thank you. And Teddy, his grandkids, and I nearly died in South Texas! Why the hell should I trust either of you?" Without a breath, she added, "I want to go home. Now!"

Quinn barked a laugh and lifted the water bottle in a mocking toast. "Saved your assets at the church. You're welcome."

Jack bulldozed on. "After South Bend, Quinn disappeared with the help of Wong. Now she's beholden to the organization, made to do some pretty bad things." When September would have interrupted, he held up a hand to silence her. They had no time for this! "Never mind the details. Quinn wants out, and I agreed to help her by bringing down the organization."

"Why? What's in it for you?" September stood, putting hands on hips, defiant.

He took a breath, and his voice briefly shook. "Kaliko Wong killed my sister, Rina. I want to return the favor. And I want your help."

"Me? How could I…why should I help you? She sounds like a terrible person, but I did nothing to this Kaliko Wong."

Jack tipped his head to one side. "Maybe you don't know what you did. But the witch seems to think you did something. And that's why she keeps trying to kill you and your cop boyfriend. As long as she's left alone, she'll keep coming for you. Welcome to your future, September Day."

Chapter 31 – SEPTEMBER

September hugged herself hard. The bomb blast should have killed her. It probably burst her eardrum, but Combs had saved her life by knocking her away from the blast. While she could still hear from the other ear, everything sounded muffled, and sort of crunchy like a defective MP3 recording.

"Mr. Glass, if Combs hired you, you answer to him." And Combs would have told her if he had planned this.

He shrugged. "Technically speaking, that's true."

"I want to speak with him. Now."

Jack shrugged. "I'd like to speak with him, too. I'm waiting on word from the hospital."

September's heart raced. "He's one of the injured? How bad? Who else? Tell me!" Her words tumbled out and she crossed her arms again. While she trusted Combs to hire the right people—

And where had Quinn left Shadow? "You tell me to trust you. Yet you have given me no reason to, no way to feel comfortable about this whole situation. You want me to trust you? Get me my dog. And figure out a way to get Combs on the phone."

Jack's explanation made no sense. September had watched over her shoulder, taken extreme steps to protect herself, and for weeks and months nothing had happened. Yes, Teddy monitored internet chatter and threats. But a person could take only so much before having to live her life. Nothing this pair said convinced her to throw in with their bizarre plan. "Well?"

He checked his phone. "We'll have a few answers in a minute." He looked sharply over at Quinn. "They've scheduled a press conference."

September sat up straighter. "Press conference?"

"Look, we don't have a lot of time. Kaliko Wong runs a criminal empire she inherited when her husband died. I don't know why she targeted you. It seems personal. And based on your recent history—two attacks in one day—all the precautions in the world haven't kept you safe." He grabbed his own bottle of water, screwed off the cap, and downed the entire contents.

He said she'd killed his sister. Jack had a reason to hate the woman, and that colored everything. "How do you know it's her?"

"I know."

The girl sitting on a countertop kicked her feet, the thumping rhythm a counterpoint to September's pulse. "Tell her about the money."

Jack nodded. "My team has been tracking this organization for years. Your friend Teddy knows. We just knew where to look earlier and more thoroughly, but now he's watching the same activity."

She drew in a deep breath. She trusted Teddy with her life. It had come to that more than once. "Tell me." She whispered words.

Quinn answered before Jack had a chance. "As soon as word spread about the explosion, the floodgates opened. Money streamed in from all around the world."

"I don't understand."

Glass glared at the girl, before focusing once more on September. "Your death means a big payday for Kaliko Wong." He summarized the information he'd gathered.

September's mind whirled. "They paid her to kill me?" She took a breath. "The woman who shot up the spa, that was Kaliko Wong?"

He cocked his head at that. "Maybe. Probably. She started out as a high-dollar prostitute and graduated to paid assassin. Then she married her boss, and after he died, she ran everything. But we're not sure yet whether outside forces directed the hit, or the witch set things up herself."

September shook her head. "Turn everything over to Combs—to the authorities if he's injured." They still hadn't offered details about his condition.

Glass was right about one thing. They'd been running around in circles, not knowing where the next bullet would come. Jack could have saved them time and pain…and maybe lives.

"Please, tell me what happened to Combs. And get me my dog." She fingered the sweat-damp dress that clung to her body. But her next thought made her wobble: something convinced the bad guys to move the money to Kali's accounts. They had a body.

What had she done by insisting the wedding go on? *Somebody died in my place. Oh god oh god oh god.*

Jack looked at his phone once again. He hesitated, then offered it to her. "We need your help. Kaliko Wong thinks you're dead or wants confirmation. In either case, you're a blind spot with the witch. I don't know about you, but when people I love get hurt, I don't just sit still. I hit back."

September took his phone. He'd cued up a live stream video from the lobby of the Heartland hospital. September searched the faces of the people standing around. Police officers, some in uniform, some plain clothes. Captain Gregory stood at the mike.

"This evening, what should have been a celebration turned into a tragedy. At approximately 7:30 PM local time, unknown suspects attacked a wedding party using a combination of an IED and gunfire from an armed drone. Casualties include some of Heartland's finest. We are saddened, and our sincere sympathies go out to the families who have lost loved ones. We have enlisted the aid of both local and federal authorities to bring these criminals to justice. As we continue to sort out exactly what happened, we'll release further details once families have been notified. This press conference serves to offer assurance that we expect no further danger to the public. The attack specifically targeted individuals involved in the wedding party." The captain drew up to his full height and looked around the room. "I will take some questions. But I'm not at liberty to answer medical questions."

September's hands turned white as they clutched the phone. *Please please please…*

Gregory acknowledged the first reporter. "I understand that this was the wedding of Detective Jeffrey Combs and September Day?" A pause. "Can you give us any names of victims? Or the extent of the injuries of those who survived?"

"Yes, it was the Combs and Day wedding." Gregory cleared his throat. "The HPD is a family. We celebrate happy milestones together, so many of our officers and their families attended the ceremony." He rubbed his eyes. "Most of you know September Day's name because she has helped to solve several notorious cases in the past couple of years. That is how she met Detective Combs."

Other reporters lost patience and shouted out questions.

"Did she survive?"

"How many dead?"

"What are the casualties?"

The captain sighed. "We cannot confirm or offer details until family members have been informed. That said, pending autopsy confirmation, September Day is presumed dead. Her family is aware of the situation."

Gasps all around the room. More shouted question.

"Autopsy? You mean, her identity isn't…"

"Why can't you confirm…"

Gregory raised his hand to stop the questions, looking pained. "The explosion made visual identification impossible. DNA will confirm identity."

September's hands shook. She braced the cell phone on the kitchen table, afraid it would slip from her wet palms. It was surreal. They had declared her dead.

But Captain Gregory mentioned other victims. All her family, all of her closest friends, had attended. She held her breath, wanting to pray, but not knowing what to say. *Please, please, please…* Who should she wish dead instead of…

Reporters' voices raised, talking over each other, shouting questions, demanding answers.

"Who else?"

"How many victims?"

"What about the bridegroom?"

Captain Gregory closed his eyes. He took a deep breath and whispered into the microphone. "Just before I came out here, I was informed by the medical staff that Detective Jeffrey Combs has joined his bride."

"No-no-no-no-no-no!" September threw the phone across the room and collapsed to the floor.

Chapter 32 – SHADOW

Shadow paced the cement run. He needed to get out and find September, but he knew better than to try digging through the cement. The people here had been kind, but they didn't belong to him. He also worried about the enormous boom that started these upsetting events.

In the wire run on one side of him, a big dog with short black and tan fur watched quietly as Shadow walked back and forth whining under his breath. She didn't seem upset, and even wagged once or twice when Shadow looked her way. On the other side, a black dog that looked like a smaller version of Shadow matched his pacing. But Shadow ignored the other dogs.

He padded to the bowl of water and lapped it dry for the second time. After barking so loud and long, trying to get September's attention in the car, Shadow's mouth felt like he'd eaten socks. At least the temperature inside the dog run wasn't too hot, but Shadow still felt like he had run a marathon. The small door on the wall would open soon and he'd race outside to *take a break*. Shadow knew it would open because one of the other dogs next door had just come in and the little door remained open. The ground outside was perfect for a dog's claws to dig.

The young woman who had led Shadow here entered from the long hallway. She stopped in front of his kennel and cocked her head. "Poor Baby, you look upset. Let's see if we can't get you feeling better. That's Keighley on one side, and Max on the other. They'll keep you company." She opened the gate to the outdoor grassy expanse. Outside lights clicked on to light up the area. "Go do your business, Baby. You've got twenty minutes before lights out."

Shadow bounded through the small door, hurrying before the woman changed her mind and closed it. His kennel sat near the end of the long line of kennels.

He'd dig out, find September's scent, and play the *seek* game to go after her. September didn't want him digging holes all the time, but one time he had to dig her up when she fell into a hole and got covered with dirt. It was a good dog's job to fix things for September.

Shadow bounded to the far side of the space and pressed against the wire. He sniffed the corner of the enclosure, noting several other dogs spent time here before him. Reflexively, he lifted his leg and left his own sign. He'd been too busy with all the people coming and going at September's house to *take a break*, or to eat. Now his tummy rumbled in protest. The lady had left a full bowl of kibble inside, but some things were more important than filling your tummy.

He found a place where another dog had clawed the dirt. Shadow put his nose to the spot and explored diligently. The dog hadn't dug very far, so Shadow would have to enlarge the hole before he could squeeze underneath.

Concerned the lady inside might try to stop him, Shadow

glanced over his shoulder and kept his ears alert for her approach. He had to dig fast, and get out quickly, before she understood what was happening. Sometimes a good dog had to disobey to do the right thing.

He put his head down, braced his shoulders, and dug. The earth smelled hot and dusty; the surface baked hard from the sun. A few cracks snaked along the surface where the other dog had begun his excavation. Within several paw swipes, Shadow's claws hooked on something hidden deep under the ground. He tipped his head to one side, pausing in his efforts, and whined. He sniffed the metal latticework, so very similar to the barrier that spread upwards and enclosed the kennel. The sides of the chain-link fence extended deep underground to block a good dog's paws.

Shadow grumbled deep in his throat but moved across the kennel to a new spot. This ground hadn't been touched by any other dog. Short grass grew from the hard pack dirt, but within moments, his claws had ripped it off and made progress into the soil. He grunted, front paws churning and tossing hummocks of grass and clods backward between his legs. But again the metal webbing stopped his progress.

He whined in frustration. Shadow sniffed the edge of the kennel wire, examining the entire perimeter of his kennel one more time. He knew what to look for now. Without exception, the metal grillwork extended deep into the ground, turning a corner once hidden to prevent a good dog's paws from tunneling out.

Shadow barked at the pockmarked excavations, as if yelling at the ground would cause it to open. He couldn't dig his way out. But he had to get out, had to find September.

Keighley appeared in the small gateway leading from her interior kennel. She cocked her head, bewhiskered face looking wise, then trotted into the outdoor area next to Shadow. Two layers of chain-link separated Shadow from the Airedale, so they couldn't do a proper nose-to-nose greeting. Despite that, Shadow appreciated her friendly overture of an offered paw.

Max came out to watch from his run, too. His short black fur shone like silk in the moonlight. He panted softly, eager to join in whatever fun might develop.

Shadow made full eye contact, and Max averted his own eyes in a polite show of deference. Shadow whined again, and licked his lips, turning away from Keighley and Max. He liked friendly dogs but had no time for introductions and play.

Sniffing from her own side of the fence, Keighley investigated Shadow's efforts to dig under the chain-link. Her tail wagged faster and faster. A low, delighted growly sound erupted from her throat. Inspired by Shadow's efforts, and her terrier heritage, she also attempted to dig. But her paws proved no more fruitful than Shadow's.

With a sigh, Shadow sank to his tummy and set his chin on his front paws. He watched with interest as Max made the rounds of his own enclosure. The other dog trotted over to Shadow and pressed his nose against the wire, wagging happily, tail churning the night air.

Then the dog whirled and raced around and around his pen. It reminded Shadow of the way Macy-cat zoomed around the house, up and down stairs and across the furniture. On the third lap around the kennel, the smaller dog leaped up, his paws grasping the chain-link, and rebounded off.

Shadow stood up abruptly, interest piqued. He cocked his head, watching the other dog repeat the maneuver.

Around and around Max ran, picking up speed and kicking up tufts of grass in his wake. On the third zoom around the makeshift course, he leaped high in the air, claws clutching the chain-link, and rear paws scrambling for purchase. Max climbed three-quarters of the way up before reaching the wire overhang topping his structure. He dropped back to the ground.

Shadow woofed softly and his hackles bristled with excitement. Max sought to fly out. Well, not like a bird. But if Shadow couldn't go under the fence, maybe he could climb like Max.

Panting with excitement, Keighley took a turn. She zoomed around and around her enclosure.

Max showed the other dogs what to do. After three quick laps to gather speed, the Kelpie leaped at the corner of the fence, hooked front and rear paws in the chain-link, and climbed up the side like a ladder. He stretched up to reach around the lip at the top, and scrabbled until he pulled himself over. Max landed with a soft thump, his white toes paw-dancing impatiently for the other dogs to join him.

Keighley barked with excitement. After her fourth lap she launched herself at the corner of her kennel. The angle gave her paws the leverage she needed, and pushed her higher. She glanced over one shoulder, panting happily as she looked down at Shadow, then scrambled up and over, dropping softly onto the grass beside the barrier.

Whining with excitement, Shadow stood on his hind legs, claws up against the chain-link where the other dogs stood. His new friends bounced up and down, excitedly yapping and encouraging Shadow to make his own effort.

Shadow knew how to climb ladders. September had taught him. He was smart and had learned all kinds of ways to get out and under and over. This skill, though, was new to him. Shadow trotted to the far end of the kennel, turned around, gathered his haunches, and launched himself. He leaped high, front paws reaching to catch hold of the top of the barrier and rear paws scrambling for purchase. But he fell back, unable to maintain his grasp.

"OK dogs, time to come in." The woman called from inside the kennel building, and the outside lights flashed on and off. "Hey Baby, I'm picking up your food too. Come on inside now, time to sleep. Hey Keighley! Max, Maxy Doodle! Everyone inside now."

Shadow took a lap around the kennel, picked up speed on a second lap, and finally flung himself up the corner of the chain-link, reaching far as he could. One paw topped the barrier. His rear paws caught, and he braced himself, balancing his weight as he scaled the wire webbing. Finally, grunting with effort, Shadow pulled himself to the top.

"Hey, where are you? Bedtime, come on let's go." A gasp. "What're you doing? Get back here! Max, you know better. Max, come!"

The sound of the interior gate opening alerted Shadow to hurry. With a final desperate push, Shadow launched himself up and over the top of the chain-link to land next to his new friends.

Max whined, licked first Keighley's then Shadow's face.

"Max Power, get back here right now. Don't give me that 'judgey' face, either." A pause. "Wanna play with the Chuckit toy?" Her voice wheedled.

The black dog looked back at the woman, clearly torn, but reluctant to follow his training. Without a backward look Shadow and Keighley took off. Decision made, Max raced after the pair, and all three disappeared into the night.

Chapter 33 – KALI

Kali smiled as she listened to the press conference confirming the deaths of September Day and Detective Jeffrey Combs. She felt a weight lift off her shoulders, one that had followed her ever since she'd learned September had survived childhood. Already, funds were being released. Yes, she'd miscalculated. Some in her organization plotted for alternatives rather than allow Kaliko Wong to head the organization.

Now they'd come full circle. Nearly thirty years ago, she had first met Myrina. How ironic that her elimination began Kali's ascendancy. Myrina had agreed to anything—money, influence, information—to ensure family safety. *Stupid woman.* After that, Kali had smooth sailing for decades.

But her husband tried to tie Kali's hands, and she couldn't allow that. So, she had had him killed—blaming others, of course—and expected full power to come into her hands. Instead, foot dragging, excuses, even threats had plagued her due to rumors she believed long dead. New York probate trundled along as legally required, but higher hurdles followed from constituents around the world. They tied her hands even more than her dead husband. Kaliko Wong was used to getting her own way, and it took all her willpower to not turn a flamethrower on her opponents. A more selective approach meant removing her competition from the equation. Because if Kali found that the rumor still lived, it was only a matter of time before her enemies also discovered that connection.

Now she felt vindicated. A small, precise bomb nestled inside the bridal bouquet added just the right frisson to the operation. Even better, September's brother, Mark, had delivered the bouquet. Kali smiled again. He knew his guilt. She just needed to persuade him to do the right thing.

Mark January had gotten too curious, and that had tripped the just-in-case warning she'd set up all those years ago. Kaliko congratulated herself on her foresight. She'd already given instructions to collect him.

The evidence was out there—never gone once on the internet—but only for those who knew where to look. Myrina was long dead. Nobody important remembered her. Nobody but Kaliko Wong knew where the bodies were buried, literally. She had everything to gain—money, power, influence—and her life to lose, should anyone dig up the truth.

Kaliko stretched like a cat, nearly purring with satisfaction. The tray of sweets on the table didn't tempt her appetite. Neither did the imported cigar awaiting her. Those were for later. A successful operation always left her starving. But not for food.

She sent a text to her driver describing in graphic detail what she wanted. What she needed. For the next hour, she would give herself over to the exquisite release she craved… and deserved.

Chapter 34 – MACY

Macy pushed away from the boy. Much time had passed since the boom. Steven still lay with his arms covering his head, scooted to the far corner beneath the bed. Macy's ears twitched. The sundered window changed everything. Each hair on his body detected differences in air movements, smells spilled into the room, and intriguing sounds made his ears twitch: creaking tree limbs, tasty crickets, and more.

His tummy pinched, reminding him he hadn't eaten in many hours. He needed to hunt one of his treat puzzles. September filled his mouse toys with yummies and scattered them around the house. Mostly, she put them on tabletops, inside boxes, and other places that Shadow couldn't reach. Otherwise, Macy had to punish the dog when he stole the cat's food. Macy had already finished the puzzle toy treats in this room.

Macy slunk out from beneath the bed then sat in the very center of the room. He began washing himself, licking his right forepaw first, and then scrubbing that side of his head and face. The space under the bed had collected lots of dust, and it now clung to his long bushy tail and belly fur. Macy couldn't abide that, so he attended to his bath, straightening, and tongue-combing the dark fur that matched the color of the wooden floors. He paid special attention to his snowy ruff and felt his heart rate slow with the self-imposed massage.

Bath finished, Macy crossed to the closed door and meowed loudly. A strong, strident meow usually opened a door, but this time nothing happened. Macy meowed again and pawed at the wooden base of the door. When nothing happened, he flopped onto his side and stretched one paw as far as he could reach underneath the barrier. Again and again, he meowed his request.

His bowl waited downstairs, on top of the cold metal box that held September's food. And it was time for Macy's pill. Every night September called him to the kitchen, asked him to leap onto the counter, open wide, and take a pill. After that, Macy got the best treats ever, and his bowl filled up with soft, stinky food.

But nobody responded to Macy's plea. Finally, he withdrew his paw. The busted window drew his attention. If he couldn't get through the door, maybe the window offered a way out. He padded across the room, weaving between the bits of glass that littered the wooden floor.

He delicately sniffed the hot night air spilling through the broken window. Macy stood on his rear paws, bracing to jump up on the narrow windowsill. He enjoyed visits to the garden, usually wearing a harness attached to his leash, and accompanied by September. But she wasn't here. She didn't open the door or call him to give his pill and special treat. He couldn't hear anyone downstairs He couldn't hear or see anyone in the garden either. No human to hear his meow demands.

Macy hopped onto the windowsill. He paced up and down, carefully judging the distance between where he stood and the roof.

His tail painted figure eights in the air, a testament to his reticence. He purred, the rumble a self-calming sound, gathered himself, and lightly jumped down to the slippery tile roof.

He lowered his head to sniff the surface. The material had cooled, but still radiated heat stored from the sun. His purr increased, liking the warmth against his paw pads. From here, he looked down directly on the patio. A double door opened into the house from the patio. He carefully crawled down the slanted roof, claws extended to give a better grip. Soon he reached the very end of the steep pitch, relieved to stop in the gutter where he could more easily perch.

Again he meowed loudly. He could jump the distance with no problem but would prefer September or another trusted human to come get him. His tummy urged him to hurry.

Macy was a cat of habit. Anything that threw off his schedule made him uncomfortable. It was bad enough that strangers had invaded his house and his territory outside the windows. Anything he could see belonged to Macy. He jealously guarded his territory, sharing it only with a select few trusted creatures, like September and Shadow. And, more recently, the boy hiding under the bed.

September didn't like Macy going outside unless he wore his vest. But September wasn't here to put on his vest or lift a smart cat down from the tall roof. So Macy would have to do it himself.

He paced the length of the gutter and back again, looking for just the right place to make his descent. At one end, another piece of metal spilled down the wall to the ground below. A vine climbed up this natural trellis, the leaves hiding its presence until Macy sniffed it out.

He had clawed his way up trees before, but going up differed greatly from getting down. Carefully Macy placed first one paw and then another against the vegetation. His hips flexed with anticipation, bracing himself to hold his weight back, until all four paws found just the right purchase in the vine. He stretched forward and downward, one forepaw at a time, until only his haunches held him in place. Below, the brick patio gave way to a flower bed, where this vine began. Without further hesitation, Macy launched himself, four paws contacting the metal downspout, almost as if defying gravity to run straight down.

He landed with a soft thump. Breath whooshed from his chest, and he sprang forward a few more steps. Macy stood, panting softly, shook himself hard, then sat down and licked himself all over to slow his rapid heartbeat and cool his body temperature. He stood, stretched, and made his way to the patio door.

But it also stood closed. He meowed over and over, and stood on his hind legs to peer through the glass. He could see through the empty living room to where the front door of the house beckoned. Just as his ears and nose had already told him, the house was empty.

Macy hunkered down against the patio door, tucking his feet underneath him, and wrapping his long, fluffy tail around his body. He meowed once more, but softly, no longer expecting any response. Then he heard a car door open and slam at the front of the house.

Macy leaped to his feet. He again placed paws on the door, digging at the glass even though he knew he couldn't claw his way inside. Macy wasn't a fan of car rides but knew that September and Shadow traveled in the big metal boxes. His meows grew louder, lower pitched, and more demanding as he saw the front door swing open.

And then he hissed, shrank down to make himself invisible, as the strange black dog raced into his house.

Chapter 35 – TEDDY

Teddy parked in the now-deserted field and watched as Lia opened the front door to September's house. Captain Gregory had called ahead to the cop on duty to let them in, with the admonition they steered clear of the garden. He watched Lia send Magic inside to clear the building, a technique she'd learned from Shadow and September.

"Oh September, I'm so, so sorry." His knuckles whitened on the steering wheel. He willed himself to stay strong. The two kids with Lia would need his strength.

Ethel had agreed to the ruse at the hospital. As a cop's wife, she'd had to buck up more than most people and wanted to protect Combs. Asking her to lie to these children and to Lia wasn't fair. Not when she was mourning her husband's death.

So Captain Gregory put protection on Combs's room and Ethel stayed with him. They wouldn't need the fiction of Combs's death for long—not if Teddy had anything to do with it. He hadn't been able to protect September, but, with the help of that mysterious texting insider, Teddy would do anything, everything, to keep the rest of their friends safe.

He opened the door to the RV, blocking Meriwether's attempts to exit. "You've already been fed. Hang out here, and I'll check back later." Teddy strode up the brick driveway, coming abreast of the trio just as Magic returned to the front door with a happy wag. The group trudged inside.

The two kids still wore their wedding attire. Melinda walked slowly with shoulders hunched, mascara turning her eyes into raccoon circles. Willie scuffed his shoes as he crossed the threshold.

Teddy met Lia's eyes. The kids didn't know yet. They hadn't seen the press conference, and if he had his way, Teddy would confiscate their phones for as long as it took. They were due some luck. He wanted the fiction of Combs's death to expire before his kids heard about it. Melinda kicked off her shoes, and ran to the overstuffed sofa, sinking into it and tucking her feet underneath her. "Why can't we stay at the hospital?"

"'Cause we're not doctors, that's why, and we're not cops." Willie spoke with the know-it-all confidence of an eleven-year-old boy. "We don't want to be a distraction. Not when they're taking care of Daddy." He found a perch beside his sister, and she wrapped an arm around his shoulders, pulling him close.

"It's been a long day and it's getting late. Melinda, why don't you take your brother upstairs and help him get ready for bed." Lia's jaw worked; Teddy could tell she struggled to hold back tears.

Melinda would have objected, but saw the look on Teddy's face. She accepted her role as big sister and comforter-in-chief. "Come on kiddo, the hospital will call with news. They'll tell us more as soon as they know." She glared at Teddy and Lia, making it clear there'd be hell to pay if her words weren't heeded.

The pair clumped up the stairs, and Teddy sighed with relief.

He still needed to fudge the truth with Lia. But at least she was an adult and eventually would understand the necessity of the lie.

The big black dog crossed to Lia, pushing his broad muzzle against her thigh. She dropped one hand to his massive shoulders, and Teddy could see she took strength from Magic's presence.

"Look at that." She waved at the dining room table, stacked high with gaily wrapped wedding presents. "They waited so long for this day. All of their friends wanted to celebrate with them. And now this?" Her breath caught. "Mercedes Gonzales lost her husband. She's got two kids to raise without a daddy." Her voice dropped to a whisper. "And those kids upstairs lost their dad, and September—they loved her, too. What's going to happen to Melinda and Willie? Ethel would take them, but with her husband laid up for who knows how long, I don't know what she'll do. And me…I have enough trouble taking care of myself."

"I got no answers." He shoved his glasses back up his nose. His fingers drummed the air, eager to be back on the keyboard, into the dark web, to find the killers. He considered how much to tell Lia. She might have some insights, but she couldn't know that Combs was still alive.

Magic grabbed the hem of Lia's wedding outfit and tugged. She absently stroked his brow. But he dodged away, sat down in front of her and pawed her leg again. His broad head tipped from side-to-side, as if willing her to read his mind.

"What?" She cocked her head too, an odd mirroring of the dog's action.

Teddy watched, bemused. Witnessing the bond between Lia and Magic hurt his heart, imagining how Shadow must feel after losing September.

Lia's eyes widened, and she abruptly strode across the room to the patio double doors. Magic followed close behind, then—

without a word from the woman—he sat and waited. She flipped the wall switch, flooding the patio with bright light, and peered out the windows, first one direction then the other. Teddy heard a quiet indrawn breath. "How the hell..." She glanced over at him. "The cat got out."

"Macy?" He took hurried steps to join her at the doors. September would have secured him inside. "We need to get him back inside." The least they could do was keep September's cat safe, with her dog already in the wind.

Lia rubbed her face and turned away from the doorway. She led Magic back to the center of the room and placed him in a down and stay. "I'm not so great with cats, Teddy. And Magic probably looks scary to him, a strange dog so different from Shadow. You know Macy better than I do. Maybe the cat will come to you."

Teddy nodded. He spotted the mound of coffee-colored fur snuggled up tight against the far corner of the patio. After living with Meriwether for half a year, he knew better than to make a direct approach. "Watch for me. Call out if he takes off."

He hurried to the kitchen, knowing the rear door opened out of sight of the patio, so less likely to spook the cat. The caterer's bounty remained on countertops, covered and ready to serve. They'd need to deal with that, too.

Teddy snagged a large dish towel and grabbed a chicken nugget from one of the dishes—better offer a high value bribe—before slipping out the door. He pitched his gravelly voice as high as he could as he reached the corner of the house. He'd read somewhere that cats responded best to singsong baby talk. The hand towel September used carried her comforting scent. Teddy was no behavior expert, but he'd been around her enough to pick up a few pointers. The cat knew some commands, but Teddy doubted Macy would respond to anyone but September under the circumstances.

"Macy-cat, want a treat? Macy, come." Teddy stopped as soon as the cat came into view. The cat's head came up, ears tipped forward, and he let out a small tentative meow. Macy stood, gave three quick licks to his white ruff, then padded swiftly to meet Teddy. He sat in front of Teddy's leg and meowed again. Teddy offered a shred of chicken, and the cat delicately took the morsel then patted his leg for more.

With a smile, Teddy dropped several more pieces on the ground in front of the cat. As Macy munched, Teddy bent down, draped the towel over the cat's back, and gently scooped him up. Teddy turned to the patio doors and nodded at Lia to open them.

Before he reached the door, an odd noise came from above Teddy, and his arms tightened around the cat's fur. He looked up.

A pair of small, thin legs dangled from the edge of the roof: Steven perched like a baby bird poised to fly from its nest.

Chapter 36 – SEPTEMBER

Shudders shook September's body, curled into a fetal position on the floor. Sobs stole her breath. Painful hiccups made her clinch her midsection. Warm hands grasped her shoulders. She screamed and recoiled. "Get off me! Don't you dare touch me."

Her mind was a jumble of incoherent memories. *Dead? Combs dead?*

She wanted to scream, rail at the sky, rend her clothes, tear her hair. In a moment, her bliss transformed to pain greater than she'd ever experienced, and September was no stranger to pain. After waiting years to find happiness… she'd pushed it away, kept Combs at arm's length for months… until he wore her down, and convinced her she had the right to be happy. She'd clung to that notion, and the belief she needed to satisfy some prerequisite to qualify for a happy ending. A wedding to satisfy her dead mother, her sisters and family, even the public's perception.

She'd insisted on the wedding. And caused his death. *Repeating the past.*

Her first husband had tried to save her, too, and she'd really tried to find happiness with him. But when Chris died, September dug a hole for herself in Heartland, locked the door and threw away the key. Combs broke down the door. He unlocked her heart. And now…

All her past failings flickered past her mind's eye, so many secrets, pain upon pain, bad choices, hopes, and dreams gone… Mourning wasn't enough. Not this time. Tears solved nothing. Anger born of despair choked her throat. Enough!

The rules protected the status quo, and September's life was anything but normal. People she loved paid for her mistakes, this time with death. Enemies followed no rules. Neither would she.

September sat up and knuckled wet from her eyes. No more would she rely on others. No more running. Or hiding. No more waiting for terror to catch up to her. With Combs dead she had nothing to lose. Nobody else to protect. And if she died going after Kaliko Wong, at least her death would not be in vain.

Focus, she needed to focus, despite the ringing in her ear and a shattered heart. She wanted Macy's purr, his soft fur in her arms, to bury her wet face in his ruff. But she couldn't function without Shadow. He'd keep her focused, prevent her from falling into that deep well from which she couldn't escape. She pulled herself upright and clung to the chair back to steady herself. *Vengeance has no time for panic attacks.*

"Mr. Glass—"

"Call me Jack."

September ignored the outstretched hand offered to steady her. "Okay, Jack. And Quinn. You say that Kaliko Wong just killed my fiancé." The grief threatened to surge once more. She couldn't even call Combs her husband, with vows left unsaid…

Jack nodded. "All our intelligence points to Kaliko Wong and her operatives. She's watched you for months. Something triggered this all-out assault, though."

September brushed off his last comment. Motive didn't matter. "Where is she?" She'd pick their brains but had no desire to join this motley duo.

Quinn shrugged. "Don't know, but she won't leave until she gets confirmation you're dead."

"Exactly what do you expect of me? Not that I'm sure I should help you, after kidnapping me, and leaving Shadow God knows where—"

"We saved your life. Had you stayed, the drone would have taken you out once they realized the bomb had missed. We share a common enemy, joining our team increases the odds of success."

September pressed her hands to her face, rubbing her eyes, and wishing she could wake up from this nightmare. "Takes more than two to make a team."

Quinn smirked. "Not everyone's here. The virtual tea—"

Jack held up a hand to cut her off. "We have a web of partners. That's how we knew you were at risk. We've been tracking Wong for years, trying to get ahead of her influence. Her focus on you made her ignore any other threats, like us."

September's eyes narrowed. He'd used her tragedy for his own twisted goals. "So glad I could help." The sarcasm cut sharper than a razor.

He didn't flinch. "I tried to stop this. Multiple warnings, in person and texted anonymously, were ignored. So, I joined your security team." He brushed his hands back and forth in a gesture that basically said I wash my hands of you. "But you aren't a prisoner here. Leave, if you want the witch to continue to stalk your every move—"

"I'm leaving, but not without Shadow." September crossed her arms, hugging herself. "You don't understand what he means to me. He's not a pet. He keeps me grounded. So I can function." *And survive.*

"He's your service dog, right. Everyone knows you're inseparable." Quinn grabbed her phone when it rang, then walked away into the other room to take the call.

"You need to stay hidden, but your dog gives you away. Wong has operatives everywhere. We have gone to a lot of trouble to make her think you died, to give us some breathing room. Time enough to take her out."

"Without knowing her location?" September paced from one end of the kitchen to the other. Her balance was returning as she adjusted to the odd inner ear issue on one side of her head.

She couldn't dismiss their help. Barefoot, wearing only the skintight under-dress, she couldn't take on a trained assassin. They clearly wanted her as bait. But only they knew where Shadow was. *Play along until she got her dog back. Then all bets are off.*

She couldn't afford a meltdown, so she stifled a choked sob, gritted her teeth, and tamped down her emotion. Until she thought about Combs's kids. Who would take care of Melinda and Willie, if not her? She knew that's what Combs would want. Heartland PD would take care of their own, but that didn't replace a parent.

September had never wanted to be a parent. But life happened. And in more ways than one, she'd been forced to face her fears, rise to unwanted challenges, and her life was better for that. Combs didn't need her anymore, but his children did. Maybe she had something to live for, after all.

But that wouldn't stop her from seeking retribution and justice for the killer who had tried to destroy her life. She'd go after the witch all right, to protect herself *and* the kids. She'd live to talk about it, to make a new life for them all.

Deep breath. *Trust only yourself. Lie, if you must—everyone else lies.*

"Before I can help you, I need clothes. And my dog." She raised a hand when Jack would have argued. "Not negotiable. One more thing. I need a name. One name, someone on your team that will convince me to join forces. Get me those three things, and I'll consider joining your cause."

He nodded. "Quinn has your go-bag. She lifted it from your car." He smiled at her look of surprise. "Yes, Quinn is very resourceful. I suspect she's on the phone arranging to pick up Shadow. I think it's a mistake, but as y'all say in this part of the country, it's your rodeo." Jack dropped his voice. "I'd rather Quinn doesn't know, but much of my online team knows me as Kid Kewl."

"Quinn mentioned that name earlier. You are the team leader?"

"There are many people on my team. You probably know Steven Childress the best."

September's jaw dropped. She'd heard some of the kids mention that name during the pill fiasco. And the anonymous texts also mentioned Steven.

Quinn interrupted as she entered the kitchen. "We have a problem, Jack. Got hold of the boarding kennel. Shadow went AWOL with two other dogs." Quinn looked at September, no apology in her face. She shrugged. "Seems like your dog's too damn smart for his own good."

At the look on September's face, Jack backed away. He suddenly understood why Kali had such respect and antipathy toward September. The news of Combs's death broke her… The loss of Shadow enraged her.

Chapter 37 – TEDDY

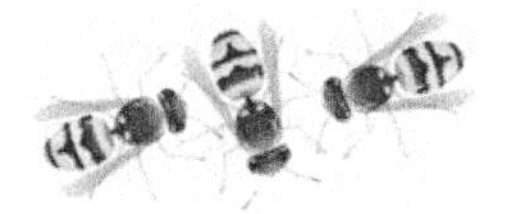

Teddy squeezed so hard, that Macy squealed. He rushed through the door as Lia opened it, moving with swift determination to the kitchen. Teddy placed Macy on the floor, hesitated, then put the bowl of chicken nuggets in the refrigerator before he closed the pet gate securely. They didn't need a cat sick from eating the buffet on top of everything else.

"What's going on?" Lia moved out of the way as Teddy rushed by her.

"Steven's on the roof." At her expression of dismay, Teddy added, "He's sitting on the edge of the gutter, swinging his feet, and looking at his tablet of course."

"How'd he get up there?"

"Same way the cat got out, I guess. But a little boy landing on his feet won't come out as well as a cat." Teddy hurried back to the double doors and started out onto the patio. "We must get him down. September should have a ladder somewhere. Maybe in the garage?"

"I think so." Lia rushed out, heading for the carriage house that served as a garage to the old-fashioned house.

He needed to keep the boy calm. Teddy didn't know much about Steven, only that the child loved electronics and software. They had that in common. But Steven didn't communicate like other children his age. Teddy didn't want to say something that would set the boy off and end up with an injured child on top of the rest of the day's tragedies.

"Hey Steven, what are you doing up there?" He watched the boy's feet swing back and forth, shiny tennis shoes sparkling in the bright floodlights.

Steven shrugged. He kept his head down, eyes focused on the tablet under his busy fingers. "Big boom. Need room. Window glass shattered fast."

Teddy nodded. The boy and cat must've been in one of the bedrooms. He wondered why April hadn't taken Steven with her when she left.

"You want to come down from there? Wait right there. Lia will bring a ladder and we'll get you down. Do you know how to climb a ladder?"

He nodded. "But the cat-cat-cat doesn't climb like that." He looked up briefly, then his eyes slid away from Teddy's, and he focused once more on his tablet. "Kid Kewl needs news. There's lots-lots-lots to lose." His fingers flew over his tablet. "All along, it's been Wong."

Teddy wrinkled his brow, wondering at the reference. Maybe Kid Kewl was a cartoon character. "Once we get you down, you can share all the important news with Kid Kewl." He wouldn't tell the kid, but right now, the entire world was full of wrong.

Teddy heard the rattle of metal and saw Lia struggling, half carrying and dragging, a tall ladder. He hurried to meet her, then grabbed one end, leading the way back to the patio. Quickly, they placed it beside Steven's swinging feet.

"Steven? Can you climb down the ladder yourself, or do you want me to help?" Lia stood, hands on hips, reluctance obvious in her voice. Teddy didn't want to think what might happen at the top of the ladder, should the boy object to Lia's close presence.

Without answering, Steven tucked his tablet into the waistband of his pants and turned around, placing his feet on the top rungs. Teddy steadied the ladder as the boy scrambled quickly down the metal stairway. A slight trickle of blood ran from one of Stephen's knees. "You cut yourself?"

The boy nodded his head, one quick jerk. He pulled the tablet back out, immediately engrossed again in the information on the screen.

"Probably when he climbed out the window." Lia motioned the boy toward the open patio door and followed him inside. "I'll get something to clean him up."

Teddy didn't bother asking Steven about his mother's absence. Either the child wouldn't know, or Teddy would have a devil of a time understanding what he said. He knew Steven was brilliant. A lot went on inside that blond head, but the rhyming words made conversation nearly impossible.

As Teddy closed the double doors he heard Macy meowing, followed by September's voice, saying, "Hungry." He started and peered into the other room.

Macy sat beside a group of brightly colored panels in one corner of the room, right beside his oversized litter box. Each of the panels contained a large button that looked like the "Easy Button" found in so many television advertisements. As he watched, Macy again pawed one button, and September's pre-recorded voice repeated the demand. "Hungry, hungry, hungry." He moved to another button, and pawed it too. "Pill time," said the recording. Macy trotted to stand in front of the closed pet gate and stare at Teddy.

"Lia? The cat's talking to me." Teddy shoved his glasses back up the bridge of his nose.

She smiled. "Oh yeah, September got some of those buttons a while ago. I didn't know she'd started using them. Shadow didn't take to them. Macy seems to know what they mean." She crossed into the kitchen, past the pet gate, found the cat's medication, and ask him to jump onto the counter. Macy obliged. She said "pill time" like the recording, and the cat opened wide. After taking the pill, the cat pawed Lia's arm, and she gave Macy the expected treat, filled his bowl and set it on top of the refrigerator. Macy leaped to the tall perch and settled down with a purr.

Teddy watched, no longer surprised by the things that September's animals could do. Each button must have a recording device inside, to allow a word or short phrase recording. They had used a similar technology for nonverbal people for some time.

"Know the reason, maybe treason?" Steven scurried into the dining room area, set his tablet on the table, and began combing through the pile of wedding gifts. "Blood will tell. Break the spell." His singsong child's voice made the hair on the back of Teddy's neck stand up. He shivered.

The boy found a fancy envelope amidst all the gifts on the table. He cocked his head, one finger following the writing on the label, then nodded.

Lia reentered the room and crossed to the boy. "Oh no, Steven, leave the presents alone. Those were for your Aunt…" She swallowed hard, being unable to finish the words.

Teddy knew how she felt. So many things to take care of, and returning gifts was the least of their worries. But when Lia tried to take the envelope from Steven, he pulled away, free hand flapping in the air at her to keep her away. "It's proof-proof-proof. Saw it on the roof-roof-roof." He backed away.

"Lia, do you know how to get hold of April? How long until Doug comes home? Lordy, does he even know? Somebody needs to take charge of Steven." Teddy drew near but hesitated to put hands on the boy. He pointed to the tablet that Steven had left on the dining room table. "Can I look at your tablet? I promise I won't hurt it. I like computers too."

Steven shook his head precisely three times. He dashed forward, grabbed his tablet, and ran across the room, finding a perch in the corner of the overstuffed sofa. He huddled there, staring from the information on his tablet to the fancy envelope in his other hand.

Well, forget that. Teddy sighed and slowly followed the boy. Steven probably had no clue where his parents were, anyway.

Lia crossed her arms. "I bet his grandfather would know how to reach Steven's parents. We can call Lysle to come pick him up." Her eyes narrowed, taking in the details of the present that Steven had culled from the stack. "Steven, that's from your Uncle Mark."

Steven nodded once. His eyes filled with tears. But he didn't bother to brush them away as they streaked his cheeks. "The assault." He waved the envelope in the air. "Her fault."

Teddy felt the words like a punch in his gut. The poor little boy might not express himself clearly, but he understood what had happened. Hell, in a way, he agreed with the child. It was September's fault. If she hadn't been so hardheaded, refusing to cancel the wedding, she'd still be alive.

Lia sat down next to the boy. "Honey, it's not your aunt's fault. She didn't want any of this to happen. Some terrible people made this happen, and I promise the police will make them pay."

He shook his head again, frustration coloring his face. "Not

September, please remember. It was Wong, all along." He stabbed a finger at his tablet.

Her brow wrinkled. "Yes, I know it was wrong."

Teddy gasped with sudden realization. Steven didn't speak with a lisp. For a young boy, he had an uncommon vocabulary and always clearly enunciated. He wasn't mispronouncing the word. He'd said the same name twice now.

"What the hell does Wong Enterprises have to do with this?"

"Wait, the same Mrs. Wong who put me and Tee 'on ice' last year? Oh, my God." Lia shook her head slowly. "But why would they go after September? My father will spend the rest of his life in prison for killing her husband, Simon Wong." She swallowed hard. "Maybe his widow can't touch my father, and instead goes after those he cares about? Maybe September wasn't the target. Maybe Kaliko Wong wanted to kill me."

Chapter 38 – KALI

Kali wandered around the house, not at all impressed with the down-home comfort touches. She much preferred shiny glass and metallic surfaces that fit her idea of cutting-edge comfort.

This three-story bed-and-breakfast boasted floor-to-ceiling windows on the ground floor, mullioned windows on the second story, and an eight-sided tower room on the third floor, accessed by a circular metal staircase, which served as a cutesy third-story study above the master bedroom. She stopped at the largest windows on the ground floor, gazing across the moon drenched lawn to the pier jutting out into the man-made lake. Her driver stood as a black silhouette against the silvery water, keeping watch and patrolling the perimeter.

No one of importance knew who she was, nor cared why she was here. All of Kali's enemies sniffed after her from across the seas. Yes, some domestic rivals continued to dog her heels, but soon she'd neuter them. With the funds unlocked, and her influence rising, nothing would stop Kali from controlling the

Wong dynasty.

Her dark hair spilled over her bare shoulders, and she idly played with the long tendrils. The water looked tempting. Her scalding shower had cleansed her, and the interlude with the driver had left her skin flushed. Even the overheated lake water, courtesy of this oppressive Texas climate, would feel cool. Kali had massaged banana-scented lotion into her skin, starting with her slender feet and legs, until her whole body smelled of ripe fruit. She wanted—needed—to expend the energy that burned within. Nothing, not even bloodletting, sated the hunger like it had in the past.

She'd been hungry since the day she was born. Sold into servitude, she'd risen through the ranks because of her natural intelligence, vicious skills, and appetite for death. She learned along the way how to manipulate others, bend them to her will without their knowledge, and ultimately ascended to the highest position within the Wong dynasty: chief consort. As his lover, she'd garnered information he did not know he divulged. She smiled at the pleasant memory. When you nurture a snake in your own nest, you have no one to blame when the snake eats your young.

Kali kept a list, a mental balance sheet of those who had done her wrong over her decades of life. Many she'd already disappeared from the landscape. Those who agreed to her will gained influence and wealth. If they knew Kali's origin story, they dared not speak of it. Once she had secured her power, she'd eliminate them as well.

Judges, senators, even congressmen did her bidding, some with full knowledge and others through manipulation. But she had her sights set on higher goals. Kali didn't need public acclamation. It was enough to pull the strings from behind the black curtain. She had worked for years to set everything up, then presented her accomplishment as a gift to her husband.

Simon laughed at her. Said she reached beyond her station. That his business ran without issues, and he forbade her to proceed, fearing the public scrutiny that would follow. His laughter cut worse than any of Kali's knives. And signed his death warrant. It took very little for her to arrange his death and lay it at the feet of a ne'er-do-well.

Beyond the legality of the inheritance, the old-fashioned hierarchy of the Wong empire demanded certain concessions. She'd assumed it would be a formality, but set triggers in place, that would warn Kali of any threat to her ascendancy. One alarm had rung several months ago, precipitating this escalation.

A new text message dinged. Kali crossed to pick up the phone.

>Located September's dog. It's on the move.

Kali had wondered what happened to the dog. Find the dog, and you'd find September—if she still lived.

<Find the dog.

She'd kill it in front of September.

Chapter 39 – SEPTEMBER

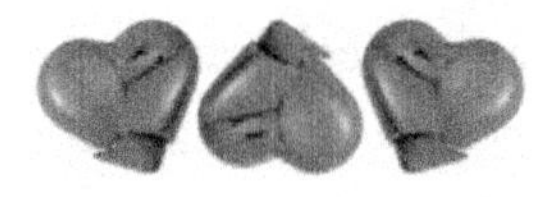

"What the hell were you thinking?" September fought to control her rage. "Shadow escapes all kinds of enclosures. Nothing will stop him from returning to me."

Quinn stumbled to put distance between them, stuttering uncharacteristically. "I told the owner to make sure he was in a contained enclosure. I told her."

"Where's my go-bag? Give it to me. Now!" She had a change of clothes in the bag. She speared Jack with her gaze. "Soon as I'm dressed, we go find Shadow." She couldn't think about anything else until they were together.

Quinn hurried to the car and returned with the bag. September grabbed it and pulled out the clothing. She ducked into the bedroom to pull on calf-length dark green tights and a tank top, adding a loose shirt over top. The sweat-soaked wedding slip she left in a pile on the floor. Returning to the living room, September laced on scuffed shoes. This outfit matched what she wore during her self-defense classes. It would suffice for the work at hand. She stood. "Let's go."

Now, with a goal, she didn't hesitate. Find Shadow. Then track down Kaliko Wong. She paused at the door, turning back to stare at the pair. "What are you waiting for?"

Quinn shrugged. "I can get you back to the kennel, but how are you gonna find the dog after that? I mean, you gonna use a bullhorn or something and yell for him to come? Here puppy, puppy, puppy…"

September rounded on the girl. "Shadow's collar has GPS tracking. I can—" Her throat tightened. She didn't have her phone. She leaned against the doorway, grabbing the handle to keep herself upright. "Oh no…" At top speed, a German Shepherd could reach 30 miles an hour. If Shadow had any inkling of where to go, he could be miles away from the kennel by now. And without her phone, she couldn't find him.

"Is the tracking app on your cell phone?" Jack looked thoughtful.

Her dog had to be found. She'd already lost Combs; she couldn't lose Shadow, too. "Lia's dog has some tracking skills. You met them. He's the bomb dog that probably saved a bunch of lives."

Jack shook his head. "And just how am I supposed to explain I know where to look for your lost service dog?"

"We can trust Lia." But could they? Lia's bomb dog allowed the explosion to happen. Her voice faltered on her next words. "She's like a sister to me, probably closer than any of my sisters except April." September's heart clenched at the thought of what April must be going through, thinking she had died. And to think Steven had worked with this man—Kid Kewl—for months. Creepy.

He pulled out his own cell phone. "We can always bring in

more help later. But for now, let me work some of my magic."

She slowly returned to Jack's side and saw he had typed in her own telephone number. "I could hack in and get the info, but we'd waste time." He thumbed through the phone, finding the screen he wanted, and handed it to her to fill in access information. Within seconds, she had logged into the geo-location app.

September could see the small colored dot that showed Shadow's presence. "Brilliant! Let's go." Again she headed for the door.

Quinn looked from Jack to September and back again. Jack nodded and handed her the phone. "This is my spare. Find her dog, then get back here ASAP." He looked directly at September. "That is, if you want to stay alive."

"You're not coming?" For a moment, September debated making a break for it, once away from this strange and dangerous man. She probably had a better chance of getting away from Quinn alone than the two of them together. But right now, Shadow was her priority.

Jack didn't bother to answer. He'd already pulled out another phone and was busily tapping the interface, communicating with one of his team members.

Quinn grabbed September's go-bag from the floor. "Take this. Who knows what we might find out there. I don't want to be the only one with firepower."

September shivered but accepted the bag. Besides her gun, it contained extra ammunition and a host of miscellaneous helpful items. With any luck, she wouldn't have to use it. But she wouldn't hesitate to shoot if it meant protecting Shadow. Or herself.

Quinn and Jack, though, were on their own.

Chapter 40 – SHADOW

Shadow loped along the highway, Keighley shoulder to shoulder with him. Max trailed behind, stopping now and then to investigate intriguing scents. Shadow didn't mind the company so long as they didn't interfere with his search. Shadow wanted to find September.

He had trotted around the front of the enormous kennel to pick up the scent of the car that brought him to this place. Everything had a signature odor and cars were no different. But on the hot pavement, scent quickly dissipated.

When forks in the road appeared, he slowed to check the turnoff. At first, he could easily tell which route the car had chosen. But the last two times he checked, too many cars had followed this car path for him to be sure. At the thought, Shadow whined deep in his chest, the uncertainty gnawing at him the way you chewed a bone.

Shadow heard a car driving along the pathway and quickly padded to the side of the road so that the underbrush would hide him. Keighley didn't follow. She and Max had found an interesting smell on the side of the road. Happily panting, Max rolled onto his side, digging his shoulders into the scent to perfume himself.

The car's eye-lights speared the dark, shining twin spotlights on Keighley. She wasn't frightened by the car, and simply waited for it to pass. But the car didn't drive on. It slowed, the driver rolling down a window to point with his hand. The car stopped. Max clambered to his feet, and shook himself. Keighley approached the car, tail wagging in anticipation of a friendly human.

Instead, the pointing finger made a loud pop-pop-pop sound.

Shadow barked, recognizing the scary sound. Keighley yelped when dirt and pavement splintered as the bullet struck nearby.

Guns were scary. Shadow hated guns. Guns reached out from a distance to hurt. Even though the gun hadn't aimed at Shadow, he didn't want any dog to get bitten by a gun.

The arm holding the gun steadied to point again, but Shadow didn't wait. He sprang from the undergrowth, and leaped, muzzle connecting with the gunman's wrist and knocking aside his aim.

Max barked with excitement and raced around the motionless car. He raced around and around, dodging from Keighley's form to Shadow, and back again.

The man cursed. He shifted, and again pointed the gun. This time at Shadow.

Max mirrored the big shepherd's earlier behavior. He leaped, jaws wide, and crunched the wrist.

The man's shriek split the night. The gun dropped.

Keighley whirled, barking loudly with excitement.

Max immediately released the man's wrist. Shadow figured the Kelpie didn't like the taste of blood, either. The two black dogs spun in tandem, and dashed back off the road, disappearing into the scrubby trees and grasses.

But Keighley remained on the highway berm, her barks and snarls increasing with agitation, as she jumped and pawed at the man's car door.

The gun had fallen to the hard pavement of the car path. But the bad man wouldn't get out to retrieve it while a dog yelled at him. Shadow hoped his friend wouldn't get bitten by another gun. He wished Keighley would hide with them.

When the car drove away, it raced so fast, it kicked gravel into the air.

Shadow crept out of the brush and returned to his friend's side. Keighley licked Shadow's muzzle, and Shadow acknowledged the gesture with a slow wag.

Max joined them, the fur still bristling his shoulders. He nosed the gun lying on the hot pavement and lifted his lips in a silent snarl. The smell rode the air, the stink making a good dog's hackles rise. None of them would forget that smell.

But now Shadow didn't know which way to go. If they continued the path they were following, they might catch up to the bad man. But the other direction took him farther away from September. What should a dog do?

Oh how he wished September was here. People knew things that dogs didn't. September would know what to do.

The moon shine gave more definition to the road and the pathway they traveled. Two more cars passed by but the dogs dodged off the road to avoid any more gun-pointing people. Neither slowed down, so Shadow's hackles smoothed quickly after they passed.

When a third car appeared, the three dogs again dove off the side of the road. They crouched low and waited. But this one slowed down. Then stopped.

Shadow's ears slicked tight to the back of his head. A low

growl bubbled, too low for any but himself and the other dogs to hear.

"I don't see anything. But the app says he's nearby."

That voice… The breeze picked up a scent and brought it to Shadow's quivering nose. Her smell!

Joyful whimpers spilled from his throat. Shadow exploded from the hidden gully. September had come for him!

He didn't wait for her to leave the car when the door opened. Shadow leaped into her lap, turning, rolling upside down, burrowing into her shoulder, and crying with joy.

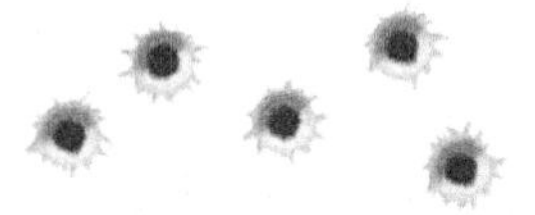

Max sheltered in the undergrowth at the side of the road, watching and listening. He immediately realized the person in the car belonged to Shadow. Their reunion prompted small whimpers of his own, but he refused to emerge from the darkness.

He liked adventure, enjoyed new dog friends, loved challenges like escaping a fence. But the scary gun, the dangerous stranger, unfamiliar night sounds and smells… Max missed home.

Max remembered the before-times, when he lived all crowded together with many other animals. Smells of desperation and sickness, constant cries of despair, little food, and never enough attention. Nobody to pet him, scratch itchy spots, or share fun games. Scared all the time.

Then people came for him. He remembered learning to trust. And for the first time, Max felt safe. And loved.

Out here in the middle of nowhere, darkness all around with gunshots and strangers, Max didn't feel safe. He wanted his person, too. Wanted to snuggle into her arms, tease his sister-dog by hiding toys, and play until his legs couldn't run anymore. He whimpered, watching Shadow, and yearning for his own reunion.

Max ached to go home. How would his person find him out here?

She always collected him from the kennel. Yes! He'd wait for her there. If he climbed out of the kennel, Max knew he could climb back inside. And while he waited for his person, maybe he could play the promised game of Chuckit . . .

With a soft woof of decision, the black Kelpie whirled, retracing his paw steps, and became one with the shadows of the night.

Chapter 41 – TEDDY

Teddy removed his glasses. They weren't smeared, but polishing them helped him think. "Lia, I don't think we know enough about Kaliko Wong to guess her motives." He turned to Steven, careful not to make eye contact. He learned the boy didn't like that any more than Macy the cat. "That's who you meant, wasn't it? Kaliko Wong caused all the bad problems? Right, Steven?"

Steven nodded once, emphatically. "Kaliko Wong all along." He stabbed his Uncle Mark's wedding envelope at his tablet. "Answers here, it's very clear." Steven huddled at one end of the sofa, staring at his tablet and fiddling with the paper clasp on the envelope.

Melinda trudged down the stairs and joined them in the living room. "I got Willie settled. I wanted him to take a shower, but he refused and went to bed in his wedding clothes. Said he doesn't want to change anything until we hear from the hospital." She shrugged. "I kind of feel the same way, like it'd be bad luck to change anything until we know Dad's okay." She hesitated. "Have you heard any news?" Her voice sounded like a tentative child, not the forceful young woman Teddy knew.

Lia looked away, seemingly afraid to make eye contact with the girl. "No word yet."

Teddy wanted to shake Lia, tell her to put on a better game face. They didn't need these kids going through the additional trauma. If Steven was right, Teddy knew the Wong organization had unlimited resources and reach. Hell, she could have an assassin poised outside and ready to breach the house all over again. At the thought, shivers traveled up the back of his spine.

But Melinda didn't seem to notice. Her focus was on Steven. "Where'd he come from? I thought Steven was with his mom." She crossed to the boy, cocking her head to peer closely at the envelope in his hand. "What's he got?"

"Melinda, do you have April's phone number? Or Doug's?" Lia asked.

Melinda pushed auburn hair out of her eyes. "No. But I bet it's on September's phone." She gestured with one hand, and Teddy saw the cell phone. "This was in her bedroom. I heard it making a funny noise. Oh, and the window up there blew out. There's glass all over the floor."

Teddy took September's cell phone from the girl. It vibrated in his hand.

Melinda sat next to Steven and got a closer look at the envelope. "Did you take that from the table? That's a wedding present. Steven, that doesn't belong to you. You don't take other people's stuff." She reached for the paper.

Steven gripped the thick paper. He dropped his tablet in his lap, so that he could hang on with both hands to his Uncle Mark's present. A brief tug-of-war ensued, the little boy making a high-pitched keening sound as the much larger girl muscled the package away from him.

"No-no-no, you don't know, but the blood will show." Stephen's voice went up two octaves, making Teddy's ears hurt.

"That belongs to September and my… my dad." Her face flushed.

Lia grabbed the envelope from Melinda. "What does it matter? Let him have it. It's not like they have any use for presents anymore."

A beat. Silence. Sudden understanding.

Melinda's face crumpled, the knowledge making her melt from the inside out. "But, but you said… Oh no. Daddeeeee!" She threw herself on the other end of the sofa, sobbing.

"Lia, give the present back to Steven. Steven, it's okay, we'll figure things out." Teddy settled on the sofa in between the two children, feeling helpless.

But once Steven again took possession of the envelope, his keening shut off like a faucet turned hard. Teddy glared at Lia, but he couldn't really blame her. They were all out of their element. He just didn't want Willie to wake up and add to the distress.

"Melinda honey, I know it's not the news you want. We have to count on you right now to be strong for your little brother. Can you do that? I promise, things are going to get better."

"How can you say that? Nothing's ever going to be all right again. I wish Dad never met September. She's the reason…" She pulled out of his arms and ran for the stairs, still sobbing.

The girl was right. Things would never be the same. Yes, Combs's death was a fiction, for now, but he might yet die. Ethel had promised to keep him posted. The last he'd heard, Combs had a broken leg, a head injury, and was unconscious.

At least Steven had calmed down. The little boy opened the wedding present and appeared to read it. He set the pages down on the sofa cushion beside him and began to type.

With a sigh, Teddy turned attention back to September's cell phone to find April's number. It had stopped making the odd buzzing sound. Maybe September had left it unlocked.

One app was running a program. Teddy recognized it, and suddenly realized what it meant. When September first installed the geo-location for her beloved dog, he'd hacked the system to track Shadow. Now somebody else was doing the same thing.

Who but September would have an interest in recovering her dog? Teddy shivered. Could it be possible? Was Combs's death not the only fiction being played?

He didn't dare hope. But Teddy made a note of the dog's last location. He'd check it out and find Shadow. He owed September that much.

Chapter 42 – SEPTEMER

September's face glowed from a combination of tears and Shadow's licking tongue. He kept trying to push his 80-pound weight into her chest, turning somersaults in her lap as she sat in the vehicle's backseat. Whimpers of delight and distress continued gurgling from the dog's throat, and September reached her arms around the dog, trying to hold his wiggling body still. The weight and warmth of him gave her the anchor she desperately needed.

"Close the door." Quinn hissed the words, glaring at September in the rearview mirror. "If we can track your dog, so can other people. Who knows how many operatives are watching us?" Her hands drummed a rhythm on the steering wheel, and she revved the engine.

September debated running. But she didn't have a lot of choices, and with Shadow by her side her brain kicked back into gear. "Thank you, Quinn." She couldn't help the ragged sound of her voice. She had to get a hold of herself—no time for mourning, not yet. September hugged the big dog one more time and pushed him out of her lap. "Good dog, Shadow, now settle. Yes, you're a good dog, I missed you so much. Now settle."

She reached out to pull the rear door shut, but another furry face pressed into the space before she could slam it.

"Who are you?"

"The door, September, close the freaking door. In ten seconds, we're going whether…"

"Wait Quinn. There's another dog." September gave the hand signal for Shadow to wait in the car's backseat as she stepped out. The other dog whined and backed away. Her paws danced without music, like Shadow himself did.

In the backseat, Shadow whined. September looked at him over her shoulder.

"Is this a new friend?"

Shadow barked agreement.

The car crept forward. September hit Quinn's car door with her fist. "Give me a second. We can't just leave this dog here."

Quinn blew out a breath but stopped the car. "What do you think you're doing? This isn't a stray dog rescue. People with live ammo want to un-alive September Day. And you're messing around with some mutt?"

September glared at her. "Shadow knows this dog. We're not leaving her out here in the middle of nowhere." She backed away, presenting her side to the dog, while holding the car door open. "Come on pooch, jump in. Kennel up." The dog stared at her, tail still wagging but not making another move. September glanced at Shadow. "She's your friend Shadow. We must go."

Shadow woofed under his breath, danced forward on the car seat, and lifted one forepaw to wave at the other dog. Then he backed up into the car, giving space for the other animal to jump in. Without hesitation, the dog vaulted into the backseat and settled beside Shadow. She licked Shadow's muzzle and settled down with a groan.

September shook her head in amazement. But she shouldn't be surprised. She'd got those talking buttons to give Shadow a way to communicate more clearly. But truth be told, the dog made his needs and desires known without the help of pre-recorded voices.

She slammed the rear door and raced around to climb in the car's passenger side. "Let's go."

Quinn zoomed down the road almost before September had the door closed.

They rode together in silence for a little while. September held her left arm between the seats, wanting contact with Shadow's warm fur. "What can you tell me about Jack Glass? How did you meet? What's he get out of all of this?"

The younger girl glanced quickly at September, then back to the road. The bright headlights illuminated the gloom on the twisty road, as the girl took corners much faster than September preferred. She had to brace herself against the door to keep from rocking back and forth. She winced when Shadow and the other dog slid in the back seat.

"Just met him. Connected by one of his online team, the guy running the whole shebang calls himself Kid Kewl."

"He works with my nephew. You know Steven is a little boy. And autistic?"

Quinn shrugged. "Kids have their reasons. I know I did." She turned up the air conditioner, and the icy breeze felt good against September's bare skin. "Maybe he calls himself that because he's working with kids. But if they're kids, they're genius kids. There's one tracking finances. I heard Jack muttering to himself the other day about Tracy's number jumbling, whatever that means. Sounds like a kid thing." She leaned into another sharp turn. "Your nephew

Steven, he a genius too?"

September had never thought about it that way. "He loves computers."

"So does Jack. You saw how he hacked into your phone to find your dog. He does stuff like that all the time." She glanced at September, hesitated, licking her lips, and then with a what the hell expression, added, "I think he's Kid Kewl." At September's expression, she smiled. "He told you that already, didn't he? I knew it."

September's heart thumped louder. Shadow's cold nose pressed into her palm, and she stroked the dog's face without looking at him. "Kaliko Wong really kill his sister?"

Again, Quinn shrugged, and kept her eyes on the road. "Don't know. Don't care. She helped me, and I'm grateful. But it comes with too big of a price attached." She arched an eyebrow at September. "You can ask him."

September bit her lip. Jack Glass acted in control, but wrath simmered beneath the surface. He said he'd tracked the witch for years. She didn't want to be on the receiving end of his rage. No, better to play the game the same as Quinn, and let the man keep his secrets.

September had enough reasons of her own to hate Kaliko Wong. The time for hiding, for letting others protect her, had ended with the attack on her wedding party. "What's the plan?"

Quinn grinned. "Kill her ass." She laughed out loud. "I got trained by the best. She said I reminded her of herself. So now, the student goes after the teacher. There's a word for that…"

September shivered. "Irony?"

"No. I think the word I'm looking for is *justice*."

They had traversed one side of the man-made lake and Quinn slowed to find the small access road, then turned with a jerk of the wheel that left the dogs in back sliding and yelping for purchase.

When they pulled up by the small cottage, Jack opened the door and waited impatiently for them to join him. September climbed out, shouldering her bag, and unlatched the rear door. Both dogs hopped out while Quinn strode ahead.

"Picked up some extra baggage." Quinn pushed past him back into the house.

He didn't say anything, just stared at September as she drew close, with Shadow pressed hard against one thigh, the other dog trailing a few steps behind. He stood aside to let her enter, and his jaw flexed when Shadow spent a moment sniffing both of his pant legs before walking stiffly inside, hackles raised at the familiar scent.

"Shadow wouldn't let me leave his friend behind." She smiled when Shadow thumped his tail against her thigh, and she moved into the kitchen area to sit at the small table.

Jack pulled up a chair and scooted close. He held his phone and gestured with it. "I feared this would happen. Tracking your dog tripped an alert somewhere. We've got eyeballs watching."

"I don't care. I'd rather die with Shadow by my side than be separated and live without him. We're better together, and he's all I have left." With Combs dead, Melinda and Willie would blame her—rightly so. She had no claim on them, not without Combs. But she could avenge his death. Melinda at least would appreciate that. September saw a lot of herself in the young girl. "I promise you, if we have any chance to succeed against Kaliko Wong, it'll be because Shadow's by my side."

He blinked, face expressionless. "Glad you're so passionate. You're going to need that determination. We must attack tonight."

September drew in a surprised breath.

"We have no choice. They'll perform the autopsy this morning. And they'll know it's not you."

Quinn cursed under her breath. "But surely it takes more time to run tests to confirm identity. With the bomb damage to the body, I mean. Bring in more help…"

Jack shook his head. "Three of us, that's it." Shadow barked. "Okay, four of us—maybe five, if that new mutt has skills."

September shuddered, a hollow feeling making her teeth chatter despite the unholy heat. "Quinn's right. It takes at least a week to get DNA results, and that's on a rush."

His icy expression slipped. "I'm sorry, September. They'll know it's not you. You never had a kidney transplant."

Oh God…no, no, please no. *April?*

He gestured with his phone again. "I lost Rina because of the witch. Now she killed your sister, too. She must pay. Tonight."

Chapter 43 – KALI

Kali sneezed and dabbed her eyes and nose with a tissue. Her eyes had burned ever since September splashed salon product into her face. Plus, nasty Texas air swam with pollen, mold, and God knows what other impure substances. Vermin, like the cats that had lived with the previous homeowner, gave her fits. The sooner Kali got out of this awful state, the better. Back to her high-rise apartment in New York City, complete with air purifiers, air conditioning, and staff to keep things tidy—and the rats, roaches, and pigeons far, far away. She'd had enough of those living on the streets as a kid.

This house looked clean enough, but Kali heard the skittering footfalls of four-pawed creatures and the plaintive meow that sounded from window to window. Her lip curled at the thought, placing cats only slightly above the vermin they chased.

From the rear door, Kali signaled to her driver. He stood in the backyard, pretending to enjoy the night air. There was nothing enjoyable about it. Just opening the back door made Kali's throat tighten from the smell of brackish water lapping the pier, and the creepy cricket and froggy chirping, which city noises thankfully drowned out, made her skin crawl.

A haunting sound echoed over the open water. An animal, maybe a bird? Kali backed inside and waited for the driver to join her. The driver had been with her for more than a decade, fallen in and out of favor, in more ways than one. Currently in favor, his steadfast loyalty brought comfort that Kali couldn't discount. Many of her operatives had worked for her late husband. She'd inherited them, but not necessarily their loyalty. This man she brought on board herself. Bought and paid for, in more ways than one.

"Prepare for a guest. A reluctant one. Nothing you can't handle."

He smiled and nodded. A man of few words. One of his best traits.

"Also, I keep hearing an animal around the house. Take care of that for me."

He tapped the gun at his side with a questioning arch to his eyebrows.

She tipped her head. "Quietly, we don't need local yokel audience. Understand?" Her voice sharpened. He knew better than to just deny her request.

His eyes lit up, and she could imagine his thought process. Another reason she recruited him. He had an incredible capacity for creative mayhem. He probably practiced on such creatures, although the idea repelled Kali. No, she much preferred targeting two-legged quarry.

September had talented resources among her friends. If the woman still breathed, and had reunited with her damned dog—her operatives had failed in that effort—then she was hidden away.

With her cop lover dead, the only thing the woman might vaguely care about was her brother. If that didn't flush her out, nothing would.

A soft whoosh-thump hit the side of the house, followed by a hiss and yowl. Kali smiled and headed for the small kitchen on the other side of the house. The thought of shedding blood, even that of an animal, made her hungry.

Chapter 44 – NEBULAE

Nebulae hissed and dropped into the undergrowth beneath the window. When the tall man approached, she trilled, willing to forgive the scare. But she stayed in her hiding spot, just in case, puzzled at the recent turn of events.

In all her six years, no one had tried to hurt Nebulae. The people she'd met in the big house constantly changed. But they all gave her lots of attention, yummy food, and shared pillow snuggles with her at night. She enjoyed the occasional excursion outside to play in the grass, chase and catch tasty bugs, climb trees, and play zoomies around the property. But Nebulae always returned inside, especially when night fell, and the coyotes sang their threats and boasts over the shiny water.

When her owner brought out the carriers, she watched the other cats being stuffed inside and carried away, except for Sunset. The orange cat escaped upstairs, to hide in the study high above everything.

Nebulae didn't like the carriers, so she hid inside a cabinet. Then she dashed out the door when she got the chance. But now, after several days outside without any yummy food or attention—and the chorus of howls growing ever closer—she wanted back inside. To make friends, get yummies, and pets from the visitors, like before. Sunset, inside, must get all the food. Not fair!

Many people had come to stay in the big old house. Nebulae liked them all, even the children that chased her. Mostly, she liked the ladies because she could snuggle up next to them once they fell asleep, and comfort herself with their body warmth. They never stayed long. But they all played fun games with her, Sunset, and the other cats. The red dot tag game was something she loved to play. She hadn't caught the red dot, not yet. She sometimes captured whirring feathers flitting on the end of strings. Oh what fun it was to leap in and grapple the toy at the end of the line.

So when this man made a silvery line fly, and the confetti fluttered around like fireflies, Nebulae chased it with delight. She grabbed the clattering shiny metal on the end of the wires when they bounced against the floor near where she sat.

And it bit her paw! Her short tabby coat stood erect all over her body in reaction.

Coyote howls made her stomach shrivel. But that feeling paled compared to the toy betrayal and the man's laughter. Nebulae didn't know why the man wanted to hurt her. The man didn't give warning howls like the coyotes, but Nebulae knew he posed a greater threat. Maybe that's why Sunset stayed hidden from the people inside the house. The old building had cubby-holes near the ceiling in some of the rooms, perfect for cats to play hide and seek, or simply hide from scary things.

Nebulae watched until the man gave up his search. Her silver fur finally smoothed when the stranger disappeared around the other side of the house.

Nebulae crouched down low to the ground, hugging the

foundation of the old house, and made her rounds. After grooming each tabby stripe to calm her nerves, Nebulae once more claimed her windowsill lookout, watching the lady inside move from room to room. She quelled her desire to meow-beg. And Sunset stayed hidden, nowhere near to hook the door handle for entry.

These strangers weren't friendly. They liked to hurt cats. She purred to soothe herself, not understanding any of it.

Patiently she waited, crouched on the windowsill, motionless and invisible to all but the most discerning eyes. Eventually, the sound of tire treads crunched on the pathway leading up to the house. Nebulae hopped down from the windowsill and melted into the shadows. She waited next to the steps in a pool of darkness no human eye could penetrate.

The car pulled up in front of the house. Two strangers got out of the front, then opened the rear door and pulled out another man. He slumped nearly to the ground until the first two men grabbed his arms, and dragged him toward the house.

Nebulae watched and listened with interest. The escorted man mumbled and mewed like a kitten calling its mother. Nebulae wanted to run to the man, rub against his ankle, and climb into his lap with lots of purrs, to chase fear away.

But the other two men frightened Nebulae, especially when the scary man joined them. She didn't want to get bitten again. So she stayed silent as prey, and watched while they pulled the mewling man into the house, then slammed the door shut. A short time later, two of the men left, climbed into the car and drove away.

Nebulae stood up and shook herself hard. She licked each of her soft gray front paws and scrubbed her face, white whiskers, and neck on each side. Then paused. Now that all the strangers had retired inside the house, she could hunt.

A bright moon glowed overhead, sparkling the water. Nebulae had to do something to fill the void growing in her middle. One time, Sunset caught a vole. He brought it into the house to share, but the people screamed and threw it away. What a waste… So, after that, anytime the cats managed to sneak outside and capture a treasure, they munched it without offering to share.

Next to the pier, the water ran clear and deep. At the thought, she stalked down the grassy yard. Nebulae stayed low to the ground, a wraith like smoke beneath the moon glow. She bent low, lapping quickly to slake her thirst. It wasn't food, but it filled her empty belly.

A shiny motion flicked beneath the water. Instinctively, Nebulae's paw flashed down, dipping beneath the surface, and flipped the small fish out onto the grassy bank. With delight, she pounced, yowling loudly with excitement.

The lights came on, flooding the back yard. Nebulae froze for three heartbeats, then grabbed the fish by the head, and dashed into the undergrowth. She growled, the fish in her mouth muffling the sound. Once her heart stopped racing, she released the fish and paw-smacked it several times.

Once it stopped moving, she cleaned herself from nose tip to tail end. Only then did she crouch over her prize and fill her belly.

Chapter 45 – SEPTEMBER

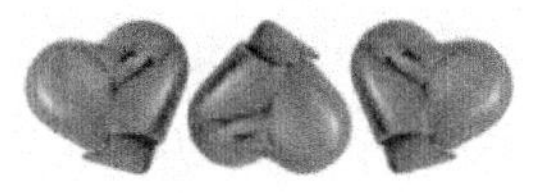

September walked from the kitchen to the sofa in a daze, the latest revelation making her want to curl up into it and disappear. Shadow did his best to climb into her lap, and she opened her arms to hug the dog close. She shuddered, but no tears came. The well had run dry. All that she had left was grim determination to make the killer pay.

They'd swapped wedding clothes, changed their hair at the salon, even traded bouquets. Of all her siblings, she'd felt the closest to April, who had been there when September needed her most. They shared so much, including the secret blessing that had completed April's life.

And now that life had ended.

April wasn't the first family member to suffer because of September. A magnet for mayhem, she could track turmoil from point to point. No, she hadn't asked for this. And yes, she wanted Kaliko Wong to pay. But more than the vengeance, September wanted answers.

Her life began with such promise as a cello prodigy, touring at age sixteen with a trusted family friend as a chaperone. His betrayal continued to haunt her, but April helped September escape the aftermath. Chris, her first husband, and Dakota started to heal her pain, but she lost another part of herself with their deaths. Then April gave her a reason to bring Shadow into her life, which led to meeting Combs.

Someone reached out to foul every chance for happiness. So, September had pushed and pushed, then pushed some more, refusing to delay embracing her one chance for happiness.

Was Kaliko Wong to blame for it all? Jack and Quinn certainly believed so. They wanted her stopped, the organization destroyed. Jack clearly had no intention of enlisting the authorities, so she didn't trust him. But *the enemy of my enemy is my friend.* Until he proved otherwise.

She pushed Shadow off her lap and practiced her breathing until her heart rate steadied, then called to the kitchen. "I'm in. Now what? Where is she?"

Jack strode into the living room, Quinn following. "She's still in the area." His eyes glinted. "Some on the inside want her gone as much as we do."

"So she's a criminal. Doing what?" *Know your enemy.* "Drugs, money laundering, prostitution?"

Quinn pulled her feet away from the guest Airedale dog and made a shooing gesture. "All the above. Also trafficking, influence peddling—"

Trafficking? A case with Lia and Tee last year involved trafficking. September had been recuperating at the time and had only peripheral knowledge of the situation.

Jack's forehead wrinkled. "Hard to keep up. Wong Enterprises operates around the world. Kaliko Wong dipped fingers in every dirty pie imaginable."

Shadow nudged September's hands to continue contact, tapping her leg with one of his scarred paws. Shadow had survived a wildfire during a tracking event in which Lia went missing. "Lia doesn't talk about it much, but her father was convicted for Simon Wong's murder."

Jack whistled. "Sounds like the witch's claws bloodied everyone around you."

She gritted her teeth, recognizing the truth of the statement. September didn't know her mother's story—that is, her adoptive mother who raised her like her own. Rose had taken many secrets with her to the grave; September wondered now if one of those secrets involved the Wongs.

"How do we find her? Where is she?" Quinn's lip curled in distaste. "Dog, get away from me."

September patted her thigh for the Airedale to join her and Shadow on the sofa. She raised her eyebrows at Jack.

"Right over there." He pointed out the window toward the lake. "She thinks you're dead, September. Even if she suspects otherwise, she'd never expect you to come after her. You've locked yourself away or run like a rabbit from every threat."

"What's over there?"

"Wong Enterprises owns a hotel in Dallas, and we watched for her there. She never showed. Then one of the Wong subsidiaries bought a house right over there. That's why I rented this place. To be nearby. Just in case."

Quinn made another face when the dogs brushed up next to her bare legs. "Wonder why she didn't kill the owners and squat for the duration." At September's look of disgust and dismay, Quinn said, "That's who you're dealing with."

Jack motioned with his phone. "Transaction went through

under the table, with a cash transfer and paperwork hidden from the casual observer. It won't show up on tax rolls, at least not for a while. Yes, the syndicate has a talented stable of financial wizards, plus bought and paid for influence on multiple levels." He snorted. "My team confirms she's there."

"House on the water? Or back from the shore?" A calculating expression darkened Quinn's face. "Trees surrounding the dwelling? How many stories? Roads going in or—"

"Quinn thinks like a sniper. Line of sight, escape routes, but we don't need any of that." Jack spoke over Quinn's protest. "Oh, you'll get your shot—literally. We also need your insights to get into the witch's head. She trained you, after all."

"You knew where she was, before she bombed my wedding, killed Combs and April and…" *Damn him to hell!* At his expression, her voice rose. "Call the authorities! Local cops, sheriff's office, FBI, or ATF…I don't know, whoever has jurisdiction." Oh, she wanted justice. But dropping a bomb on Kaliko Wong made her no better than the witch.

"They've had plenty of time to take her down. She's got layers of legal protection, financial influence, political support. She'd never serve time—or if she did, would continue running things from the inside. You can't be that clueless." He crossed his arms.

September remembered the legal and political entanglements she'd discovered on her trip to South Bend. Chris had left her a box full of information about her past, but the documents disappeared, stolen by bad actors. She'd first met Quinn there—or the girl Charlie Cider, anyway. Another connection to the syndicate she couldn't deny. "She'll have guards and security; drones like at the wedding. We three can't compete with that! She'll kill us before we get out of the car."

While September wanted the woman to pay, offering herself

up for a suicide mission made no sense. "Oh. You want me to lure her out, be a decoy?" Calm descended with the understanding—followed by acceptance. If it brought Kaliko Wong to justice, she'd take the risk. She dropped one hand to stroke Shadow's brow, and the dog's warm presence helped steady her nerves.

Quinn put her hands on her hips, her lithe physique emphasizing her athletic ability. "An assassin stays nimble, no excess baggage. She went alone to the salon, and if not for pure dumb luck you'd be dead already." She nodded at Jack. "Kali will be alone except for a driver, and he'll double as muscle."

"She's never failed, so she thinks she's invulnerable." September slowly nodded. Overconfidence could bring Kali down.

"Killing you has become a point of honor with her." Quinn kneed the Airedale away from her. "What the hell does he want? He won't get off me."

"It's a she. Her name's Keighley, according to her collar tag, and she just wants attention, probably missing her person." If they survived, they had to return the dog "You want me to knock on her door, then run, and hope Quinn gets a shot?"

"Something like that." Jack motioned to her go-bag. "You supply the distraction. Plenty of stuff in there to get creative. Your swim training could come in handy."

He wasn't serious. Hell of a joke. "You expect me to swim across the lake, sneak up to the house, and murder this woman?" *Was it really murder, to defend yourself?*

"Don't be silly. We can't drive you up to the front door, true, or have you exhausted after swimming across the lake. But a short distance, that's doable. She won't expect incoming from the lake." He jerked a thumb toward the back window again. "You'll use the kayak."

Chapter 46 – TEDDY

Teddy scrolled through September's phone for April's number, hitting *call* when he found it. She must've asked someone to take charge of Steven. Then, in all the confusion, they had left the little boy behind. He listened while the phone rang and rang. An echoing sound came from upstairs.

He glanced up when Melinda reappeared, clutching another phone. Her eyes were nearly swollen shut and she spoke in a whispery croak. "Is that you calling? It says September."

Teddy grimaced as Lia collected the phone from Melinda. "Sorry. I called on September's cell trying to reach April." *So, April also left her phone behind in the bedroom.* He scrolled further and found Lysle January's number. He'd know how to reach Steven's parents, or at the very least, could pick up his grandson.

The man picked up on the third ring but didn't speak at first. Teddy belatedly realized he called from September's number, which no doubt showed on her father's phone. "Mr. January, this is Teddy Williams. Yes, I'm calling on September's phone. So sorry for the late call. I didn't know how else to reach you, and we found her phone here in the house."

"Yes?" He cleared his throat before speaking again. "We're a little overwhelmed here. What can I do for you, Mr. Williams?"

In the background, Teddy could hear the voices of somber conversation of subdued adults—September's siblings and their spouses. Teddy couldn't imagine the horror, grief, and shock they all felt. "My deepest sympathies to you and your whole family. September felt like part of my family, too." He cleared his throat. "I have a bit of a situation here, though. May I speak with April, please?"

Silence. Then: "Isn't she with you?" Teddy could tell he pulled the receiver away from his mouth, covering it to call to the assembly. "Quiet down everyone. I'm talking here."

Teddy's stomach dropped. "April isn't here." He watched Macy leap over the kitchen's pet gate, stride across the room, pause before Steven, then vault onto the sofa cushion beside the seated boy. The cat settled down next to his thigh, only the barest contact between the pair. Macy washed himself, and a purr rumbled so loud Teddy could hear it across the room.

"When she didn't join the rest of our family, we figured April took Steven home. Or she stayed there to help with Combs's kids. You haven't heard from her?"

Teddy took off his glasses, rubbing his eyes, and trying to fit the pieces together. "We haven't seen her since the wedding. But Steven's here." *Now what?* "We've got our hands full with Melinda and Willie. You understand. I'm here with Lia Corazon. But youngsters, especially kids like Steven, are a bit outside my wheelhouse."

The silence stretched to nearly a minute before Teddy prompted the man. "Can someone come and get your grandson?"

Lia startled as the phone—April's phone—in her hand jangled.

She crossed to Teddy, showing him the phone's caller ID. June, one of the sisters with Lysle January had just tried to call April.

"Mr. January, June just called April's phone. She left that here, along with Steven." He swallowed hard, wishing to heaven he knew what to say or do. Finally, Teddy offered: "I can drop Steven off at your house if you're having problems coordinating rides."

"No, no, please keep Steven with you for the moment. We'd appreciate that very much. I'm sure you understand, Mr. Williams. Steven has never stayed here alone, never without his mom or dad. We aren't equipped… That is, Steven isn't the easiest child to manage. And we have a lot to manage right now. The grandkids, my daughters, and their families…"

"But Mr. January—Lysle—he's your grandson, too."

Heavy breathing, followed by angry, pain filled whispers. "I raised Rose's children as my own. I love them all, but I never signed up for September's troubles. Rose wanted to do right by her, and ended up dead! April nearly died because of her, but forgave September. Now April's disappeared in the middle of this mess. Everyone is scared to death, cut and bruised, damaged hearing, awful things." He choked on a sob. "God forgive me, but I don't want Steven here." He took a ragged breath. "I'll reach out to Doug about April. And they can collect the boy and move on with their lives. As should you." He disconnected the call.

Teddy stared at the silent phone. Then, without a word, he set it on the table.

Lia touched his sleeve. "I overheard some of that. Was he serious?"

Teddy shrugged. "Grief does weird things to people." Maybe Lysle would change his mind. For a while, Teddy had resented September after his own wife's death, although she had nothing to do with the chain of events that hurt so many. Had September lived during the Salem witch trials, she'd already have burned at the stake.

Now what? Teddy felt compelled to find Shadow. But he might need Magic to do that. He didn't know how to get a dog to track, and Lia wouldn't let the dog go by himself. They couldn't leave three kids alone in the house, in the middle of the night, especially after the tragedy.

None of these kids had parents right now. He prayed Combs survived his injuries so he could reverse some of the awful news. Ethel hadn't sent the promised update yet.

He walked past Steven, who still sat on the sofa clutching the papers from the gift envelope with one hand and typing on his tablet with the other. Yes, dealing with the young fella could be daunting, but this was a child. A brilliant child who spoke his own language. The big sable and white Maine Coon cat blinked at Teddy as though agreeing.

Teddy opened the patio door and stepped outside. He motioned to Lia, and she understood, staying near the boy to supervise. Teddy didn't think Steven would become upset, as long as he had his tablet, although Teddy worried a bit about what would happen if the battery ran out. Surely the boy would eventually nod off, with it so far past his bedtime.

He dialed and Ethel picked up almost before the first ring sounded. "Any word?"

"He's still unconscious. The doctors say he is stable, but the explosion burst both his eardrums, he has a concussion, and bruised lungs. His broken leg will heal, but it's high—near his hip—so he'll need a lot of rehab to regain full use. They're keeping him sedated as they're concerned about spinal injury, too." Her voice caught. "Until he wakes, we won't know a lot more."

"So terribly sorry. What we've asked you to do, the captain and

I, it's not fair. I know that."

She whispered back fiercely. "If it keeps others safe, it's the least I can do. Gotta protect those that are left." She sniffled. "Felix posted a detail outside, and Stan's in the next room. So I can stand vigil for them both."

He closed his eyes. Dare he ask more of her? He had to push past the discomfort. She knew what self-sacrifice meant, and when it really mattered.

"I have another hard ask. This time, no arm-twisting, no arguments to convince you otherwise, just a simple yes or no, and I'll respect that."

"Go ahead."

He took a big breath, glancing through the double doors to be sure Lia's attention was elsewhere. "September might have gone into hiding."

She gasped. "Still alive?"

He backpedaled quickly. "Not sure. But somebody tracked her dog, using her phone app."

"… And who besides September would do that? Or could."

Teddy smiled, liking how quickly Ethel grasped the essentials of the situation. "I can track the dog, too. Maybe it will lead to September, or at least some answers, and maybe…"

She breathed heavily. "How can I help?"

Teddy sighed. "Thank you. I'm here with Lia, her dog, and Combs's two kids. And Steven."

"And you can't leave those kids alone. Wait, Steven's there? Where's his mom?"

Teddy considered what to say next. If September didn't die, then the body might be April. He quickly shared his thoughts, and some of the phone conversation with Lysle. "I think Lia suspects the same, but we haven't had that conversation. Can't say much around the kids. It'd help a lot to have her and Magic along. But like you said, we can't leave the kids."

"You need a babysitter." The words sounded brittle and harsh, but he didn't blame her. "I'll do it on one condition."

"Of course, Ethel. Anything."

"Nail the bastards who did this."

Chapter 47 – SHADOW

Shadow watched September open her bag and pull out various items. He sat as close to her as he could. He could sense her heart rate, faster than normal but steady, so she didn't need his touch.

Keighley paced around the small cottage, sniffing the floor, and exploring nooks and crannies. When she got too close to September, Shadow lifted his lip in a silent snarl, cautioning the Airedale to keep her distance. He didn't know Keighley well enough to trust her with September. Nor did he trust the two other people in the room.

He remembered Quinn. They'd not had much contact, but he remembered she liked cats. Shadow liked cats too, so he figured she wasn't a bad person—even if she stole September away and left Shadow at the kennel. After all, she brought September back to collect him. His tail thumped the floor at that thought.

The big man called Jack worried Shadow. He'd been in the

garden when a loud boom shook the house and hurt a good dog's ears. He'd taken September to the car. Shadow knew that Jack talked with Combs. He also knew Combs always protected September. The man loved September almost as much as Shadow did. Shadow wondered why Combs hadn't joined them here.

"Want to play the *show me* game?" September stood up from the sofa and grabbed the leash she had removed from the bag.

Shadow jumped to his feet, paws dancing with excitement. The *show me* game made him feel happy and accomplished. He already knew many words but always wanted to learn more.

Quinn stood at the kitchen table, checking her equipment. Shadow didn't know what everything was, but it smelled like heavy oil and reminded him of guns. He turned his attention back to September's bag of objects and recognized the gun in her own pile of equipment. Shadow whined.

September picked up a square box from a nearby table. She held the coiled leash in one hand and the box in the other, standing easily with each hand outstretched.

"Shadow, this is leash." She lifted the hand holding the coiled leash. He panted happily, watching her carefully, and ears twitching. "This is picture." She presented the picture frame in her other hand and waited until he woofed softly under his breath. "Shadow, show me *picture*."

He bounced forward, nose poking the picture frame in her hand.

"Good dog, Shadow." September pulled another item out of her bag, and Shadow recognized it; his ears pricked with interest. They'd played with buttons before, but they weren't much fun. Macy played with the buttons to get good stuff, but most of the time, Shadow got what he wanted without pawing buttons. Maybe this time would be different.

Jack looked up. He'd been staring into his phone and making faces. That's how Shadow knew he felt unhappy, worried, and angry. His smells changed, especially with the anger. Shadow stayed alert to prevent the anger from spilling toward September or himself. That was his job.

"Why the hell are you wasting time playing games?" He crossed the room to loom over September. "We have the house floor plan."

"You want me to lure Kali out of the building, right? Get Quinn a clean shot." September jutted out her chin. "I don't particularly want to get myself shot, or knifed, or whatever deadly assault she has planned for me."

Jack crossed his arms. "Isn't it a little late to train? And I thought you'd already trained him."

Shadow looked from the big man to September and back again. He pawed her leg, wanting the game to continue.

She blew out a breath. "You've never had a dog, have you? Shadow knows many words and has lots of behaviors on cue. For something new, we build on existing knowledge and chain a series of behaviors together to build the new action." She held up one button. "You wanted distractions? How's this?" She fiddled with something on the button then spoke into it the way she did her phone. "This is September. You want me, come get me." She fiddled with the button again, and this time September's voice came out of the button, repeating the same words.

Shadow wagged. He'd seen that trick before. People could do amazing things that dogs couldn't understand. But people always had their reasons.

"We use the buttons to record my voice, your voice, Quinn saying things, maybe even announcing the police have her surrounded and to come out. Whatever you want."

His eyes narrowed, something people did when they had to think really hard. "The plan was to make a noise in the boat, far out in the water, away from the house. Then dive under to stay safe."

Quinn blew a rude sound with her lips. "Kali could shoot the head off a butterfly in the middle of the lake. Floating in a boat? That's an invitation to target practice." She turned to September. "I like your idea. If you've got the guts to set those buttons close enough, where she can hear them. At windows, doors… Jack, you said you have a floor plan of the house?"

Jack nodded. "But she'd still have to get past Kali's driver. He won't let her get that close. Even if he did, how do you trigger them?" He stared at Shadow so hard that it made his lip curl up in protest. "Is your dog gonna run from button to button, paw punching them one after another?"

"Maybe. You have a better idea?" She didn't want to put Shadow at such risk, but nobody would expect or look for a dog. September turned back to Shadow, still clutching the picture frame in one hand and the sound button in the other. "Shadow, this is picture, and this is button." She held both objects out in her hands, one on each side. "Show me *button.*"

Keighley dashed in front of Shadow and bounced to nose boink the button, triggering September's recorded message:

"This is September. You want me, come get me."

Chapter 48 – SEPTEMBER

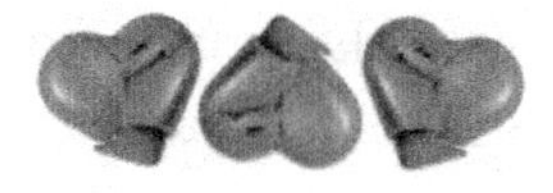

September quickly gathered her thoughts and reassessed the Airedale. "Let's see just how much you know, Keighley."

Quinn stared, challenge clear in her expression. "Do we really have time for this? No need to complicate things. Just get me in position, make some noise to lure the witch into range. I'll do the rest." She slapped her palm down on the table, and September flinched at the sharp noise.

Jack held up a placating hand. "She's the dog expert. And it's her life on the line. The sun rises a little after six, so we have a bit more time for prep if she thinks it's necessary." He looked at September. "I'm sure you're a terrific trainer, but in that time can you teach something new?"

September shrugged. "She already has skills. Someone taught her how to learn. Otherwise, she wouldn't have responded so quickly just by watching Shadow play the *show me* game." She turned to the guest dog. "Let me see what else she knows that might help us. Otherwise, we'll need to confine her here. And based on her partnering with Shadow, betcha part of her skill set includes escape."

September put Shadow in a down-stay and stroked his arched neck to soothe him. He didn't like all her attention focused on any other dog. "Baby dog, this isn't about you. Just chill. *Go to* couch." He thumped his tail against the floor, hopped up onto the sofa, and sighed, before resting his chin on his forepaws.

September ran through half a dozen commands, putting the Airedale through her paces. She had a solid sit, down, stay, speak—and she wriggled with delight when asked to fetch just about anything. Shoe, phone, book, and pillow were all names she knew. Keighley curled her lip when asked to fetch her gun. Instead, she grabbed the pillow again and tried to shove it into her hands.

Pursing her lips, September tried another angle. "Keighley, *nimm* gun." She spoke the German word used when training Schutzhund techniques.

Gingerly, the Airedale grasped the gun, obeying the "take hold" command. That could come in handy, especially since the trained skills included learning to guard—*pass auf*—and attack—*fass*—on command.

"She's had some serious training. We don't have time to teach new skills, but we can use a shortcut." She rummaged in her bag and brought out the laser pointer on a key ring that held various assorted items, including a lock pick, corkscrew, and knife. She flicked on the laser light, showing the dog the red dot on her palm. She asked the Airedale to nose touch the dot, and she did so immediately. *Target training, check.* September directed the laser pointer at her gun, and again asked for fetch. This time, Keighley followed the pointer, but after fumbling with the weight of the piece, gingerly picked it up and brought it to her.

"Good dog. What a good girl." September wrinkled her nose, thinking. Many pet dogs, as well as service animals, learned the *go to* command. Shadow knew it. Coupled with his *settle* request, she could ask him to *go to* a location like the couch, bed, crate, or another room. With as much training as this dog already showed, September believed she also understood the *go to* command. But she might not generalize or understand the concept except in her own familiar home.

Maybe partnering object names with the joy of fetching, and chain it with the *go to* command… They just might have a long-distance answer for deploying the talking buttons.

"*Go to* bed." The dog looked around the room, as if searching for a familiar sleeping place. That told her the Airedale at least recognized the *go to* command. They could work with that.

September showed the dog the laser dot on her hand again and ask her to touch, and after she did, September swung the pointer to the far corner of the room, swirling it on the floor. "*Go to.* Touch."

Shadow whined and raised his head from his paws. September glanced at him, and slightly shook her head; with a sigh, he resettled his chin onto his paws.

Keighley dashed across the room and nose-touched the red dot on the floor. She panted happily, tail shimmying. This dog clearly lived for performing, had a hard time sitting still, and acted energized by learning. September knew the versatile breed could do virtually anything, from protection work to service dog partnerships.

Although the terrier had already showed she understood the name of the button, September reinforced the notion by swirling the laser on the pre-recorded button. "*Fetch* button." She watched the dog prance forward, gently pick up the plastic talking button, and bring it to her, offering to drop it in her hand. September shook her head. "*Go to* bed." The dog looked puzzled for a moment, until she swooshed the red dot back into the corner and repeated: "*Go to*. Go to bed."

September could almost see the wheels turning in the Airedale's head. Still carrying the button, Keighley spun and carried it to the corner of the room. "Good dog. Drop it." She did, and the recording sounded as the button thumped the floor.

Jack looked properly impressed. "Neat trick. But there's still the matter of getting you and the dog… two dogs?… to the house, with no one seeing." He looked at Quinn. "That kayak just got awfully crowded."

September shrugged. She was making things up as she went along. There was no guarantee that any dog would perform a known command, let alone something new, under pressure. But she had nothing to lose. Except her life. Since that was nearly a given, teaching the tricks might be the last chance she'd have in this lifetime. It'd be worth it to see Kali taken down. "Let me see the floor plan, or any kind of landscaping, so I can better prep the dogs." She motioned to her bag. "I can pack everything in there. But if it gets wet, it'll sink to the bottom of the lake. And what about the guard? Anything I do will alert whoever's inside the house. Then, like Quinn said, Kali plays shooting gallery from her perch inside." September still doubted her ability to shoot somebody in cold blood.

"Same as for the witch. Lure him to a spot where I can neutralize him, no noise, no fuss. I have a suppressor on my weapon." Quinn shrugged again. "Be flexible, though. The situation is fluid."

Jack opened his computer. "I have an aerial view from Google Earth, and a virtual tour of the house itself, although that's from a couple of years back when the house was on the market." He stared at September as if he could hear her doubt. "If someone points a gun at you, you won't hesitate. And I have a dry-bag you can use. If Quinn can't nail the guard, you'll need to do the honors before putting on your canine circus. You approach from the water side. I'll be at the other side of the house, ready to knock out drones or any other contingencies we've missed."

"We prepare for anything and everything. Build in redundancies." Quinn grinned and fondled her sniper rifle. "That's what Kali does."

September squared her shoulders. "I'm doing this, not for Jackson Glass retribution, nor for Quinn Donovan's freedom, not even for September Day's vengeance—although God knows I hunger for that—but to protect the future victims. She's done damage for many years?"

"Decades, yes." Jack confirmed.

"She won't quit. If we don't stop her, it goes on and on. If I die getting this done, promise me…" Could she rely on his promise? Did she have a choice?

"Your condition?" Jack's lips twitched into the semblance of a smile.

"Build in redundancies, you say. So, Jack, promise to put the police on notice." She held up her hand to stop any protests. "Consider the police a backup, just in case everything goes sideways. You texted warnings to me that not even Teddy could trace. Use those skills, get the cavalry on speed-dial. Do that, Jack, or you finish this project alone, and Shadow and I will take our chances leaving."

He laughed—the first time she'd heard that sound—and picked up his phone, typed a message then stabbed *send.* "Done and done. Now saddle up, September, we've got a witch to burn."

The words chilled. Shadow rose and followed her to the table, where the team assessed the aerial view of the viper's nest. They had only a few hours before sunrise, barely time to drill both dogs once they'd agreed on the plan.

She prayed she was a good enough trainer to keep them all safe.

Chapter 49 – TEDDY

Teddy opened the front door and stood aside to let Ethel enter. The small woman carried herself with the stiff military posture befitting the wife of a fallen officer. He admired her stoic demeanor.

He still mourned his wife, Molly. The pain never left, although it sometimes softened with memories of happier times. Ethel's loss of Stan had happened in a heartbeat. Teddy's loss took months, as Molly's memory evaporated day by day. He suspected Ethel's shock still muted the full pain, and his heart hurt for what he knew she'd experience.

"Thank you for coming." He closed the door and gestured toward Steven, who still sat on the sofa, engrossed in his tablet. Teddy whispered, "Can't get the tablet away from him." Macy was still nestled beside the little boy, making biscuits with his paws on the soft sofa cushion.

"Gives the child something to do." Ethel glanced up the stairs and raised her eyebrows.

Teddy nodded. He could still hear Melinda's intermittent sobs, but he hoped Willie slept soundly. There'd be hell to pay when Melinda discovered their lie. He looked forward to telling her that Combs survived. *Please let it be so.*

Lia entered from the kitchen, closely followed by Magic. It hadn't taken much for Teddy to convince Lia to accompany him on the tracking errand. "Hi Ethel. How's Stan?"

Teddy winced. But Ethel kept her composure and maintained the fiction. "I can't do anything for Stan. He doesn't know I'm there." Her voice hitched a bit. "The doctors know best and promised to call me." She took a seat beside the cat. "At least here I can feel useful."

"Lia, give me ten minutes, then bring Magic over."

Teddy left Lia chatting with Ethel. He needed to secure Meriwether in the RV before Magic appeared. While the police dog should be immune to the wiles of a teasing feline, too much was at stake for him to risk even a minor disruption. He set Meriwether in his carrier and shut the door. "Complain all you want, but you're not getting out."

He had the information from the mysterious search by whoever remotely opened September's phone app. They'd start there. The signal had a limited reach. Unless Shadow traveled outside that range, they would track him down. Teddy prayed they would find September as well. He'd drive and Lia would monitor the app once they reached the origination location.

Lia tapped on the door and Teddy let her and the big Rottweiler inside. The dog trailed his leash when Lia dropped it, immediately heading to the back of the RV to snuffle around the cat's carrier. Teddy congratulated himself on his foresight.

"Magic, leave Meri alone." Lia had swung into the passenger seat and accepted September's cell before Teddy noticed the fancy envelope she also carried. She handed it to him. "Yeah, Steven had put the papers back in the envelope and Ethel got it away from him. She has a way with that little boy. Anyway, Ethel recognized the present. Said that Mark talked with her before buying it."

"You know what it is?"

She shook her head. "Didn't open it. Ethel seems to think it might have something to do with all this." She made a vague waving gesture to encompass the last few hours.

He glanced at it then tossed it on the dashboard to look at later. They had more pressing matters.

Lia braced herself as the RV swerved on the narrow road. "You think September's alive, and took off with Shadow? If we find her alive, I'm gonna kill her. After I hug her neck."

He ducked his head in complete agreement. But he wouldn't blame her if she had. Her car hadn't moved, so maybe she was working with somebody else. Heck, maybe Combs set it up. There was so much about the situation Teddy didn't understand. Somebody had pulled strings—a lot of them—he just didn't know whether it was the person targeting September or someone else.

First things first. He hoped finding Shadow would answer a lot.

They drove in silence for about twenty minutes, until they reached where Shadow's GPS last registered on September's phone. Teddy pulled to the side of the road, parked, and took the phone back from Lia. He accessed the app and waited for the locater to update.

Lia broke the silence. "Magic tracks people. I brought one of the hand towels from the kitchen for September's scent. But he won't be any good at tracking Shadow." She didn't apologize. She had trained the dog for tactical police skills, but she continued to beat herself up over missing the bomb. The police would track down who assembled the bouquets and every other angle.

Teddy had mixed feelings about tracking Shadow. If alive and in hiding, September had good reasons for doing what she was doing. He didn't want to increase the danger by revealing her location, but he cared too much to ignore the opportunity to help.

He returned the phone to Lia. She knew the area better than him.

Lia squinted at the screen, mumbling to herself, and adjusting the view on the phone screen. "That blinking light, is that Shadow? It's not moving. He's at Turtle Lake, an area with lots of little rental cottages. Only about three miles from here." She peered closer. "There's an address."

Teddy shoved the RV into drive and left skid marks on the narrow country road. Magic yelped, then trotted up to the front to press himself against Lia's side.

"Hey, what happened?" Lia tapped the phone. She tipped it to face Teddy.

He took his eyes off the road briefly as the screen went black. "The app was just deleted."

"Lucky we got the location first." Lia wrapped her arm around Magic's broad shoulders and pressed her cheek against his head. "It's okay, boy, you want to go to work?"

The dog whined eagerly, trembling with excitement. Teddy thought Lia should have left the dog with the veterinarian, but she swore he'd got a clean bill of health.

Magic had acted dejected all night, almost apologetic. Teddy didn't ascribe to giving human emotions to animals. But the relationships he'd seen between September and Shadow, and Lia and Magic, sometimes made him rethink what he knew. Animals understood more than humans gave them credit for. It was humans that had problems understanding animals.

As they drew closer to their destination, Teddy lightened his foot on the accelerator. It wouldn't do for him to put Nellie Nova into the ditch, and they needed to approach with caution.

They passed a few small cottages, most with overgrown scrubby trees shielding the drives. Probably best to go in on foot, and be cautious until they knew what to expect.

When they reached the designated address, he parked the RV, pocketed the car keys, and pulled his gun out of the glove box. Lia had her side-arm and disembarked holding Magic's lead to keep him close. She carried the hand towel in her other hand. Her youth and training trumped his arthritic knees and iffy eyesight, but he could still serve as a backup with the best of them.

They approached the drive and saw a car parked beside the small cottage. Lia offered the towel to Magic and waited as the dog huffed the scent off the fabric. His tail stirred the sultry night air, and within seconds of receiving the cue, Magic's head swiveled, nostrils whiffering the oppressive atmosphere. Lia allowed the dog to tug her toward the parked car, while Teddy stood rooted in place, afraid to breathe.

Magic sniffed all around the small vehicle, paying particular attention to the trunk. He sat and then turned his big head to meet Lia's eyes.

She raised her hand and pumped her fist with triumphant excitement, but made no sound, and Teddy knew: *September was here!*

He motioned toward the house. If here, it might not be by choice. Until they knew for sure, they couldn't let anyone know about their presence.

Lia went left, and he walked right, as quietly as possible, to reach the windows. No lights were visible due to shutters, but he heard nothing. Lia silently moved to the door and tested the knob. Unlocked. She made a *wait there* signal to Teddy, then unlatched the door and opened it just enough for Magic to slip inside.

Magic knew September. Teddy didn't worry the dog would injure her. The same wasn't true for strangers, whether they offered September help or confined her. God help the person who tried to go up against Magic. Lia waited at the door, then quietly followed him inside.

Teddy heard paw treads running from room to room, searching the building. He felt his own heart speed up, not sure what he hoped the dog would find. September alive would be wonderful. But what that meant made his heart ache. She'd let them think she was dead. Why?

Lia returned to the front door and swung it wide "Nobody's here."

Teddy gritted his teeth, frustration making him want to scream.

The dog sniffed the air, looked up into Lia's eyes, then strode purposefully off the porch and around the building. Still holding the scented towel, Lia followed the dog. "He's tracking."

Teddy stumbled after the pair. The rear of the property butted up against the lake. A ramshackle pier jutted out over the water in one corner of the unkempt yard.

They followed Magic when he crossed the grass, not bothering to lower his nose to the ground. He reached the pier and snuffled a wet rope that coiled, snakelike, at the end of the pier. Magic sat, alerting on September's scent.

Chapter 50 – SHADOW

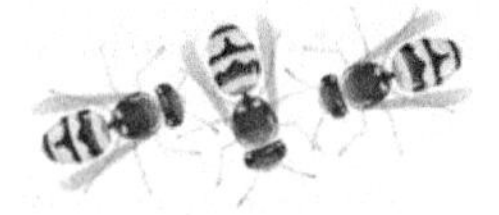

Shadow took turns with Keighley, retrieving the talking buttons and carrying them whatever place September told them to. They practiced the *show me* game, and he knew that meant to paw the button. September and the other two spoke into lots of buttons, so September's voice, Jack's voice, or Quinn's voice repeated the words just by punching a button. He didn't understand the point of the new game, but if it pleased September, Shadow happily played along.

His tummy rumbled, and he wondered when his next meal would come. It'd been hours since he ate. At the thought, his mouth watered.

He wondered why September spent so much time with Keighley. After all, Shadow did everything she asked the very first time. He was smart that way. Keighley took several repeats to catch on, but then played the game okay, though not as good as Shadow.

September raised her eyebrows when Keighley headed into the kitchen. The Airedale tipped her head one way and another, and then lay on her side to paw at the freezer door. September watched with amusement when the freezer opened. It was empty. She checked the rest of the refrigerator.

"Do you have anything to eat?"

Quinn laughed. "I'm surprised you've got an appetite."

September made a face. "Not for me, for the dogs. The cupboards are bare." She looked inside her bag and pulled out a cellophane wrapped treat. Shadow sniffed excitedly, detecting the odor of peanut butter. She peeled back the cover and broke off a piece. During the next set of exercises, she shared the yummies with Shadow and Keighley each time they got the game right.

If anything, the snack made Shadow even more hungry. He licked his lips, wishing for more peanut butter. Maybe when they went home—he'd really like to go home—September would give them more. Or bacon. That would be even better.

Now that both he and Keighley understood the new game, September turned it into a contest. She'd done this before, with Willie's dog Kinsler, and with Magic. He watched her unwrap a second bar and licked his lips. Shadow always won the contest with Kinsler. Magic was younger, and bigger, and sometimes he won. But Magic wasn't here, and Shadow planned to win whatever game September offered to get all the peanut butter treats for himself.

September lined up a half-dozen of the buttons on the kitchen floor. "Fetch button."

Each dog grabbed the closest button. Then September directed them with the red dot, commanding, *go to.*

They raced each other, Shadow vaulting over a chair, and Keighley nearly taking down Jack in her run to the other side of the room. "Drop it. Fetch button."

Shadow released his button, whirled, and raced back to retrieve another. Keighley moved at a more leisurely pace, and Shadow wriggled in place, knowing he'd won the contest.

September waited until the Airedale had reached the correct place with the second button, then asked each dog to drop the object. She gave Shadow half of the treat. "One more time."

Jack stepped in. "Time's up. It's go-time. Whatever they know, use it. But ditch the dogs if they get in the way. Take out the guard first, then set up the lures to get Kali into the open."

Quinn also spoke, her voice high-pitched and excited at the prospect of whatever was to come. "You ever been in a kayak?"

"A little late to ask, but yes." September stroked Shadow's face, bending down so that he could lick her neck. She hugged him close for a moment. "Who knows about the new dog? But Shadow's never been on a boat." She whispered into his ear. "Trust me, baby dog. We'll get through this together."

Chapter 51 – JACK

Jack drove down the narrow lane with lights off to remain unnoticed. As he turned a corner, in his rearview mirror he saw a large RV pulling up to the cottage he'd just left. *Interesting.* Points to the geriatric hacker for tracking them down.

He hadn't sent for the man, or any other law enforcement, despite his promise to September. He controlled the end game. He didn't want the witch arrested. Her lawyers and money would ensure she escaped the punishment she deserved. Jack wanted her dead.

The dog in the back seat barked and yapped, bouncing from window to window.

"Shut up." Jack had no confidence the dogs could help. September had insisted Shadow accompany her in the kayak with Quinn. The two-seater open hull boat, styled more like a sea kayak, barely fit two humans and Shadow had to sit on September's lap. A second dog wouldn't fit in the craft.

He intended to get as close to the target house as possible without alerting surveillance. His virtual team continued to monitor internet chatter and warnings, while he interfaced with both women. Once Quinn secured her sniper position, and September signaled readiness, he'd release the mutt for the first round of distractions and draw out any external security. If the witch tried to dodge out his side of the house—and he hoped she would—he'd destroy her.

Rina, I will keep my promise. Sorry it's taken me almost three decades. The dog barked again, and Jack clenched his jaw to keep from snapping.

September had packed the dry-bag, including the extra burner phone they'd use for communication. If the guard killed September, Quinn could still take him out, then target Kali. And if Quinn got neutralized, Jack would get his turn.

The kayak trip would take twenty minutes, or longer; skirting the shore as a straight shot across the lake made them too big of a target. The gibbous moon brought a lot of light to the darkness. The topography from the satellite sources might not be as accurate as they needed, so they'd reassess as needed.

Jack reached the lookout, grateful the dog had stopped yapping. When his phone pinged, he startled, thinking September had messaged him too early. Quinn wouldn't let her bail. Harder to back out when you shared the boat with a trained killer.

But the message came from neither of the women… *What are you doing up so late?* Steven had every reason to lose sleep this night after the traumatic day. All too soon he'd understand he lost his mother. Jack regretted that. He knew how it felt to grow up without a mother. His brow wrinkled as he tried to decipher the boy's rhymed text message.

>I know why she had to die. Wich just sour she loses power.

He texted back a questioning emoji. And Steven immediately replied.

>Had to wait to send so late. Teddy gone and work gets done.

An attachment followed.

>Clear as mud just look at blood.

Jack sighed, but he had another few minutes to wait. He enlarged the jpg to read. His eyes grew wide and he choked back a gasp of sudden understanding.

It made perfect sense. And changed everything. Jack pounded his fist on the steering wheel, wanting to turn back the clock to give himself time to process.

He had to stop September. Her death would betray Rina all over again.

Chapter 52 – SEPTEMBER

September knelt in the midsection of the small kayak, with the dry-bag between her knees, Shadow perched like a figurehead squeezed up before her. Quinn crouching behind her made September's palms sweat, and Shadow whined, conscious of her distress. This homemade boat looked nothing like the kayaks she'd used before. Three crowded the tiny craft, but they had no choice.

The vessel bobbed like a leaf riding the tide and was nearly as fragile. This wasn't like the modern fiberglass boats she'd paddled on the Great Lakes. No, this homemade boat stretched treated canvas over a wooden frame and ribs, like skin on a whale carcass. Someone spent many hours designing and building this watertight craft. Even the double-bladed paddle looked ancient. One end had a chip in the blade as if a lake creature's jaws bit out a chunk, while the other boasted many nicks and gouges, probably from pushing off shorelines or rocks. The battle scars told of old adventures, but she doubted any came close to the coming showdown.

Only the dip-pull of the paddle disturbed the glassy lake as the kayak skimmed the water's surface. She paddled with caution until muscle memory kicked in: left side dip-and-pull, right side dip-and-pull. The alternating strokes moved the boat with the smallest effort, despite the heavy load. The paddle's length kept them several feet away from the shore. Only a few trees curtseyed over the water to offer shelter. She hoped their silent motion remained unnoticed, at least from a distance.

As the target house became visible, September confirmed what the schematic had shown. The builders had flipped the design so the front of the structure faced the water. A veranda wrapped around the front door and sides of the house, while an octagonal tower boasted four large floor-to-ceiling windows. She knew the dining room had two more windows, including the one facing the roadway where Jack watched. When first built, they might have doubled as doorways when the bottom sash opened fully. She suspected renovations since then had changed things.

According to the floor plan, the back of the house, facing the roadway, featured a stone terrace in front of a family room with sliding glass doors. A single-car garage also gave access to the house proper.

Shrubbery in front of the veranda railing partially hid the downstairs windows. That made it difficult for September to discern movement inside. She counted on the reverse being true, with the vegetation helping to shield her presence. When the sun soon rose, the house would cast dark shadows across the grassy shoreline. The unfettered views from the second story windows was a concern.

The grassy yard sloped from the veranda to the water's edge. No place to hide, nowhere for shelter. But the undeveloped lot next to the mowed expanse boasted a large tree, a pecan with arching limbs that had a natural perch. September paused in her paddling and glanced back at Quinn, cradling her weapon with an air of palpable excitement. September pointed from Quinn to the tree and raised her eyebrows.

Quinn's eyes narrowed. Then she offered a sharp nod in agreement. She moved in her seat, and the kayak tipped precariously.

September hissed and leaned the other way to counterbalance. Shadow whined and rose to his feet. September reached forward, placing a calming hand on the dog's flank. She spoke in the barest whisper. "Shadow, settle. Good dog."

She resettled herself for a few more strokes, then shipped the paddle. The kayak glided to shore, bumping through scrubby cattails and lily pads festooning the shallower water bordering the undeveloped part of the property. The scrubby vegetation might provide some cover. A fallen tree limb clawed the lake's face and September grabbed one gnarly branch to steady the craft.

Shadow leaped out, aiming for the marshy shoreline, but splashed into deeper than expected water. He yelped.

This time Quinn hissed for silence. She followed Shadow, stepping from the boat into ankle-deep water, then carefully trudged to solid ground. Within seconds she'd disappeared into the undergrowth.

September tied off the kayak to the bobbing tree limb. Shadow stood on the scrubby shoreline, pacing back and forth, but keeping his vocal comments to himself. September signaled him to *wait.* He yawned widely, turned his head to the side and licked his lips, behaviors signaling stress. She hated putting him through this, hated that she couldn't explain. Shadow trusted her with his life. They had to succeed.

She waited in the bobbing kayak, her attention swiveling between the looming house and the empty boughs of the pecan tree.

An enormous figure appeared around the corner of the house, making his rounds. He walked down the green lawn toward the pier, a weapon at the ready.

September froze, held her breath. She repeated the palm-out *wait* to Shadow. And she prayed Quinn delayed her ascent to the pecan tree perch. With nothing but crickets and tree frogs commenting on the night, scrabbling up the tree would shout for attention.

The man continued his approach.

Shadow yawned again and sniffed the air. His ears came forward, hackles raised at the stranger's presence. He stared at September for direction.

The guard drew closer. Something had alerted him and he was clearly prepared to use the gun.

September lay down on the kayak's bottom. She bobbled her body to one side until her weight tipped it enough to fill with water. She capsized the boat, and hidden underneath, September and the kayak sank beneath the surface. The canopy of kayak canvas captured and held air, allowing her to lurk there, breathing quietly.

Shadow yelped as she disappeared. The man's steps pounded closer and closer.

Chapter 53 – SHADOW

Shadow barked, and barked again, when the boat tipped over with September inside. A strange man carrying a gun—he could smell the oil and rank odor—tromped too close. Hidden in the nearby tree line, Shadow heard Quinn. She had a gun, could help September, but instead moved stealthily away.

Shadow wanted to dive into the water. But September had told him to *wait.* Maybe she had a good reason, but his hackles refused to smooth. The man with the gun could hurt September, hurt Quinn, even hurt a good dog.

What to do? Go into the water after September? Chase Quinn so she'd use her gun to protect September? Would the man find her in the lake?

As the man drew near, his slinking posture changed. He stood tall when he saw Shadow, and pointed his gun.

Lifting his lips in a snarl, Shadow stepped forward, stiff legged and bristling fur, ready to meet the man with his teeth. But September told him to wait. He hesitated.

All around them, leaves rustled in a hot wind that breathed

hard as the sun peeked above the nearby house. Shadow backed away from September's watery hiding place, drawing the man into the sapling stand. His paws squished in the soggy marsh, more fit for frogs than a good dog's feet.

"Well, what have we here?" The man whispered, almost as if he knew September hid close by. "A black German Shepherd. I know somebody that has a black shepherd named Shadow."

His ears twitched at his name. Shadow ramped up his growl.

"Does that mean a certain someone still lives?" His tongue made a tsk-tsk sound. "I thought she would be smarter than to show up here." The man circled, until Shadow stood between him and September's invisible form.

Shadow heard an intake of breath underneath the boat, so quiet only a dog could hear. His growl rumbled, and he bounced forward to warn the man to stay away, before retreating to guard the water's edge.

He whispered again, but with more urgency. "I got your dog in my sights. I'll give you the count of three before I put a bullet between his perky black ears. Come out quietly, and I promise I won't hurt you. We have business to do, and you're worth more alive than dead. One…"

The man raised the gun. The pointed end looked like a tiny eye staring directly at Shadow's face.

"Two…"

Shadow heard September's movement under the boat and whined. He didn't want the bad man to hear and go after her. He backed up as far as he could, staying between the gun and the hidden boat. His rear paws sank up to his hocks in the water, while his forepaws braced against the soft mud of the brackish shore. The boat bobbed underneath the surface only a couple of dog lengths away.

"Three—"

September burst from the water, brandishing the long paddle. The man stepped forward, surprised determination on his face. She wound up and swung it around like Shadow's Frisbee. The blade connected with a melon-like thump against the man's face.

His hands arched up and out in a belated defensive posture. The gun dropped and splashed into the water. The man stood upright only a moment before he collapsed forward and didn't move.

Shadow's hackles bristled. He cautiously sniffed the prone figure, but from a distance, leery to get too close and have the stranger grab at him.

September stepped onto marshy ground, water cascading from her form. One hand still held the paddle, the other clutched the dry-bag with their supplies. "Good dog Shadow. Good wait."

He wagged, and his fur smoothed. Shadow stood back to give September room to climb out of the wet.

Chapter 54 – SEPTEMBER

September held the double-bladed paddle like a spear, ready to smack the big man again if he so much as twitched. She'd flattened his nose with the same stroke that clobbered his chin, but she doubted he'd be out for long.

She pulled a pair of zip ties from the bag. September trussed his wrists together behind his back, and raised his head enough to tape his mouth, and wrapped it around the back of his head. Finding a nearby rock, she propped up his head so that he wouldn't suffocate in the muck. She'd reluctantly come to terms with how to deal with Kaliko Wong, but she would not murder a bound, disarmed man. The police could pick up the trash later.

And Jack would help her disappear. She and Shadow would have nothing left to go back to. Even if she didn't pull the trigger, she'd be prosecuted for her part in dispatching the evil that had haunted her life.

Toggling the com-device fitted in her good ear signaled Quinn she'd disabled the guard. Immediately, the undergrowth rustled as the young woman scaled the pecan tree quicker than a cat. Once securely seated on her sniper perch, the girl shot September a thumbs up.

September examined the big man. She took his Taser, retrieved her own weapon from the dry-bag, and snugged it to the small of her back. Adrenaline made her nerves thrum.

Then she knelt and opened her arms wide, and Shadow pushed into her embrace. Oh, how she needed that. She steadied her breathing, timing it to the dog's soft panting breath, until they breathed in tandem. One heart. One purpose. No words needed. She knew he'd do his part, anything she asked, and more. *Please God, let us get through this.* And if not, let them go together.

September pulled out the burner phone, and, feeling like she was leaping off a bottomless cliff, texted Jack.

<Ready. Send dog.

The canine duo would need to work quickly to distribute the recorded buttons to the windows and doors. If a dog dropped one, the recording sounded prematurely. Once placed the two dogs would trigger pairs in tandem, on opposite sides of the house. The more confusion, the better.

But Jack's response surprised her.

>She knows you're there. Too dangerous. Pull back, wait in boat.

Her jaw clenched. What the hell? She punched in the text reply.

<Driver disabled. Quinn in place. Go-time.

>Stand down.

Something had changed. He hadn't cared about her safety before. If anything, he'd treated her as expendable.

The longer Quinn sat perched in a tree, the greater the chance of discovery. If the young woman had a clear view of the house, the reverse was true as well.

Combs died, and April died, and how many others died because of this woman? No, she refused to sit on the sidelines, not anymore.

<Send Keighley. Or we'll go it alone.

Chapter 55 – JACK

Damn it to hell!" Jack slapped the flats of both hands against the sides of his head, wanting to punch something, punish himself for not recognizing the reality sooner.

Steven's message made horrible sense of the increased interest in September, the extraordinary monitoring of the woman's life, and repeated assassination attempts. He finally understood Kaliko Wong's world was at stake. This wasn't an assassination hired from outside sources. No, this was about preserving a legacy. Wong's legacy. And Kali's control.

The dynasty, built on tradition, meant power and influence stayed in the family. As Wong's wife, Kali had wielded great power and influence, and as his widow, she had merged and expanded her following. Yet a more traditional faction, those with a long memory, nipped at her heels. They never accepted Kali as a leader, only tolerated her while she had the support of her husband. With him dead, they wanted no part of the outsider.

The dog in the back seat paw-danced on the upholstery. "Shut up, dog." He could turn the animal loose to raise the distraction level as planned. But would it help September survive?

Rina had never been a threat. She knew nothing, cared nothing about the business, only devoted herself to her family. Her husband had used her brilliance to amass unimaginable wealth and influence. And now here they were, an end game Jack should have expected.

A new message came in from his team.

>Three drones monitoring house.

"Dammit!" Under whose control, Kali's or her traditionalist opposition? That might explain how September so easily disarmed the guard. With a start, Jack understood something beyond the obvious. Killing the witch would not free September from the past…

And Kali understood as well. Her lack of entourage wasn't so much overconfidence as a distrust of her cohorts. September's very existence threatened everything, but September didn't know she held the keys to bringing down the entire sinister crime syndicate.

If September wouldn't call off her attack, Jack had to improve her chances of survival. And escape. Then he could build a partnership with September, and they could do more than avenge Rina. Together, they could make things right.

The dog whined again and clawed at the window. Jack pulled out his night vision binoculars and focused on the house. The silhouette of a dog padded across the terrace. September had already sent Shadow. He paused at the sliding glass doors, dropped his head, then whirled to race back to September. If Shadow had already reached the rear of the house, he'd already left three or more talking buttons at the front.

"Son-of-a bitch, the training actually works." He lowered the binoculars and turned to the dog in the backseat. "You want to join the party?" Too late for the dog to help with the buttons, but she could cultivate additional distraction. That raised the odds of survival in September's favor.

With enough distraction, Jack could get into the house and take care of the witch himself. That's what he should have done all along.

Chapter 56 – TEDDY

She's alive!" Teddy steadied himself to keep from pitching into the water. September had been at this cottage. He knew dogs could detect scent days, weeks, sometimes months after someone's presence. But in this remote spot, and on the wet boat rope… He knew they had just missed her.

Lia's eyes filled with tears. She fell to her knees and hugged Magic, smoothing the short, silky fur on the top of his blocky head. She murmured softly, and Teddy knew she needed a moment to steady her emotions, just as did he.

Shadow must have been in the area with September. She'd traveled with someone else, leaving everything behind, maybe intent on disappearing to protect the rest of them. She had help. It hurt that she left him out when he would've done anything to help. But the knot in his chest relaxed enough for him to breathe, knowing she still lived.

"She's playing dead." Lia sprang to her feet, staring around as though answers to their questions beckoned, if they only knew where to look. "She knows the threat isn't over." She cocked her head. "So, who died in the blast? I mean, besides Combs and Gonzales." She scrubbed the tears from her face and cleared her throat. Teddy watched her shake off emotions and put on her professional attitude. "We need to call for backup. If we found her, the people with drones and bombs can find her, too."

Teddy agreed. But flooding the area with police would warn whoever was after September. He stared across the open water, wishing he'd brought his binoculars from the RV. "She took a boat. What does that tell you?" Maybe Lia's younger eyes could detect more than his in the dawning light.

She twisted, hands on hips, scanning the area. The sun painted the water red. "She needed to get from here to there." She made a general waving motion toward the far shore. "Wanted to stay undercover and approach without detection. Otherwise, she'd take the car. I'd hug the shore and get as close to my target as possible to keep from alerting anyone."

He nodded. If she meant to disappear for good, a boat would've been the last place he'd expect to find evidence of September. She would've headed for DFW airport, changed her appearance, and been gone. Taking the boat meant a destination. And a purpose. What—or who—awaited across the lake?

Teddy spun on his heels and hurried back to Nellie Nova. September had gone after someone, probably whoever she believed bombed the wedding. He needed to check properties bordering the small lake, so the police knew where to send help.

They all piled back into the RV. Teddy clicked into his computer and brought up the satellite image of the lake. Lia stood behind him, peering over his shoulder. "Do you think she knows?"

"Knows what?" He continued refining his search. It made sense September's attacker stayed in the area until an autopsy confirmed her death. He could ask Captain Gregory to keep the result quiet and fake her death like Combs, but such information rarely stayed private for long. The killers would redouble efforts to hunt down September. Maybe she'd finally had enough and turned the tables.

"Do you think September knows Combs is dead? She lived for the wedding, couldn't wait to start a new life. They deserved some happiness, especially after all they had gone through."

His lips tightened, agreeing with Lia's assessment. If September saw the press conference, Combs's death could well have pushed her to jump off this cliff. He sighed, staring at the computer screen. "There must be forty houses abutting the shoreline of this lake. Tiny cottages, small lake houses, estates with acreage, even a bed-and-breakfast." It would take hours to check each one.

Teddy's phone chirped, announcing a text.

>This is Jackson Glass, part of September's protection detail.

Why the hell was the man contacting Teddy now? Before he could reply, another text arrived.

>She's alive but on a suicide mission. At the Cat's Cradle B&B.

>On Lakefront Road.

Teddy's jaw dropped. He didn't question. It came from the same number as the cryptic warnings yesterday. He remembered the odd-looking albino man and knew he had skills. If he'd partnered with September, but now asked for help, they had no time to waste.

"Lia, call Captain Gregory."

Chapter 57 – KEIGHLEY

The door… The door the door… The man had to open the door. Keighley pawed at the window, turning her plaintive whine into a more demanding bark. Maybe the man would understand that.

She had helped Shadow break out of the kennel, and ever since, had enjoyed nonstop action. The training games made her tail wag faster, and she couldn't remember a time when she'd had more fun. It had been so long since Keighley wowed the crowd in the show ring. She'd missed the challenge of competition, although she enjoyed working as a therapy dog.

Chasing in tandem with Shadow brought a new joyous bounce to her paws. Now she was locked inside this car with the dour white-haired man. She grew more and more frustrated, especially since she could tell the man's anger threatened to erupt. Keighley leaned forward, and cold nosed the man's muscled arm, but the man flinched away.

She couldn't understand that. Every person she had ever met crooned sweet words to her and offered to cuddle. She enjoyed pets especially with her boy—even though he'd grown up and left home. That made Keighley sad. But now adventure called. She could hear and smell Shadow outside the car, not too far away. She knew Shadow played the game, another contest. Keighley was good at contests. She wanted to play, too.

Open the door-door-door!

She could barely contain herself when the man climbed out of the front of the car and did just that. As soon as the door cracked open she shoved her nose in the gap and leaped out of the vehicle.

Off like a shot, her tan paws made little noise as she ran to reach the terrace where she had last detected Shadow. She sniffed around the button that sat in front of the sliding glass doors. It smelled like Shadow. She wagged happily, and as she'd been taught, Keighley pawed the button.

But nothing happened. Her paw flipped it, and it skittered across the paving stones into the brush beside the terrace. With frustration, she tried to dig it out, but the recorded voice sounded muffled in the dirt. "Come and get me!" September's voice sounded from the button, and Keighley pawed it again. "Come and get me!"

That was no fun. So, she barked to tell it so, then she dropped her nose and followed Shadow's scented path to the next window, where another button rested. Before she could paw this button to make it talk, a lithe striped silver-furred figure slunk around the far corner of the house. The dog's head came up, her neck arched with interest, and she inhaled the rich smell. Cat. She liked cat smell.

Hissing, the cat arched her back and dashed away. The dog followed, the instinct to chase overwhelming any other training or desire. Her paws thundered on the wooden treads of the veranda, and the cat leaped high onto the railing, then posed, a teasing torment out of nose reach.

Keighley barked again, dancing up and down on the creaky wooden flooring. She heard a strange humming sound underneath the floor grow louder and louder. The cat ducked her head and walked daintily along the railing to the far edge of the veranda.

Something bit Keighley on her muzzle. She snapped at the air, caught the buzzing insect, and yelped when it bit her tongue, too.

Down near the water's edge she caught the scent and the motion of Shadow. With insect pursuers hectoring her retreat, Keighley streaked across the lawn, yelping with each galloping paw thump.

Chapter 58 – SEPTEMBER

September kneeled on the hard-pack dirt, still hidden in the rough vegetation next to the mowed grass expanse. Shadow had just returned from placing the last button.

"Good dog." She mouthed the words and gave him a thumbs up, the silent signal for *good dog*. He'd taken all the buttons they'd prepped, and she hoped placed all where needed. She'd seen Shadow deposit the most important ones.

She checked Quinn's position. Now came the most dangerous and important part of the plan: luring Kali out the door and down the steps of the veranda. If the buttons didn't flush her out—

A yelp sounded near the house. She squinted as the Airedale pelted toward her, then at the house, where a shadowy cat form perched on the railing.

September groaned. The cat canceled any training the dog had learned. Forget the talking buttons. Keighley's cries easily got the attention of anyone inside.

The dog barreled into September, whimpering and howling.

"Hush, settle. The mean cat can't get you." She crooned so

softly she could barely hear. She opened her arms, despite Shadow's half growl of dismay, to cuddle the other dog.

She immediately recoiled, slapping away a stinging insect that squirmed in the dog's wiry fur. She picked up a twig to flip another out of the dog's coat, but it returned to target her own bare arms. After half a dozen slaps in the air, September finally nailed the yellow jacket.

No wonder the dog ran from the house. She couldn't send Shadow to paw the buttons, not now that those inside would be watching for any motion. Kali or her operatives would easily pick off anyone—dog, or human—who ventured across the grassy yard.

As the dog's whimpers faded, September stared at the distant house. A light flicked on in the tower's top room. A shadow moved across the window. September glanced at Quinn and motioned toward the distinctive figure's silhouette.

But Quinn shook her head. She pantomimed listening to a phone, and following the hint, September reached for hers. Jack had sent a text.

>Wait. Please. I'm going in.

Quinn couldn't shoot at the tower window, or she might hit Jack.

Chapter 59 – JACK

The dog's barking gave Jack the opportunity he needed. He couldn't risk entry through a window or even the sliding glass doors. Too obvious, and possibly booby trapped. He'd go into the garage and disable the car before going after her.

Jack had already straightened and bent a metal clothes hanger into the hook he needed. He snaked it into the gap at the top center of the garage door, wiggled it a bit, and captured the release cable. With the dog still barking loudly, Jack risked a sharp hard tug to disengage the door.

Then he lifted the door just enough to roll inside, and let it slide back shut. He continued to roll, sheltered beneath the parked vehicle for just a moment, breathing slow and steady. He listened carefully, and hearing nothing, rose to his feet. Opening the hood of the car to disable the engine would take too much time, and risk noise, so he did the next best thing and punctured all four tires.

Now inside the building, drones couldn't see him. The same wasn't true for September, or Quinn. If he gained control of Kali, it eliminated any tactical drone surprises she controlled.

Jack hurried to the door into the house. Most homeowners didn't lock these doors, relying on the garage door for security. Kali knew better, but he had come prepared. Within moments, his picks opened the five-pin tumbler lock, and he slipped inside. The door opened into the family room he had spied through the sliding glass doors.

In a low crouch, with weapon drawn, he moved through the kitchen to the dining room and into the living room to reach the staircase. All were deserted. He heard nothing from the upstairs, but that was the only place the viper's nest could be.

Jack didn't like stairs—a shooting gallery with him the sole target. Besides, old houses were notoriously creaky, especially staircases. But he had no choice.

He slowly and carefully stepped onto the first tread. Jack kept his back to the wall as he ascended step-by-step up the twisting staircase. He held his breath with each careful step, ready to dodge in the opposite direction of any unexpected sound.

When he reached the midway landing, where it turned back on itself to reach the second story, Jack finally heard voices above him, probably from the third-floor.

"You don't have that long to live. So, make your peace, if there is such a thing." Kali laughed, the voice taunting, and as sharp as the knife she used to torment her victims.

"Admit it. You hate September, too. She's why your husband died. She got all the accolades over the years—a brilliant prodigy, a pampered daughter, never mind her artistic little brother. And now even my organization turns on me and wants her." Her voice dripped with sarcasm. "What a shame you blew her up when you delivered the flowers."

Chapter 60 – KALI

Kali jumped back from the window after sneaking a quick glimpse. But the barking dog she'd heard must've been a stray. It looked nothing like the mutt September ferried around. Kali was very conscious of the target she made. She had the overhead lights on to flush out any enemies, like a moth to the flame. So far, no takers.

The highest point in the old Victorian, the study above the master bedroom, was accessible only by a narrow curling stairwell. And thick antique glass panes made it difficult for a sniper to see through for an accurate shot.

Kali itched to dispatch Mark January. He represented everything she disliked about the world. People who believed they deserved special consideration but didn't have the guts to stand up and demand, nay, take it for themselves. He pretended it didn't matter, but of course it did. Why should September get all the attention and accolades for her music when his artistic ability also shined, albeit differently?

Kali had never been given anything. Everything she attained, she won in battle. Those who looked down on her then, looked up at her from their graves today. Had she complained? Hidden her resentment like this man? No, she took what she deserved.

"You achieve success by recognizing opportunities and grabbing them by the throat." She paced around the man. Until she got confirmation of September's death, this man served as her insurance. The vendetta not only eliminated September, it flushed out defectors within her organization, so she could eliminate them and strengthen her position. *Wheels within wheels.*

"You have it all wrong. I love my sister. I didn't know about the flowers. O God, if I could change things…" He sobbed.

The man didn't even have the balls to struggle against his restraints. He sat, hands zip-tied behind his back, ankles taped, and a noose around his neck. She'd attached the rope from it to the enormous ceiling beam at the top of the tower. He pretended not to know what was going on. *Liar.*

The traditionalists had already made a deal with him in case they couldn't reach September. He knew what was at stake, and he'd sold September out. And now he wanted absolution.

She snorted. "Do you have any idea what you set in motion with your little wedding present?"

"September never saw it. Nobody knows." He raised his head, jaw stiffening, and met her eyes with an expression of cold steel. "You killed my sister, not me. Maybe you'll kill me next. But someone will come for you. You can count on it."

Suddenly Kali could see the family resemblance. She straightened her spine, ignoring the frisson that clenched her gut.

A clinking on the metal stairs betrayed the intruder. Kali spun into a crouch, weapons appearing as if by magic in each hand.

Overhead, a cabinet door squealed open, followed by a hiss and spit.

The sudden unexpected noise jarred Kali's aim just as she fired down the stairwell, the burst of automatic fire spraying the metal rungs of the staircase. The thump of a falling body followed.

Kali looked up toward the cabinet. Nothing there.

Chapter 61 – SEPTEMBER

September pulled away from the Airedale and gave the hand signal for *down.* Shadow responded immediately, flopping to the ground and licking his lips. The combination of behaviors self-calmed canine stress, and when the other dog saw Shadow *down* on command, Keighley copied the behavior, and the agitated whimpers slowly declined.

September knew the stings hurt. Fur had protected the terrier from the worst, but yellow jackets were vicious little beasts. She must have agitated them.

Once again, September raised her binoculars. The cat hadn't moved from the veranda railing.

Improvise September, improvise.

Toggling the laser pointer, September reminded the two dogs of the earlier game they played. She shined the light against a nearby tree trunk and mouthed, "Shadow, *show me.*" He rose to his feet, quickly trotted to the tree, and did a paws-up to punch the light.

She repeated the exercise, this time designating the Airedale.

Like a star, Keighley performed the exercise flawlessly.

Next, September took out another of the talking buttons, with no recorded message. She placed the button on the ground, and first with Shadow then his new friend, shined a laser pointer on the button coupled with the command, *show me*. Again, each dog performed perfectly.

Finally, she repeated the exercise, this time without the laser pointer, and simply stated, "*Show me* button." Shadow paw punched the button. The other dog looked puzzled. But when she shined the light, the Airedale immediately responded correctly.

Dogs usually generalized commands once they became entrenched. Shadow had had years of experience with the *show me* game, but the new dog not so much. September needed the dogs to play the buttons in tandem, on opposite sides of the house—Kali couldn't shoot two places at once—but it required skill and discipline to perform at a distance from the handler.

Shadow always performed his service dog skills near her. He never needed distance training. He also knew when to disobey. She hadn't taught him that. September worried that if she left him out, trying to keep him safe, he would take on the task anyway and get himself hurt. Better to give him a specific direction, hopefully one that would keep them both safe.

The far side of the house, away from the water, offered the safest area for him. He'd placed the final talking buttons on the veranda, so she sent him back to the far side of the house.

A lump formed in her throat as she watched his swift progress, until he disappeared around the corner of the house. Still in her *down* position, Keighley nosed her bare calf. Whether the dog succeeded now came down to her ability, not the dog's.

She took a big breath, squared her shoulders as she stood, and prepared herself. *Do it for Combs. And for April. For all the people she's hurt.*

September spoke softly, but with command to the dog at her feet. She showed the laser again, ran it along the grassy incline up to the house, noting how the Airedale's attention followed it, then shined it in a swirled pattern on the front door.

"Keighley, show me button!"

Chapter 62 – NEBULAE

Nebulae liked dogs well enough. Occasionally, a dog visited from the neighbor, but usually she only saw them from inside the house through window glass. Having a strange dog thundering about on her property—this house, yard, and everything she could see from the upstairs window belonged to Nebulae—put her tail in a twist.

She still wanted Sunset to open the door, since the people refused. Then she could snuggle with the marmalade cat and share their favorite sun-soaked sleep spot in the bay window. The fish she'd eaten earlier was making Nebulae sleepy.

Now another dog thundered up the grassy expanse, ignoring Nebulae to tear around the side of the property. Nebulae watched with interest, wondering why her territory grew thick with dogs. She sniffed. Better dogs than another cat. She'd share with Sunset, but a stranger cat—no!

On the other side of the house, she could hear the dog's nails scrabble on the paving stones beside the rear sliding doors. Nebulae rose with a soft meow. Perhaps the door would open for the dog and Nebulae could take back her house.

But before she could jump down and pad around to explore this new opportunity, a bright red dot appeared on the wall next to the front door. She recognized that red dot. People who visited the house often played with the red dot so Nebulae could chase it round and round and round. The game always finished with stinky treats.

She crouched on the railing, haunches gathered and rear paws treading in preparation. The red dot traveled down the wall to a place in front of the doorway. It swirled there at the foot of the door, flickering over and around a strange object.

Nebulae pounced off the railing and stalked the red dot. The object didn't move, but the light flickered all around, tempting her to pounce, to grapple, to bite.

Pop-pop-pop-pop-pop

The burst of noise from inside the house startled Nebulae so that she leaped high in the air, coming down on top of the odd object.

"I'm here. Come and get me."

A strange woman's voice spoke from the object. Nebulae hissed and backed away. The red dot flickered again. Nebulae didn't know whether to run away from the scary popping or punish the voice coming from the button on the floor. She reached outward, paws and claws extended, and… bat-bat-bat… hit the object until it skittered across the wooden flooring and stopped talking.

On the other side of the house, the strange dog's claws danced their own counterpoint. A different girl's voice spoke from the distance.

"I'm here. I'm coming for you."

The dog's foot treads moved around the side of the house. Another voice spoke, a man.

"Karma is a bitch. Your turn."

Chapter 63 – KALI

Kali peered over the railing, semi-automatic still at the ready. Below her, splayed on the bottom step of the spiral staircase, a man struggled to crawl out of sight. His dark stocking cap had come askew, revealing his platinum hair.

"You died decades ago. Suicide after I— after your sister and parents were killed." She looked around for anyone else that might have penetrated the house. "Where's the rest of your team?" He must have intel from inside the Wong organization.

"I'm a solo act. The Day woman died. I figured you would stick around to be sure. Do you really think anyone could survive that bomb?" He moved out of sight.

She'd have to travel down the staircase, put herself at risk, to finish the job.

Kali laughed. "I thought it a nice touch, having her brother deliver the coup de grâce. He'll hang himself, out the window, for the cops to find." She paused. "You called the cops, right?"

"I know why you want them dead. The same reason you murdered my sister." He coughed, a bubbling sound that made Kali grin with satisfaction. That spray of bullets must've caught him.

He was a kid, barely a teenager back then, and he still acted like a kid. She didn't deign to answer. He understood—better than anyone—who and what September and her brother represented. This man was only the first of the roaches to directly challenge her authority. And she'd squash him, squash them all, just like bugs.

Nebulae watched the red dot skitter across the door, and travel on to the next window. Another button sat on the sill. She'd learned the game now and slunk low to stalk the teasing red dot that pointed the way. Standing upright on her rear paws, she stared through the window into the house—her house—from which she'd been banned. Nebulae's ears slicked back, wanting some way to vent her displeasure.

The red dot loomed, hovered above the button. The tabby cat hit it with one hard paw, whap-whap-whap, and when it fell, she bopped it again. Nebulae checked the next window without needing the red dot prompt.

Each button yelled different words with strange voices, making her even more aroused. Nebulae raced from button to button, paw-whapping one after another, over and over again …

"So Vanya…" Kali turned the name into a taunt.

"Jackson Glass. You're right. Vanya died with Rina."

His voice gave her the location she needed. Like a dancer, she twirled and skipped down the metal stairs, swinging her weapon to take him out—

"I'm here. Come and get me."

The voice threw off Kali's aim just enough to miss and shatter one of the bay windows in the master bedroom.

Jack dove through the broken window. He rolled onto the veranda's roof, hugging the wall so as not to give her a clean shot.

September Day's voice! It came from downstairs at the front of the house. She lived. *Nine lives, like the vermin cats she loved.*

"September?" From upstairs Mark yelled. "Oh my God, you're alive. September, run, she'll kill you!" Kali heard his thumping movement as he tried to escape from the chair.

Before she could put a bullet through the floor, another voice rang out, this time from the front window downstairs.

"I'm here. I'm coming for you."

A different voice. She'd teamed with others besides Vanya, or whatever he now called himself. Kali checked her weapons. Knives. Handgun. The semi-automatic. Plenty of ammunition. Her driver was too good for this rabble to best. He must have turned traitor.

"Karma is a bitch. Your turn."

Jackson's voice came from the side of the house—but she could still see his shadow out the window on the porch roof. Aha, a trick, then. But it didn't matter. She would defeat all her enemies.

She ran back up the metal staircase. Time to keep her promise about Mark January. Kali aimed her gun at the man.

Before she could pull the trigger, an orange spitting demon with claws unfurled dropped from above, landing directly on Kali's face. The blast instead shattered the window.

Mark screamed. Hot wind blew in.

Kali peeled the cat off her face, but before she could dispatch it, he disappeared once more into a cubbyhole in the ceiling. She smacked the man silent with the butt of her weapon, then muscled him out the window to dangle by his neck.

If anyone outside cared, his mid-air death-jig would be a distraction while she took care of business.

Kali cared about only one thing. To watch September Day die.

Chapter 64 – SHADOW

Shadow rounded the corner of the house, having pawed every button he previously placed. When he had heard the burst of gunfire inside the house, his ears went back, and a low growl bubbled deep in his throat, but he continued to work. That's what September asked. He lived for hearing her tell him, "good dog."

Overhead, another burst of gunfire followed by shattering glass split the silence. Thumping sounds overhead brought Shadow into a crouching pose of readiness. Someone had jumped onto the roof. He worried a bad person would leap off to attack a good dog. Or worse, go after September.

At the front windows, he spied the cat tap-tap-tapping one of the buttons. It fell from a window, and the cat chased its skittering form across the wooden porch. The button spun into the bushes, and the cat glanced around when she heard Shadow's approach. Immediately, her back arched just like Macy-cat when startled.

The red dot still jittered across the bottom of the door. Shadow swung his head toward where he knew September waited, hidden in the undergrowth by the water's edge. The cat didn't know about September, but when Shadow posed no threat the dancing light recaptured her attention, and she dashed to stand on hind legs and paw at the flickering light, following as it traveled to the window.

Shadow backed away and watched. September hadn't taught him what to do if a strange cat appeared. He'd have to figure this out himself.

He watched the cat discover another talking button on the edge of the window. With one lithe motion, the cat leaped to the windowsill and paw-punched the button.

September's voice spoke with the paw-teased button.

"Come and get me. Come and get me. Come and…"

Her voice made Shadow's chest swell with love, even though she wasn't here, and he knew the voice came from some human magic.

The cat flinched only briefly, then continued paw-patting the button until she smacked it off the windowsill and it rolled across the wooden floor. The cat pounced on the button, falling onto her side, and grappling the plastic toy, biting it and making September's voice sound over and over.

"… Get me… Get me… Get me…"

Shadow flinched at a distant scream, this time from the real September, not the button. Her anguished cry made him want to race back to her side. But she stepped out of hiding just long enough to give him the hated hand signal: *wait.* Then she retreated into the brush.

Shadow waited. Inside, clattering footfalls spoke of someone scrambling down stairs. A slight figure burst through the front door, teeth bared. He recognized her from the salon. She held a gun in one hand, a knife in the other. She took half a step back into the doorway to shield her body as she scanned the backyard.

The cat startled, then with a happy chirp abandoned the button and approached the woman, trying to slink into the house.

The woman's lip curled and her eyes widened when she saw the button. She kicked the cat aside, then pointed the gun at Shadow.

Without a second thought, Shadow leaped to nose-punch the gun aside. She countered. Her knife scored a searing pain on his shoulder as he dashed by.

At the kick, the cat screamed and climbed the woman's leg, sinking claws into flesh to seek a safe perch. But she slung the cat off, her knife spinning away in a clatter of metal.

"Kaliko! Come and get me. I'm the one you want!" September screamed, stepping into the light of the new day. The sparkling water backlit her figure. "Shadow, *away*." She waved and pointed.

Shadow raced to take refuge around the far corner of the house.

Overhead, the noise distracted Kali, and she glanced back. "That's your brother up there, hanging out the window, gasping his last breath. Think you can save him? You can't even save yourself, not this time." She laughed. "He wanted you dead. So I'm doing you a favor."

Her gleeful voice sounded like September's joyous tone when they played one of their games. But this was no game. In this game, the loser would lose more than a treat.

Shadow peered around the corner of the house to track the lethal woman. He ignored the hurt on his shoulder. He'd felt worse, and playing this game required all his concentration.

The red dot crawled across the wall next to the open door. It danced from one side of the opening to the other, as if trying to touch the woman hiding inside. The cat noticed, too.

Far from being defensive, the cat's dilated eyes and a strained growl announced her intent. Shadow understood.

The cat's body shrunk close to the floor, each paw step deliberate. She stalked the red dot but would make do with nailing the nasty woman, given half a chance.

The woman finally noticed the cat's offensive pose. With a snarled curse of her own, she aimed a burst of gunfire at the floor of the veranda, intent on destroying the cat. Quick as a wink, the cat dove between the banisters to safety in the shrubbery.

Shadow shivered, but not from the gunshots. A buzzing cloud of yellow swarmed from beneath the veranda to avenge their shredded nest.

Chapter 65 – SEPTEMBER

September watched as Jack struggled to keep his balance and not slip off the veranda roof as he strained to climb to reach the dangling man: her brother, Mark. She had no way to reach him in time and prayed Jack could do what she couldn't.

Keighley pressed against September's side, a low growl threatening the distant figure. She'd recalled the dog after seeing the cat play with the buttons, and felt gratified by the Airedale's protection training.

Kaliko Wong had grown to monster proportions in September's imagination. The reality looked far different. A slim ballerina of a woman, dark hair bound tight to her head, brandishing a gun that she now took time to reload, clearly relishing the entire experience.

She stepped out of the door and a shimmering nimbus engulfed her, creating a monstrous, magical aura that augmented her legend. The golden cloud followed as she skipped down the veranda steps and took a half-dozen unsteady steps toward September.

Shadow cautiously crept out to watch, blatantly disobeying September's *wait* command. Sometimes he did that. And while she appreciated his need to keep her safe, September's focus wavered when she knew his risk increased. Shadow's choices weren't arbitrary, though, so he must know something she didn't.

Kali had stopped. She waved one arm haphazardly through the air while making a high-pitched mewling sound. She turned in a half circle and caught sight of Shadow. In one smooth motion she aimed and fired her gun. Shadow yelped and danced sideways.

She missed! Clearly the stinging cloud disabled her. September grabbed up the kayak paddle, ready to finish the job. She dashed forward, then stopped when Kali braced both hands on the weapon and again took aim at Shadow. September screamed.

"Shadow, *down. Wait.*"

September raced toward the evil woman, her decades-long tormentor, determined she would not take Shadow's life!

At the sound of September's voice, Kali pirouetted, adjusting her aim. She wavered, her aim all over, and looked ready to collapse.

September brandished the paddle like her self-defense long staff. She whirled it overhead, around, and around, the whickering whine a warning to stay back, and the blur of motion disorienting the killer's concentration.

Time to roll the dice. "Keighley, *fass*!" The command to attack rolled off her tongue.

She just wanted time for Jack to save her brother, for Shadow to escape. If everything for her ended here, she'd join her sister April—*and Combs, my love*—knowing she'd done one thing right.

The Airedale flew forward, snarling, ready to engage. She leaped for Kali's arm, and swung the killer around. But the swarm turned its attention to the dog, and she yelped and dodged away.

The protection dog returned to her guard position beside September.

The dog's distraction gave September the needed seconds. The paddle blade connected with Kali's gun hand with a satisfying thwack. The weapon dropped to the ground. The stings had nearly blinded the killer—she squinted through swollen eyes, breathed with whistling wheezes. Kali's face, bare arms and thighs sported red wheals and the woman's neck had swollen to twice the normal size. The Airedale's teeth had left her mark.

Despite her distress, Kali went into an offensive posture, clearly just as lethal without weapons. September kept the paddle before her, using it like a spear, jabbing at the woman and alternating with flowing slices through the air.

Keighley raced in, and the witch produced a knife. "*Wharten*, Keighley, wait good girl!" She couldn't let the dog sacrifice herself. This was September's fight, and time to take down the snake.

The pair circled each other, Kali dodging and ducking, trying to close the distance between them. September feared hand-to-hand with Kali meant certain death.

Shadow again broke his wait command. He danced around the pair, dodging close to nip ankles. Kali turned with snakelike speed, striking with her foot and catching his hip, knocking the dog off his feet. He quickly scrambled upright, snarling but taking more care in his next approach.

A bright red dot appeared, swirling on the center of Kali's chest. September blinked in confusion. Then understood. She reflexively glanced toward Quinn's perch in the distant tree, swung her wooden paddle at Kali's head, and stepped out of the line of fire.

Shadow continued worrying Kali's feet. Terrified he'd be hit, September yelped, "Shadow *down*!" He sank to the dirt, immediately behind the woman's feet.

Kali poised to throw her knife at September …

A furry missile zoomed by, passing September just as Shadow flopped onto his tummy. Keighley obeyed her crash course in the *show me* game. She leaped high, paw-punched the red dot on Kali's chest.

The knife flew past September's ear.

Kali fell backward over Shadow's crouched form.

And Quinn's shot missed as well.

Chapter 66 – JACK

The rising sun painted a dark silhouette of the house against the grass. Jack saw the women struggling while the dog danced around the pair. Nothing he could do for September now.

Jack was losing blood from the wounds Kali had inflicted with her spray of bullets. None were lethal, but they certainly needed medical attention. He had to get Mark to safety before his own energy and willpower evaporated.

Jack drew his knife and slashed the tether leading to Mark's neck then caught the man's stiff form with one arm, while bracing against the second-story bedroom window. He'd fallen from the third story to land on the roof of the veranda, directly outside the master bedroom windows. The pitch of the roof proved difficult to navigate, but with the window already shattered, Jack's grip on the sill kept them from sliding. Mark struggled, and Jack whispered urgently: "I'm trying to save you, jerk. You nearly got your sister killed."

Not having much choice, Mark's struggles ceased.

Jack heaved the smaller man into the house through the broken window and vaulted in after him. The pair lay panting side-by-side on the floor until Jack roused enough to roll to his knees. He slit the zip ties and tape securing the man's wrists and ankles. Immediately Mark clawed at his neck, pulling loose the noose digging into the flesh below his jaw.

His voice came out a croaking garble. "Who are you?"

Jack pulled himself to his feet and stared down at the dark-haired man. "I knew your mother. Your real mom." Emotion long dead to him, and kept at bay out of self-protection, flickered—an ember that would flame to life given half a chance. He couldn't afford that. Emotions left you vulnerable and weak. The death of his family had destroyed his younger self.

He glanced out the window and saw that September had gained ascendancy in the struggle against Kali. He smiled.

In the distance, sirens wailed. Teddy had wasted no time contacting the authorities. Jack couldn't afford to be around for the hard questions they'd ask.

Mark struggled to his feet, balancing precariously, and clutching a dresser to keep his balance. "I don't understand...."

"It's complicated." At the younger man's stricken look, he relented. "There's not much time, but I'll give you the crib notes." He talked as he helped the man down the narrow stairs. "Once upon a time a beautiful innocent young girl fell in love with a powerful and dangerous man..."

Chapter 67 – SEPTEMBER

September saw divots of grass appear, indicating another silent shot as Quinn continued to pepper the area.

"Keighley, *vorhous.*" With danger over, September gave the hand signal to get the dog clear of gunfire. The Airedale barked and ran, pawed the lever handle of the front door and disappeared into the house.

Like a spider, Kali crawled on all fours, combing the grass with her hands, searching for a weapon. September stepped forward, holding the kayak paddle ready, no longer hesitant to deliver a fatal blow.

Sirens split the morning air. Jack must've called the police after all. At the thought, she hesitated, eyes drawn to the empty roof. She prayed Mark was still alive.

She looked down at this swollen horror of a person and tossed the paddle away. Kaliko Wong had destroyed her life, but she'd be damned if she let Kali turn her into a murderer too.

Kali rolled onto her back, still straining to breathe. She stared up at September through hate-filled, swollen eyes. She raised both hands with triumph, a rictus grin splitting lips. The woman had recovered her handgun.

"Shadow, *show me* gun!" He leaped, nose contacting the gun.

But Kali had learned, and her two-handed grip foiled Shadow's attempts. He barked with frustration and danced away when it aimed at him.

"Don't. You. Dare. Shoot him, you die!" September took one giant step toward the woman, and swung hard with the trailing foot, kicking Kali square in the jaw.

But Kali caught September's foot with one hand and wrenched her off balance.

September fell to the ground. She kicked and rolled, tried to distance herself from the clutching hands. But Kali held on, and pulled herself on top. September bucked her body, grabbing Kali's gun hand, and twisted as hard as she could.

She outweighed Kali by twenty pounds, but the assassin had trained for a lifetime compared to September's meager weeks of practice. She couldn't compete. And Shadow, never trained in protection, couldn't help.

She smells like bananas. September almost laughed, wondering at what the mind noticed at the moment of death.

Shadow barked hysterically, leaping around the struggling women. He jumped in to take small nips, and then bounced away, but the killer remained determined, the way she'd fought on despite the yellow jackets.

September clung to Kali's gun with both hands, intent on keeping the barrel away from her face, her torso, her dog. She felt the hard outline of an object digging into the small of her back. Her gun, beneath her. Out of reach now.

The pair panted in unison, the killer straddling her until September's strength gave out. Sleepless nights, endless wedding plans, the explosion, hope destroyed, and love lost… No amount of adrenaline could save her.

Kali grinned as she wrenched away control of the gun. She took her time and spoke through swollen lips, thickened tongue, and whistling breath.

"I want to feel your hot blood on me. Then I'll kill your dog. Barbecue him. Like a proper Texan." She licked her lips and pressed the barrel of the gun to September's forehead.

Chapter 68 – SHADOW

He didn't know what to do. Shadow yelped, and barked, eager to help but afraid he'd make the gun *pop-pop-pop*. He stared into September's face, beloved eyes raining tears. Her heart galloped faster than even four paws could run, and she stank of fear and anger and… He tensed. She'd taken a breath to speak.

"Shadow. *Play tug. Tug gun*!"

The game he loved—but loved September more—and he knew exactly what she wanted. What a good dog should do. Just like what Max, his Kelpie friend, had done.

His jaws crunched Kali's wrist. The bad woman yelled, a strangled squeaky sound because she was breathing funny. Shadow tug-tug-tugged violently in one direction and shook his head hard. September twisted the other way.

The gun went off, so close to Shadow's ear he felt the heat. He yelped and dashed away. The bad woman still straddled September and wouldn't let her up. He dodged in closer, ready to grab and tug again.

He saw September grapple at her waist. She shoved something against the other woman's bare midriff and pulled the trigger.

The woman convulsed. She shivered and shook and let go of her gun.

September pushed her off and rolled away several feet before sitting up. She pulled the trigger on the funny gun a second time. "Took that Taser off your guard, you son-of-a—"

The woman's eyes rolled up in her head. Her fingers clawed at her throat. When the woman finally stopped jerking and lay still, September dropped the gun. She turned to Shadow and whispered, "Good dog. I love you, baby dog."

Shadow pushed himself into her lap. He licked her face, tail thumping the grass beside them, knocking her back down with his relief and excitement. Her face still rained tears, though her heart no longer raced.

She pushed to sitting and wrapped her arms around him. He whined and pushed back into her embrace, anchoring her to the here-and-now. That was his job. Even if this time he couldn't wake her up to scare the nightmare away, they could cling to each other. And soon, with September's stroking hands and Shadow's steady presence, they'd heal each other's hurts. They'd made that unspoken promise long ago, never to be broken…

When they heard a tread on the veranda, he felt September stiffen. She pushed Shadow away with one hand, and with the other retrieved the gun nested in the small of her back. Shadow stood by her side to meet whatever new enemy approached.

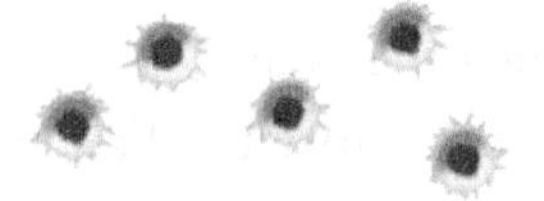

Jack winced as he climbed behind the wheel, thankful the engine turned over immediately. It had taken him longer than expected to make his way back to the hidden vehicle. He left Mark still jabbering questions that Jack didn't have the patience to answer, at least not yet.

Quinn appeared like a ghost at the side of the road. He slowed the vehicle to a crawl, and she opened the door to slide in as the car continued to roll. She whistled, and he flinched when the Airedale vaulted into the car after her.

She saw his look and shrugged. "Loose end. Better that I drop her back at the kennel. Otherwise, September will return the dog, and create even more questions."

He stared at her but didn't argue. He hit the gas and sped away from the old yellow Victorian.

She glanced at his expression. "Don't worry, September's a survivor. People that matter are counting on it."

"Are you working for the traditionalists?"

A grin lit up her face, and she shrugged. "What you think?"

Wheels within wheels within wheels…

They passed a large RV. He needed to talk with Teddy Williams. The man had skills.

Chapter 69 – SEPTEMBER

Exhausted and distraught, September held her gun at the ready, just as she'd trained. Whoever was coming to rescue Kaliko Wong, she'd shoot first and ask questions later.

Instead of the goons she expected, Mark moved slowly into view. He hesitated, as if also fearful of threat, and massaged the deep red marks on each side of his neck.

With a choked sob, September sprang to her feet and rushed to meet him. They sank together in the grass, giving the swarming yellow jackets space as they clung to each other.

"I'm sorry, so sorry. Are you okay? Oh Mark, forgive me." Shadow pressed close on her other side, and she opened one arm to include him in the embrace.

"You didn't do anything wrong. It's my fault. I should never have gone looking for answers." Mark stroked her hair, so like her own. The two youngest of the January kids, so different from the rest of the blonde headed blue-eyed siblings.

"I don't know why you're apologizing. Neither of us did anything to deserve this." The volume of the sirens increased, and she knew Kali would get arrested. But could she trust the justice system to contain the witch, and protect them from her vengeance? She kept a watchful eye on the prone figure in the grass. September felt no regret over triggering the Taser multiple times. She wouldn't become a murderer but that was the least the killer deserved.

What had happened to Quinn? She shaded her eyes. Only birds perched in the pecan tree.

Mark continued speaking, eager for her to understand. "When I got the results, I didn't know what it meant. Then people from her organization"—he nodded at Kali—"showed up to explain *the facts of life*. That's what they called it." He hooked a thumb back at the house. "Didn't that Jack guy explain it to you? He knows all about them."

"Explain what?"

He looked miserable. "After testing for April's kidney transplant, and learning we're adopted, I needed answers. Mom wasn't talking."

Her heart clenched. She'd never talk to April again. They *were* sisters, never mind about blood relationships. Chosen family mattered more. April, and Combs, and God knows how many others…She struggled to hold it together, at least until the police arrived to cart Kaliko Wong away.

Mark cleared his throat. "I sent samples to one of those DNA services. September, I found out who our parents are."

The first flashing lights were visible. Suddenly, September didn't want to know what her brother had to say. Shadow leaned hard against her. He knew the black void beckoned. She'd not had a meltdown in so long…had to hang on. She stroked the big dog's black fur, but her heart raced faster and faster. Black sparklies danced before her eyes.

"When Simon Wong died, the organization started looking for

his kids." Mark took her hand and squeezed. "Mom saved us. I mean, Rose January, our adopted mom, she saved us. Jack said everybody thought we died with our biological mother, until I sent in that sample for DNA. Our mother's name was Myrina—"

"Rina. Jack's sister." September shuddered, and hugged Mark, just as the cars stopped at the back of the house. Too much, it was too much to take in! Jackson Glass, their uncle, wanted to avenge his sister's death. He'd said family meant everything to her. He never said Rina had two children. Or that her husband headed the crime syndicate that was trying to kill them.

She and Mark were no threat, knew nothing about Wong Enterprises—wanted nothing to do with them. And yet the witch set out to assassinate September, and ended up destroying everything she ever wanted, everyone she loved.

September stared at Kali. The woman had recovered enough to pull herself, crawling, closer to the lake, closer to the pier as if still intent on making her escape. Despite every abuse poured upon her tortured body, Kali fought on. And her survival would perpetuate September's torment.

With a cry torn from the depths of her soul, September leaped to her feet and chased the escaping woman. *Stop her, stop her, stop her!* Before she had gone half the distance, familiar voices cried out to stop.

Teddy. Lia. And the barking of Magic…

The black Rottie mix zoomed past September, stopping Kali's haggard progress. The witch produced another knife from somewhere, and slashed the air, keeping the dog at bay as she continued progress toward the water. Lia raced to join her dog. Magic grabbed the woman's arm, crushing the flesh until Kali dropped the blade. Lia drew her weapon and held the killer motionless until the police officers arrived. They bound Kali's wrists behind her back and pulled her upright.

A shot rang out. Kaliko ceased struggling and became a dead weight in the officers' grasp.

Lia backed away when the police dropped Kali's body. The woman's body rolled down the meager slope, splashed, and then sank beneath the water.

September staggered backward and fell to her knees. Quinn? She looked around. September glimpsed the big man she'd left bound in the bushes before he disappeared into the undergrowth.

Teddy stumbled behind the phalanx of police. His expression mirrored her own kaleidoscope of emotions: anguished reproach, joy, sorrow, and pain.

She wilted. Shadow raced to join her. At his touch, she collapsed on the grass, curling into a fetal position. Shadow pushed as much of his black face into her neck as he could manage, trying to merge their bodies and climb into her heart while his cries of emotion mirrored her own.

Then Teddy was there. He dropped to his knees beside her, his rough hand stroking her hair.

And the grief she'd held inside erupted in gut-wrenching sobs. *The pain, oh God the pain, April gone, and Combs…* Combs who had waited patiently, who healed her heart. Never again to see his quirky smile, tease his serious expression away, hold his hand, feel his warm arms about her. He knew all her secrets—*oh God, such terrible secrets, even worse now!*—and still his love endured.

She'd caused his death, refused to heed warnings, blinded by selfishness. She'd killed him, the one human whose love she could count on.

Teddy took her in his arms. He rocked her, murmuring softly, but she couldn't hear him, couldn't understand his words over the gasping sobs and keening wail rising from deep inside, surrounding her, and echoing over the lake—spooking the water birds into flight.

Teddy gripped her chin, forced her to meet his eyes. “September honey, he’s not dead. Look at me. Combs is alive.”

She finally heard. When the words pierced her understanding, September surrendered to the spinning black void.

Chapter 70 – SEPTEMBER, TWO WEEKS LATER

In the back seat of her car, Shadow yawned widely, and stared at her in the rearview mirror. When she met his eyes, he thumped his tail on the backseat. She reached behind her between the two seats, so that he could cold nose her palm and she could stroke his cheek. Of them all, Shadow seemed the most relaxed after the ordeal. She now realized how much of a strain it had been for the dog, with the wedding plans and the crowds of strangers tromping in and out of his house. At least at Lia's place, he could play with his young son, Magic, and help train the young boarding clients.

So much had changed. As soon as she learned Combs lived, she'd wanted nothing more than to run into his warm embrace, for them to comfort each other, and put the damaged parts of their lives back together again. The doctors said his leg would eventually heal, but it would take months of rehab for him to return to mobility. Combs deeply mourned Gonzales. Captain Gregory had shared with September he doubted whether Combs would recover enough to resume his duties as a detective. Or whether he'd want to.

She had felt a weird mixture of emotions when she first saw him. Captain Gregory even deferred her debriefing when they learned Combs had awakened. She'd rushed to the hospital, put on a cheerful face—not sure what or how much to share with him—and had the decision made for her. By protecting her, Combs suffered a traumatic brain injury, wiping out all memory of the event.

At first September welcomed his memory loss, believing it spared him the pain she felt. Then she realized he didn't remember her, either. The doctors couldn't predict when, if ever, Combs would regain full memory. He might remember her tomorrow, next week, months from now, or…

Thank God he remembered his children and Aunt Ethel. Melinda didn't hold back, blaming Teddy for lying to her, September for her father's injury and Uncle Stan's death. Aunt Ethel turned her grief into helping Combs recover. He couldn't manage the stairs, so they'd set up a convalescent area in the living room. September felt like an unwanted guest in her own house. At first she'd hoped her presence might prompt his memory to return. But with so much of their history tied to painful trauma, she believed his subconscious wanted her erased—the injury granted his unspoken desire.

She ached to fix this. And didn't know how, and feared making things worse.

For both of their sakes, she moved in with Lia and took on more training and behavior work. Shadow's minor cut, and her eardrum, were mostly healed, thank goodness. It'd take longer to heal other hurts. But animals didn't care about your past, or your failings. They forgave even the most egregious insults.

Even her father—well, the man she'd always thought of as her dad—kept his distance. She'd attended April's memorial service, and none of the family except Mark wanted to be anywhere near her. Especially not Doug. He talked of moving away.

Nobody but she, Mark, and their Uncle Jack knew about their legacy. September wanted to keep it that way. "Bad blood. But that doesn't mean I let it rule me. Right, Shadow?"

He woofed, offering a happy doggy grin.

September glanced at the floorboards of the passenger seat. Her go-bag rested there, checked daily, and updated regularly with new emergency gear as she maintained vigilance. She kept it always within reach.

So far, the police ascribed the vendetta to Kaliko Wong's twisted reasoning after the events in South Bend, and September wasn't inclined to share her thoughts on the matter. Kali's operatives, or those against her, could have killed both September and Mark at the lake. They wanted her alive. Kaliko was dead, but September feared the woman's organization hadn't finished with her.

Confirmation arrived this morning. A phone call from an attorney requesting her presence at the lake house. He refused to comment or clarify, would only speak to her in person. Alone.

She brought Shadow. And her gun.

She parked the car in the driveway of the Cat's Cradle B & B. September grabbed her go-bag, slid it over her left shoulder, then collected the gun. She got out and opened the door for Shadow. Together, they crossed the terrace to the open sliding glass doors.

Cautiously, she stepped over the threshold into the family room area, checking left and right to take in the kitchen and dining room beyond. Both appeared empty.

"Hello?" Shadow pressed hard against her thigh, while

September kept her gun at the ready.

"In the living room."

September leveled her weapon and entered the room.

The man just smiled and continued sitting in the armchair, legs crossed. Two cats, one orange and the other a silver tabby, sat on the window seat of the bay window, purring in the sunlight. "Apparently, the cats come with the house," he said, waving at them.

"Who are you and what do you want?"

Shadow growled, and his hackles rose.

"Have a seat. We have things to discuss. I'm here as a representative of your organization. To share the *facts of life*, so to speak." He glared at the gun in her hand. "Oh, for heaven's sake, put that away. You're not really going to make a mess after we spiffed up the place for you. Even got rid of the yellow jackets."

Slowly, she placed her gun at her back. If he wanted her dead, she wouldn't have made it into the house. Slowly she settled in the chair opposite him, but motioned for Shadow to stay close. His low growl continued. He remembered this house, too. "You worked for Kaliko Wong?" She wouldn't trust anyone who supported that killer.

He pulled a sheaf of papers from a briefcase and spread them on the low table between them. He cocked his head. "Oh, you can call me Mr. Thomas, but my name doesn't matter. I served the Wong family in many capacities. Today, I serve as an attorney." He gestured toward the paperwork. "I've already had this conversation with Mark."

September couldn't quite wrap her brain around this bizarre conversation. Shadow whined and licked his lips, reacting to her own emotional turmoil.

"Many years ago, someone kidnapped Myrina Wong and her

two children. Mr. Wong paid the ransom, but Myrina didn't survive the exchange, and the children disappeared."

"Jack said Kali killed his sister."

Mr. Thomas didn't bat an eye. "Maybe so. Before my time. I know Mr. Wong sent Kaliko to rescue his wife and was told they all died, along with Myrina's brother and their parents." He stared at her. "Yet here you are. Mark tripped several online alerts by sending off for DNA evaluation."

"I want nothing to do with any of this."

He smiled. "You have no choice as the designated heir. You, and your brother Mark, are Wong royalty, whether or not you want it."

She rose to her feet. "I don't want it. I'll sign anything you want, renounce any claim, so will Mark. We have enough trouble living a regular life without worrying about a criminal organization."

His mouth dropped open. He laughed, louder and louder, then clapped his hands as if applauding a performance. "Oh, how very honest of you! That's right, you're engaged to a cop. What would he think? Is that the problem?" The laughter abruptly shut off.

"Don't you dare—"

"What? Say something bad about Detective Jeffrey Combs? He doesn't remember you. What will you do, September Day? Shoot me?" He spread his arms out, making himself a target. "It wouldn't stop anything. I'm not the only lawyer on call. The Wong organization, as you know, employs many with a variety of skill sets."

She felt the words like a gut punch. Maybe he wouldn't touch her, but the organization had killers on the payroll. Like Quinn. And Combs couldn't defend himself. Or his kids. Or any of her friends… Slowly, she sank back into the seat. Shadow pressed against her, she stroked his neck and concentrated on taking deep breaths.

"That's better." He returned his attention to the papers. "Now, there are a couple of ways we can do this. The Wong organization has many businesses, much influence, and a great many assets, both liquid and otherwise, throughout the world. Yes, there are some aspects that, shall we say, skirt the letter of the law, particularly those run by Mrs. Wong during her recent tenure. But most of the organization's business is conducted in the public eye. The transfer of the company's assets and control legally passes to the eldest child. That's you. And part of the public record."

September swallowed hard. Everyone would know. "If I refuse?"

"Dare to refuse, and you die. Then it passes to your brother, Mark. With both of you out of the picture, the legacy passes to your heirs. If or when you have them." He shrugged.

Oh God, he couldn't know. She licked her lips. Stared at the papers on the table. "There's no way out, is there?" Her fist was clenched in Shadow's ruff, and she had to work to relax her hand.

"Don't look so damn stricken. Your father was an astute and successful entrepreneur. He got caught up by a master manipulator, and once she got her claws into the organization, it took extraordinary effort to extract her. After she killed Simon Wong and took control, the organization went off the rails completely. It'll take great effort to repair the damage…" He stared at her. "That's why the organization needs you. Yes, you're the blood heir. But you're also a fresh face with no special alliances. You pose no threat to those who matter."

They want a puppet. She licked her lips. "There's a man in prison for killing Simon Wong." *Lia's father, in fact.*

He shrugged. "Well, Kaliko had a way of making things

happen to her benefit. But, with you at the helm, just think of all the wrongs you could right. Virtually unlimited funds and influence." He made a motion with his hands encompassing the entire house, the grounds, and the lake beyond. "For instance, this all belongs to you now." The cats in the window seat meowed, stretched, and yawned. The man smiled, face lighting up, obviously a feline fan. "The cats, too. Kaliko bought this entire property just to make sure of your death. Pretty ironic now that you get to enjoy it."

Unlimited funds. Worldwide influence. She wanted nothing to do with any of it. But she had no choice. But she could use her position to champion the innocent tipped the balance. "So, what I say, goes? I am in charge?"

"Suddenly, I detect some interest. Yes, you are in charge. Just learn from the lesson of your predecessor: choose your battles." He tipped his head, playing with a fountain pen. "How good are you at walking a tightrope?"

"Been doing it my whole life. While wearing a blindfold." *At least now they'd ripped the blindfold off.*

Chapter 71 – TEDDY

"How's he doing?" Teddy whispered when Ethel opened the door, a finger to her lips. She quickly ushered him inside, pointedly ignoring the material he carried. He glimpsed Combs on the sofa, injured leg propped up, and Macy snuggled next to him as he slept.

They quietly made their way to the kitchen. Ethel poured him a cup of coffee, then refreshed her own, before inviting him to join her at the stained-glass table. "He gets stronger every day. He still has nightmares, but vague ones, he still can't remember anything. Not like we do. He hated missing Gonzales's and Stan's funeral. But he doesn't remember April, or anyone connected to September. Frustrating for him, but maybe a relief for now. He just can't take any more."

Teddy sighed and set the envelope on the table. "Where are the kids?" They didn't need to hear this. Melinda had barely forgiven him for the deception about her father's demise.

"Melinda went with Willie to soccer practice; one of the other moms picked them up. She's really stepped up during this horror.

I'm proud of that girl." Ethel sipped from an oversized mug. "How's September?"

He shrugged. "Same, I suppose. Not saying much to me." He got more updates from Lia than from September.

Ethel sighed. "Horrible situation all around, and I know she blames herself." She spoke without bitterness, and Teddy found that amazing. "But there's plenty of blame to go around."

He shared that guilt. "She fired the security, says the danger's gone. How can she know that?" Teddy didn't think he'd ever stop looking over his shoulders.

"She knows." Ethel finally turned her attention to the fancy wedding envelope he'd brought with him. "If you've read that, so do you." The lines in her face had deepened with the loss of Stan, but Teddy wondered at her sense of peace despite her pain.

"How long have you known?"

"Not long. Mark shared his concerns right before the wedding. Neither of us knew what it meant. Now Mark has closed his glass studio and left town."

"Shouldn't Combs be told?"

"No! Not now. Maybe never." She took a deep breath and offered a quizzical smile. "Why should *that* matter to him? He can't even remember her. He needs peace if he's going to heal." Her hand slapped the envelope. "Burn it. Or give it to September, if she cares."

He'd tried that. She wouldn't return his calls. He'd driven out to Lia's place before coming here. September had left in a rush, something about some abandoned cat. Leave it to September to distract herself by focusing on the needs of animals.

"Hey, anybody here?" Combs called from the other room.

They both startled. Ethel stood, still clutching her mug of coffee. "In here, dear. Teddy came to visit." She gestured for him to put away the fancy envelope and hurried to join Combs in the other room. Teddy followed slowly.

Combs held his cell phone in one hand and turned it to share with them. "I just got this text of a video about a local news story from a couple of weeks ago. It's making the rounds on the Internet. Is this somebody else I'm supposed to know?" Deep trenches furrowed his brow. The marks had become indelible. The man had always tended toward the serious, but Teddy hardly recognized Combs now. He looked ready to throttle anyone who drew too close. Macy purred and began kneading his arm, and his expression softened a bit.

Ethel took the phone and glanced at the video for only a moment before shaking her head. She offered it to Teddy. He turned up the volume to play the short piece.

"A stay-cation at Pauline's Paw Palace last week saved dog owner Andrea Neal's life when her dog Max stopped a carjacking attempt," began the voice-over. The screen switched to a woman. "I usually board him at Corazon Kennels, where he loves the training games. But they were full, so we went with a new place," said Neal. "Max learns fast. He likes to hide toys from his sister, and play Chuckit, with the fetch ball. He learned all the basic commands, too. But nobody taught him this." She shivered. "On the way home, we stopped at a light. A scary man pointed a gun at us through the window and said *show me your keys.* Max leaped through the car window, and knocked the gun away, then barked until the guy ran. He saved my life!" The video showed a closeup of a grinning black dog.

Teddy shrugged. "I don't know them, either."

He offered the phone back, but Combs just stared, watching it play again. "That's the *show me* game. September does that with Shadow. That dog even looks like Shadow. A little. He's black, right? Doesn't he?"

Ethel gasped. "You remember?"

Combs looked up at her and saw the "Son Of A Peach" coffee mug she held. "I gave September that mug. She drinks her weight in coffee every day…"

His face crumpled. Ethel rushed to his side, took him in her arms.

"I remember." Combs sobbed. "Oh God, I remember her, I remember! Where is she?" Combs looked up at Teddy. "I couldn't protect her. Then I blamed her for all this—" He pointed to his leg. "So, she packed a bag and left, won't stay here, in her own house. She won't come near me. Do you think…will she forgive me? Would she even still want me, all banged up like this. Oh God, the way I treated her, she must hate me!" His words rushed out, fast and furious.

Teddy closed his eyes, throat tight. He didn't know who sent the video and didn't care. Max the hero not only saved his person's life, but may have just saved September and Combs's love.

He squeezed Combs's shoulder. "Talk to her. Don't wait, do it now." Life was too short to waste time on what ifs and guesses. He pushed the phone back into Combs's hand. "Call her."

Chapter 72 – SEPTEMBER

We need a name for legal purposes. To put on the documents, sign paychecks, assign real estate deeds and bank accounts, all that lawyerly mumbo jumbo, you know the drill." The lawyer paused. "It would make a positive impression with our, shall I say, *competitors*, and with the traditionalists in the organization, for the new boss to show her legitimate claim. Rumors have circulated for decades that the children survived."

She couldn't change her name, didn't want the world to know. "I refuse to use Wong, with its bloody taint."

He nodded slowly. "Your mother's maiden name was Glasovich. Your uncle changed that to Glass."

How do you choose a new name in 30 seconds? "What you think, Shadow? I promise, you don't have to change your name." The nightmare wouldn't end. But if she at least let Mr. Thomas think she agreed, she'd find a way to escape. For now, play the innocent he thought she was. "What did my mother name me?"

"Sorokin. Kinsey for short." He smiled at her expression. "It means magpie. You were a chatterbox as a kid, apparently." He gestured toward her hair. "Also, the bird has black plumes accented with white, just like your hair. Myrina had the same moon mark, I'm told, probably part of the albinism of your uncle."

What a mouthful. But it wouldn't track back to her own name, at least not at first look. She nodded reluctant agreement. "Sorokin Kinsey Glass it is."

"We'll have a history and backstory created to explain why Simon Wong's long lost child finally resurfaced." He wrote her new name on one of the page's blank lines. "We have skilled computer geniuses up to the challenge. Oh, and now that you're taking over the organization, your uncle can come in from the cold. If he wants."

She shivered, not sure if she ever wanted to see Jackson Glass again.

After the lawyer departed, taking the stack of signed paperwork with him, September walked to the lake. The sun beat down, the hot July day blistering the weathered boards of the pier. She sat on the very end, taking off her shoes, and setting her go-bag on the wood beside her. She placed her gun on top of the bag. Shadow joined her on the other side, and one of her new cats, Nebulae according to a picture in the house, paddled in the nearby water, enjoying the flitting fish just beneath the water's surface. Sunset seemed to prefer to stay indoors.

She had traded her old life for a new one. Her renovated brick house on Rabbit Run Road, planted with fresh blooms, would forever haunt her nightmares. The building still sheltered those she loved: Combs and his children, who she'd hoped to mother.

How strange to inherit this old house, complete with the cats who had helped save her life.

According to Mr. Thomas, she now had the means and

wherewithal to do anything she wanted with the assets of the organization she'd inherited. And she had no desire to do anything at all, except sit here quietly, her dog on one side, and her mind flying like a dragonfly unable to settle.

What an absurd name, Sorokin Glass, as awkward as September January or September Day had ever been. She laughed, then couldn't stop laughing. *Cursed to have horrible names.* Combs would think it hilarious…

And like that, her laughter became choking sobs.

September touched the emerald engagement ring. When Combs made it plain she meant nothing to him anymore, she had moved it from her left ring finger to her right hand, because it also represented the past. Those dreams of safety, love, and acceptance blew away in the dust of rainbow hued rose petals. She still yearned for that happily ever after. But she'd never find it in another person, place, or thing. Only inside herself.

She had to keep this new identity separated from September Day to protect those she loved, whether they remembered her or not.

September laughed when Shadow slurped tears from her face. The cat climbed into her lap with wet paws and settled with a loud purr. All right, she had no choice. So she'd take the dare or die trying. First, she needed to learn the extent of *Kinsey's* influence, resources, and power. She must make things right. Only then would September Day deserve a happily ever after.

Her phone rang. She wanted to ignore it but the ring tone… Combs.

Terrified, she answered. She'd learned that things could always get worse.

"Hello." She squeezed her eyes shut, bracing for whatever might come.

A long silence. And then she heard his voice, ragged, almost a sob. "I remember. I remember you, us. Everything. Come home, September. Honey, will you please come back?"

September touched the ring on her finger, the green sparkle matching renewed hope in her eyes. Her chest swelled until she thought she might explode with happiness. She pushed Kinsey away to consider another time.

Combs wanted her, September. She'd let nothing come between them ever again.

She laughed with delight, and scrubbed tears away. "Yes, we're coming home."

FACT, FICTION, & ACKNOWLEDGMENTS

Thank you for reading DARE OR DIE, and I hope you enjoyed this seventh book in the September & Shadow thriller series. Thank you, too, for coming along with me on the adventure. There never would have been Thrillers With Bite without you, dear reader, adopting these books. (Can you hear my purrs and woofs of delight?)

After publishing 35+ nonfiction pet books, research fuels my curiosity. While in fiction I get to make up *crappiocca*, as September would say, much of my inspiration comes from news stories, past and present—the weirder, the better. For me, and I hope for you, the story becomes more engaging when built not on "what if" but "it happened." So in each book, I like to include a Cliff's Notes version of what's real and what's made up.

As with the other books in the series, much of DARE OR DIE arises from science, especially dog and cat behavior and learning theory, and the benefits of service dogs. By definition, thrillers include murder and mayhem, but as an animal advocate professional, I make a conscious choice to not show a pet's death in any of my books. All bets are off with the human characters, though.

This story took September and Shadow—and me—in unexpected and surprising directions. Sometimes the Muse dictates what happens, and I don't always like it, either. DARE OR DIE, while shutting some doors, opens wide possible opportunities to explore with the characters, old and new. Thanks for coming along for the ride.

I rely on a vast number of veterinarians, behaviorists, consultants, trainers, pet-centric writers and readers, and rescue organizations that share their incredible resources and support to make my stories as believable as possible. Find out more information at IAABC.org, Dogwriters.org and CatWriters.com.

FACT: The *show me* game is real, created by trainer Kayce Cover as a vocabulary exercise to be used with a variety of animals, and which my own dog loves to play. See https://synalia.com

FICTION: Pet viewpoint chapters are pure speculation, although I would love to read dog and cat minds. However, I make every attempt to base animal characters' motivations and actions on canine and feline body language, scent discrimination, and the science behind the human-animal bond.

FACT: Yes, some dogs can climb fences. Larger dogs like Shadow the German Shepherd or Keighley the Airedale might have a "paw up" to leap over the top, but even smaller canines like Max learn the technique. And yes, dogs learn from watching each other. Here's a fun video of a couple of smaller fence-climbing canines: https://www.youtube.com/shorts/Hv-_kTWIs2M

FICTION: While dogs learn very quickly, especially if they've been taught to enjoy training, I've stretched reality a bit for purposes of the fiction story. I have no doubt Keighley and

Shadow could learn and execute all the commands needed to place and trigger—at a distance—the "talking buttons." But in the timeframe necessary for the story? Hmm.

FACT: The "talking buttons" are real. I've not spent enough time with my cat and dog with them yet, but they work extremely well. In fact, some pets become incredibly adept at communicating using these recorded buttons. Some like Bunny the dog even describe their dreams using the buttons. This communication tool reveals some interesting differences between dogs' and cats' thought processes in communication. Watch Bunny the dog here: https://youtu.be/z8k2upr9vCE

And Billie the cat here: https://youtu.be/aV4zo01_8Bg

FACT: Real-life pets inspired some of the animal characters in DARE OR DIE. I've held a "Name That Dog/Name That Cat" contest for each of the novels in the series. For this most recent contest I limited nominations to my newsletter subscribers (join the list on my website at Shojai.com if you'd like to nominate your dog for a future book!). I narrowed the nominations down to ten cat finalists and eighteen dog finalists. In the story, I planned for one cat hero winner and one dog hero winner but…the voting became so close, I had to expand the storyline to include more of these marvelous pets!

Congratulations to Iris Adorno-Williams from New York for nominating the winning six-year-old silver tabby cat, **Nebulae**! "She earned her name when she climbed up on my husband's back to look down in the telescope. She's always curious, opening cabinet doors to see what is behind them." Iris says Nebulae indulges in the *zoomies* and is particularly well behaved when asleep. Ha, just like a cat!

Congratulations to Judi Moyers for the winning dog, black and tan Airedale Terrier **Keighley.** "She was named *Keighley Mor of*

Briarbumble after a town where the Airedales originated in England and a Gaelic name for girl. She also was a beautiful show dog and finished her championship in six shows. We had to watch her as she could open the latch handles on the doors. She once locked herself in the pantry with cereal. She'd lie on her side and get the freezer door open to pull out packages of frozen chicken to eat!" She qualified for search and rescue training but ended up working as a therapy dog once she retired from show circles.

The contest was so hotly contested that I also included the runners up. The kitty **Sunset** is a six KG (13 pound) marmalade cat nominated by Janet Glazebrook from Canada. "Sunset walks on a leash and is usually placed in a harness in the front yard, where he hunts voles in the garden and waits for neighbors to stop and pet him. Sunset opens doors that have lever handles and lets himself out of the house if the door isn't dead-bolted."

Max the dog was nominated by Andrea Neal from Wyoming. He looks like a solid black (with a bit of white) Kelpie, and his DNA results include Border Collie, Lab and German Shepherd in his heritage. They rescued him from a hoarding situation. "I have seen Max take the ball out of a Chuckit! (fetch toy) that was hanging on the wall or take toys and hide them from his sister."

THANK YOU to everyone who took part in the contest and to all the winners. I think they all deserve treats. Maybe even catnip and bacon! To see pictures and learn more about the nominees and voting, visit these pages:

https://amyshojai.com/hero-dogs-for-dare-or-die-thriller/
https://amyshojai.com/hero-cats-for-dare-or-die-thriller/

FICTION: I made up Turtle Lake and Cat's Cradle B&B to better fit the story requirements. But there are many similar lakes in North Texas, and I don't know about you, but I'd love to stay at a B&B with cats.

FACT: The description of the homemade kayak comes from my childhood. My father built one as a boy with his dad, and then my father and brothers refurbished the frame with new canvas for our use. We use a double-bladed kayak paddle that looked like the one in the story, as we traversed the river behind our house. I think the "bones" of that old boat are still stored in the attic of my dad's garage, maybe ready for another generation of kids.

FICTION: There's no such place as Pauline's Paw Palace. But my own pets stay at a similar doggy daycare and boarding facility that, to my knowledge, has never had an animal go AWOL. Many of the best these days ensure they have escape-proof enclosures with tops or other techniques that keep boarders safely confined.

FACT: Bo fighting (a type of stick or staff fighting) has been around for centuries, called by many names. The technique not only offers terrific self-defense options, but a staff also looks less threatening but can, in fact, be lethal. It requires no ammunition or licensing. Here's a terrific overview of some of the staff techniques from around the world: https://youtu.be/Cv3ROAi7TFk

FICTION: I made up the "targeted IED bomb" in the story to keep it survivable. Also, C4 explosive smells like motor oil and comes as a moldable putty, easy enough to form into a bridal bouquet, complete with triggering devices.

A bomb causes immeasurable damage to the human body. The change in pressure from an explosion bursts eardrums, damages lungs and internal organs, and throws people far distances. If they survive the blast itself, then shrapnel driven into the body, or being slammed into buildings, increases trauma. Basically, the farther away you are from the epicenter, the greater your chance of survival. Gonzales and Combs knew that, and so did their best to move Willie and September away from where the bomb dog alerted. Falling onto the ground and opening your mouth (to help equalize pressure in your ears) lessens potential injury. A burst eardrum hurts like crazy, but usually heals quickly. Here's more about the devastating trauma potential of an explosion: https://tinyurl.com/4ytvps8y

FACT: Nearly anyone can get a drone these days, even those with a camera. Someone with Kali's resources certainly would use this technology. I may have fudged a bit on the gun-mounted drones, but it IS a thriller. And gun-toting drones are now available, even to the private sector (probably for a lot of money): https://www.bbc.com/news/technology-40901393

FACT: Texas famously has gorgeous roses available. Yes, there are roses named My Valentine and Masquerade. I know this because at one time, we surrounded our "Rosemont" home with over 700 roses, including My Valentine. Today, we're updating our garden. I may pass on getting the Masquerade rose, though.

FACT: GHB (gamma-hydroxybutyric acid) also known as one of the "date rape" drugs, does exactly what is described in the book. It comes as a liquid or powder, easily adds to liquid, and takes effect quickly within ten or fifteen minutes. The effects can last two to six hours, but the drug affects people differently. Those under the influence become giddy, compliant, and willingly do things they might not otherwise—and may have no memory after they recover.

FICTION & FACT: I'm not aware of instances where music or a sound in an MP3 track detonated a bomb, but technically it's possible. For purposes of the story, the online music track chosen for the wedding got doctored, allowing the bomb in the bouquet to trigger at the specific time in the music.

Today, we know that radio frequencies including calls on a cell phone, can trigger explosives with detonators designed for this purpose. Today, both government agencies and terrorists look to using sound as a defensive or offensive weapon. Everyday speakers can transform into dangerous devises, as outlined in this interesting (and scary) article: https://www.wired.com/story/acoustic-cyberweapons-defcon/

FACT: People sensitive to one allergen often also have allergies to multiple things. Kali's allergy to cat dander, Texas pollen, and yellow jackets (oh, those stings!) would certainly diminish her abilities.

And yes, yellow jackets build nests in the ground, under buildings, and sting repeatedly. They also like the scent of bananas. Throughout history, bees and even scorpions figured in warfare, with hives lobbed in catapults to disrupt enemy forces. That inspired the notion of including nasty yellow jackets in the story. Read about some historical applications here: https://tinyurl.com/app/myurls

FACT: Many dogs adore playing tug-o-war games, and Shadow learned the right way to play. Yes, you can include this fun game with your dog, but make sure you both follow the rules to stay out of trouble. As with anything, safety means understanding why dogs love it and how to channel the natural impulse appropriately. My colleague Trish McMillan wrote a brilliant explanation of the concept and how to play safely here: https://tinyurl.com/yhm3857p

FACT: Tasers are different from stun guns. Both produce painful shock to stop another person, either to control them or disarm and allow you to escape. A stun gun works only in close contact, but I needed something useful from a distance. The bad guy deployed a Taser at the cat—able to shoot the metal barbed probes up to 15 feet away. If September had remembered in time, she could have shot Kali with the Taser from that distance. Also, while the cat probably wouldn't receive a painful shock simply by batting them around, the sharp probe and silvery wire certainly would cause enough surprise, along with the "confetti" that accompanies each blast. This colorful paper contains the serial number of the deployed cartridge to track the source. For those interested, here's an interesting slow-motion video of a Taser deployment: https://tinyurl.com/mcj3668w

FACT: This book would not have happened without an incredible support team of friends, family and accomplished colleagues. Special thanks to my editor, Nicola Aquino of Spit & Polish Editing, and first readers Kristi Brashier, Andrea Neal, Mary Stansbury Hoge, Carol Shenold, Frank Steele, and BJ Thompson for your eagle eyes, spot-on comments and unflagging encouragement and support. Youse guyz rock!

I continue to be indebted to the International Thriller Writers organization, which launched my fiction career by welcoming me into the Debut Authors Program. Wow, just look, now I have seven books in a series! The authors, readers and industry mavens who make up this organization are some of the most generous and supportive people I have ever met. Long live the bunny slippers with teeth (and the rhinestone #1-Bitch Pin).

Finally, I am grateful to all the cats and dogs I've met over the years who have shared my heart and often my pillow. Shadow-Pup and Karma-Kat inspire me daily. And the pets who live on in my heart continue to bring happy memories.

I never would have been a reader and now a writer if not for my fantastic parents Phil and Mary Monteith, who instilled in me a love of the written word, and never looked askance when my stuffed animals and invisible wolf friend told fantastical stories. And of course, my deepest thanks to my husband Mahmoud, who continues to support my writing passion, even when he doesn't always understand it.

I love hearing from you! Please drop me a line at my blog AmyShojai.com or my website Shojai.com where you can subscribe to my PET PEEVES newsletter (and maybe win some pet books!). Follow me on twitter @amyshojai and like me on Facebook: http://www.facebook.com/amyshojai.cabc.

ABOUT THE AUTHOR

Amy Shojai is a certified animal behavior consultant, and the award-winning author of more than 35 bestselling pet books that cover furry babies to old fogies, first aid to natural healing, and behavior/training to Chicken Soupicity. She has been featured as an expert in hundreds of print venues including The Wall Street Journal, New York Times, Reader's Digest, and Family Circle, as well as television networks such as CNN, and Animal Planet's DOGS 101 and CATS 101. Amy brings her unique pet-centric viewpoint to public appearances. She is also a playwright and co-author of STRAYS, THE MUSICAL and the author of the critically acclaimed THRILLERS WITH BITE pet-centric thriller series. Stay up to date with new books and appearances by visiting Shojai.com to subscribe to Amy's Pets Peeves newsletter.